FRAUD
IN
PARADISE

PARADISE SERIES

BOOK 21

DEBORAH BROWN

FRAUD IN PARADISE
All Rights Reserved
Copyright © 2020 Deborah Brown

ISBN: 978-1-7334807-2-7

Cover: Natasha Brown

PRINTED IN THE UNITED STATES OF AMERICA

FRAUD IN PARADISE

Chapter One

"Oh yeah, she's dead," Rude Banner said in a breathy whisper that could be heard down the block as she tromped backward out of the bushes that lined the front of the two-story apartment building, wobbling unsteadily on her feet. That morning, she'd donned cut-offs, a tank top, and faded knee-high turquoise rain boots, a safari hat tied under her chin.

Cootie, her someday husband, plodded down the driveway in jean overalls over a wife-beater and craned his neck to peer over the bushes. "Oh yeah, the broad kicked the bucket all right. Anyone we know?" he shouted in a gravelly voice.

The sixty-something couple had hooked up out in the mangroves and found out that they had similar interests—a love of moonshine, big slithery bugs, and other fascinations that bonded them.

"Appears to be Pastel from unit seven," Rude yelled as she trotted over and stood next to Cootie. She bent so far over the sidewalk, she was in danger of falling flat. Cootie jerked on her matching wife-beater, and she straightened and turned. "She's starting to bloat," she said, accentuating that by puffing out her cheeks, "so she's been here a while. Must've missed her on my evening walk."

"You mean on your nightly snoop, sticking your nose into other folks' business, whether they like it or not." Cootie gave her a one-eyed squint.

"It's called being friendly; you should try it," Rude snapped.

"Okay, you two," I said as Fab and I got closer. "No fighting in front of a dead body... or the neighbors." I nudged Fab, indicating with my head that she should go and inspect said body. No one would argue it wasn't her forte. "Call 911," I threw out to anyone willing to make the call.

"Madison Westin," my bestie, Fabiana Merceau, said, shooting me a dirty look. Not sure why, since it didn't slow the sexy French woman from checking out the deceased. She took her phone out of her pocket. Another specialty of hers—pictures. The more ghoulish, the better.

What a weird morning, and it had only just begun.

The ringing of my phone had woken me up. "Dead one out front," Rude whispered hoarsely as soon as I answered. "You need to get over here pronto." She hung up.

I groaned and rolled over.

Creole's piercing blue eyes were focused on

me in annoyance. "I'm afraid to ask. What now?"

I repeated the brief conversation.

"Your family's right—it's past time to sell." He turned onto his side and pulled the sheet over his head.

I owned rental property on the other side of the Cove, and in the past, it'd attracted, to put it bluntly, nutjobs. In my defense, I did my best to block any and all attempts by said folks to move in, but unfortunately, some snuck in under the radar.

So much for my husband going with me. I scooted off the bed and crossed the room, going into the closet to change into work clothes—crop sweats, a t-shirt, and tennis shoes were a must.

Creole had bought the house from an investor looking for a quick flip. He'd knocked out the walls and remodeled it into one large open space, with pocket doors along the wall that opened to a view of the water. The mammoth bathroom with high-end finishes shared the same view as the rest of the house.

I hurried into the kitchen, which was a large expanse of stainless steel and granite, everything top of the line. The island was my favorite for spreading out paperwork, as it gave me plenty of space. I made a quick cup of coffee to take with me while sending off a text to my best friend and partner in crime, Fab. "Dead body. Interested?"

Creole stuck his head out from under the sheet and grouched, "I hope you're not bothering Fab.

Didier likes to spend mornings with his wife."
He rolled over and sat on the edge of the bed, his
feet hitting the floor.

My phone pinged with an incoming text: "Pick
me up out front."

Instead of answering Creole's glare, I poured
my coffee into a thermos. "I'll call you later." I
hustled out the door and into my Hummer.

I flew down to the opposite end of the
compound—aptly named, since Fab's father had
bought the rest of the block, including the two
other houses there, as a wedding gift and had
security fencing installed. Fab walked out of her
front door just as I pulled into the driveway. I got
out and swapped sides so Fab could use her race-
car-driving skills to scoot us across the Cove.

Tarpon Cove was located at the top of the
Florida Keys, and as we flew down the highway,
I did my best to catch a glimpse of the sunlight
gleaming on the blue-green waters of the Gulf,
which rippled today in the slight wind. A heron
glided gracefully in front of us and over to a
nearby beach.

Fab parked the SUV around the corner from
the two properties I owned. With a sense of
urgency, the two of us got out and cut down a
walkway between two neighboring houses in
time to find Rude and Cootie making their way
back out of the bushes.

"Remind me, who's the manager here?" I
pointed to the apartment building I'd recently

purchased, now certain to be the center of hot gossip. Rude raised her hand tentatively. "It's your job to call 911," I told her. Just because she ignored me the first time didn't mean I was going to make the call.

"Cootie?" Rude said in a whiney tone, waving at the man, who started walking backwards. "Hon?"

"I'm already late getting to the job site." Cootie ran his hand through his two clumps of grey hair, which stuck up on end. He grumbled something unintelligible and didn't let his work boots slow him as he ran to his pickup and hopped in. Without a backwards glance, he hit the gas and squealed off down the street.

Rude mumbled to herself, jerking her phone out of her pocket so hard, I expected to hear a ripping noise. She cursed the screen before placing the call.

A door slammed in the distance. I didn't bother to peer over my shoulder, knowing who the shoes slapping down the middle of the street belonged to—the manager of my cottages, Macklin Lane. I'd inherited the ten units next door from my Aunt Elizabeth—individual cottages built around a U-shaped driveway, which backed up to the beach with easy access. Out of view from where we stood was a large pool and tiki bar area.

"Hey." Mac bristled, skidding to a stop next to me. "There's excitement and no one calls me? I'd have called you." The overly endowed woman had stuffed herself into a body-hugging knit dress, a flamingo wide-eyed and winking on the front. The shoes that could be heard on the next block were pink slides with artificial grass growing out of the soles, the bands across the top adorned with fake flowers.

I sighed and waited while Mac blew smoke out of her ears, then pointed her in the direction of the deceased. Not to be outdone, immediately went over to where Fab was stepping out of the plants, whipped her phone out, and took her own pictures.

Shaking her head, Fab rejoined me. "Not much to see, other than that the woman's dead."

"What's your professional opinion?" I asked her. I'd give her assessment the same weight as any coroner's. Given her sophistication, you'd never guess her penchant for the morbid.

"My professional guess is that the deceased was offed several hours ago. Florida weather isn't conducive to leaving a dead body in the elements. Deteriorates fast." Fab scrunched up her nose. "No visible signs as to cause of death, but she was lying on her back and I thought shoving her over with my shoe wasn't respectful."

"That wise choice also saved you from being charged with fooling with a corpse."

Sirens could be heard in the distance, coming up the main highway through town.

"I say we go over and sit on Mac's porch and watch the drama unfold." Fab tugged on my sleeve. "She's got a good vantage point, and we won't be up in the middle of things."

I hooked my arm in hers and turned. "Let's not dawdle. When the cops get here, I want to be able to plead ignorance." I skidded to a stop and yelled to Mac and Rude, "We'll be over there." I pointed and waved.

Rude, who was still on the phone answering questions, waved over her head. Mac crossed the street to talk to one of the neighbors. Or question the woman.

Fab and I climbed the steps to Mac's house and rearranged the chairs on the porch for an unobstructed view.

We'd barely sat down when Crum, one of my tenants from The Cottages, strutted down the driveway, a stack of beach chairs in his arms. He'd been banned from wearing the underwear-only attire he preferred, and today, he'd donned a flirty skirt over his tighty-whities and paired the ensemble with mismatched, dog-eaten tennis shoes. He clunked across the street, dumped the chairs in Mac's driveway, unfolded them, and formed two rows.

"What are you doing?" I yelled, eyeing the chairs and willing to wager a fiver that they were rescues from trash day and that somehow the man was about to make money off the finds. Anyone who knew Crum wouldn't be stupid enough to take the bet.

"Good morning, ladies." Crum ignored my question and started back across the street.

"Bring back two bottled waters," I yelled at his back.

He spun around and came back, hand out. "I need the key to the office. Unless you want me to fill a couple of bottles from the hose."

Fab handed over the keys. "Cold ones, please. Unopened."

"What do I get for my benevolence?"

"Help yourself. But don't stuff your underwear." I bit my lip to stop from laughing at Fab's groan.

Crum came back five minutes later, water in hand and leading a line of people across the street. They filled the chairs just as two cop cars pulled around the corner and parked in front of the apartment building.

"What's the old goat up to?" Fab eyed the group with suspicion.

Before I could tell her to ask him, she yelled, "Hey."

Crum deciphered that one word as a complete question and puffed up his chest. "Sold prime seating to view the transfer of the body. When there's a buck to be made, I'm your man." The snooty retired college professor had enough dough to buy up the whole block, but he found it more entertaining to see how hard he could squeeze a nickel.

It was the guests from The Cottages interested in the unfolding drama who'd rented a chair. The regulars were still sleeping off their drunks from the night before, and it wouldn't be their first dead body anyway.

Out of the corner of my eye, I caught sight of Kevin Cory getting out of the first cop car. Another officer climbed out of the second one. I'd seen him a time or two but couldn't remember his name. A minute later, an ambulance rolled up.

Kevin was a local sheriff's deputy and a tenant at The Cottages who'd been snuck in by my brother. One would've thought he'd have packed his bags and moved on long ago, since we only tolerated one another. But no. He'd decided he liked the place well enough that he could ignore that I was a pain in his backside.

Folks, apparently tired of peeking out the blinds, spilled out of their houses and crowded the sidewalk, most not venturing past their driveways. A brave one or two moved into the street and closer to the crime scene for a better look.

A third cop car pulled up and blocked off the end of the street closest to us.

"You've got to admit, it was a good idea of mine to sit where, so far, we haven't missed anything," Fab said, and laughed.

"I forgot to thank you for letting me intrude on your morning. I appreciate not having to come over here by myself."

"As soon as I read 'dead body' to Didier, he started laughing and said, 'You'd never miss that.' Besides, he was headed to the office. Which reminds me." Fab pulled out her phone.

When she started speaking in French, I knew she had her husband on the phone and guessed he was getting an update.

Our husbands insisted on being kept in the loop and stressed that we choose personal safety over anything else. Or Creole used to before I bested a drug dealer in the purchase of the building next door. In retaliation, he'd kidnapped Creole and Didier. Creole came back with a head injury that he hadn't fully recovered from, although the doctors assured us it could happen any day. The actual circumstances surrounding his injury were unclear, as he still hadn't been able to remember the events of that day. Now, he never mentioned safety or calling with updates. I tried not to let it bother me.

Mac came trotting around the corner. She'd learned all the shortcuts from Fab and used one to cut over to another street and come around the back way, leaving no one the wiser that she'd looked her fill at the body. For the next few days, she'd be popular at Custer's, a seedy local bar she occasionally frequented. The retelling of the drama would get her a free beer or two. She threw herself into a chair next to me and propped her grassy slides up on the railing.

Kevin got on the loudspeaker in his car and ordered everyone out of the street under threat of arrest. The coroner's van rounded the corner and slowed in the middle of the street, taking the space that the ambulance had just vacated.

"Well?" Fab asked Mac.

"Turns out dead chick isn't Pastel, who proved that by poking her head over the railing, surveying the scene, and going back inside," Mac said. "Rude seemed to think there was a resemblance, but I couldn't see it. I imagine that when the dead woman was still sucking air, she looked a lot different."

"Got a clue as to the cause of death?" I asked.

"Gunshot," Mac said.

"How do you know that?" Fab demanded.

"Rude, uh… thinking she was alive and that it might help her breathe if she were on her side, moved her a bit with her foot and saw the blood and the hole." Mac demonstrated with her shoe.

Fab made a choking noise. "You need to tell Rude to toss the boots."

"That's a terrible idea," Mac said snootily. "I'm going to suggest that she display them on a shelf with a little placard saying they'd been to a murder scene."

I didn't bother giving her my opinion, which I knew she wouldn't want to hear, and instead changed the subject. "Wouldn't one of the neighbors have reported hearing a gun shot?"

"You're asking me?" Mac asked.

"Save the innocent face. You know whenever someone sneezes in this neighborhood, probably the entire Cove." I took her non-response to mean that no one had poked their head out their door and admitted to anything. "I expect to be kept up to date. Since you're training the new manager..." I indicated Rude, who'd rapidly overcome her reticence and appeared to be enjoying being in the center of the action, answering all the questions the cops were shooting at her. "You need to tell her."

"No need to worry on that score." Mac snorted. "I'll be telling her plenty. I'm still not over Rude calling you before me."

"Go easy on her," I said. "It's probably her first dead body, and people can get squeamish and forget to bypass the owner." Some people anyway.

We sat there for nearly an hour, and it was boring. Some of the people that paid for seating started asking when the police chase would start, a testament to Crum knowing how to sell non-existent excitement.

Fab's stomach growled, and it was music to my ears. I knew we wouldn't be there much longer. She stood and stared at me, telegraphing *let's go.*

"If Kevin comes looking for me," I said to Mac, "tell him that after I barfed in your bushes, you insisted I go home and Fab drove me."

"You might want to put on the performance of

a lifetime before you sneak your butt out of here so folks can corroborate my story." Mac waved to the guests that hadn't bailed on the drama and crossed her arms, waiting for me to put on a show.

I stood. "Let's hope Kevin doesn't ask, and if he does, you have time to make something up."

Fab put her arm around my shoulders. "Just lean on me, and we'll cut out the back."

"I'll call you and let you know how I'm feeling later." I winked at Mac.

Chapter Two

"Where to now?" I asked as Fab and I got in the SUV, even though I had a pretty good idea.

"Gunz has a job, and I need backup. That would be you."

Gunz was a client of Fab's and the problem solver for a large family. He had more relates than you could shake a stick at, and all of them together didn't have enough sense to fill a boot. Fab and I speculated that some of the people were only claiming a blood tie to avail themselves of his "clean up your mess" services, which he foisted off on Fab.

I pointed to my sweats. "I'm not dressed to your standards, unless we're running from bullets."

"Let's hope not." Fab stuck her nose in the air and took the back road to her office, housed in one of the twin warehouse buildings she owned.

Both buildings sat on one parcel, and she shared office space in one with her husband. Recently, she'd rented the other building to an associate of hers—Toady, who she used on cases that came with an element of danger, which Fab had promised her husband were in her past.

Toady didn't mind and, in fact, relished the excitement. In addition to living and working there, he had signed on as security guard for the property. Anyone who attempted to put one over on the old alligator would soon find themselves food for the ones living in nearby murky water. It was agreed that Xander, our information specialist, would share part of the space as his office, since he'd been the one to pitch the idea.

Fab punched in the code for the security gate, pulled in, and waited for it to close before driving into the garage and parking next to Gunz's Escalade. To stop me from continually asking how he managed to get inside, Fab had finally fessed up that she'd given the man a code. We got out and climbed the thirty or so steps to the second level. The door opened into one large open space decorated in chrome and glass, with splashes of color differentiating Didier's side from Fab's. I'd claimed the alcove around the corner and put my beachy stamp on it.

Gunz's large, bald bulk took up a chair and then some in front of Fab's desk. We'd interrupted him barking into his phone, and he turned and gave Fab a once-over, followed by a flirty wink. His gaze moved over me, and he wrinkled his nose. "Gotta go," he growled to whoever was on the phone.

Grabbing a water from the kitchen, I joined the two at Fab's desk, pulling a chair into the corner so I could observe both of them at the same time.

"Let me guess: I'm the last to know what this job is about. Hmm..." I tapped my cheek. "It has something to do with one of your crazy supposed relatives."

"I sort of like you. But that could change." Gunz screwed his nose up. His eyebrows might have shot up if he'd had any. I suspected they'd been waxed and were afraid to grow back. "Try not to screw up my growing affection with sarcasm."

"Sounds swell." If I hadn't been sitting, I'd have punctuated that with a bow.

"All I know is that we're boosting a car." Fab sliced her finger across her neck, cutting off my "hell no" response.

Gunz retrieved some keys from his pocket, affixing his smarmy smile in place as he bent forward to hand them to Fab. "It's all legal. I'm surprised your backup's hair didn't catch fire at your description."

I shot Fab a "hurry up with the details" glare, and was about thirty second from getting up and hauling out the door, taking my ride, and going home. That would annoy her, since she liked to drive it and refused to buy an SUV of her own. *Why,* she'd responded when I asked why she didn't just get one, *when you have one?*

"My Aunt Marsha has a friend," Gunz said.

"Who's a friend of a cousin's sister-in-law, three times removed," I mumbled.

"As I was saying..." Gunz blew out a huff of

air. One would think he struggled to be patient. "Her friend, Peg Landry, has a son…"

Rhymes with peg leg, sort of. I was certain I could remember that word association.

"…who recently turned eighteen and demanded a car for his birthday. He didn't get one. He'd threatened to steal hers and followed up on that threat a couple of days ago. My suggestion of kicking his butt to the next county was blown off. Peg thought it was unnecessarily harsh for Sonny Boy."

"We're retrieving the car? Why not the mother?" Fab asked.

That told me that, once again, she'd accepted a job without getting the particulars. "My guess—" I waved my hand. "—Mommy doesn't have the guts for a showdown with her sainted son."

Gunz ignored me, instead holding up his phone. "I'm texting you the address. It's Peg's idea that the car be picked up without her son's knowledge. She says she'll store it in her garage and her son will learn his lesson when he has to confess to her that it was stolen."

I couldn't imagine doing that to my own mother. One thing for certain: she would've killed me. "So Pegleg…" I ignored Fab's snicker, and there was that bunched skin on Gunz's forehead again. "…thinks her spoiled brat, which is a kind assessment, is going to learn a lesson? When prodigal son finds out he's been had and the car is in the garage, game on for another round of hide and go fetch."

"Listen up," Gunz grouched. "Pick up the car ASAP so Aunt Marsha will stop burning up my phone. She's a favorite, and I want to keep her happy."

"Since I do most of your jobs without grumbling, I'm hoping you'll agree to do me a favor in the same spirit," I said. Not waiting for agreement, I told him about the murder. "If you could hit up your multitude of sources and get back to me with the who and the what... and how would also be good, I'd be appreciative."

"I'll get right on it and expect the same from you."

"We're on it." I stood. "I'm going to change clothes." And shower, but he didn't need to know that. "Just so you know, you're going to need to feed me before we go get this car," I told Fab, then crossed to the bathroom, which was the size of a small apartment, with a shower that could hold a dozen of one's closest friends. It had been Fab's idea to allot me space in the walk-in closet, which now held changes of clothing for both of us. I couldn't deny that it'd come in handy at times.

* * *

After grumbling and reminding Fab that I was ravenous, I rigged a coin toss and chose mini tacos on the beach, bought from the only roach coach the two of us would eat off, as we knew the owners and that they didn't cut corners when it came to cleanliness. We claimed one of the picnic tables overlooking the water and watched the surf as we ate.

"How's married life?" Fab asked.

"Same old." A sigh escaped despite my best efforts. "The doctor said recovery from head trauma takes time and was vague about exactly how long it would take before all the memories returned. It would help if I could go to these appointments and hear firsthand, but Creole wants to manage his healthcare on his own. Doing otherwise, he says, makes him feel dependent. I did ask if he would feel the same way if it were me with the partial amnesia. Surprisingly and without hesitation, he said yes. There are times when it feels like we're complete strangers and we're getting to know one another again."

"When we're out to dinner or at a family get-together, Creole's more outgoing and funny than before," Fab said. "It's a nice change."

"It's good to see him interacting so easily with friends and family."

"You know you can tell me anything."

"I do, and I'll admit it's not easy." At home and when it was just the two of us, we were polite. If I only knew what to do for him, I wouldn't think twice. I hadn't shared my feelings of extreme guilt about how everything had played out with anyone, and the last thing I was going to do was complain about how long his recovery was taking, so I changed the subject. "You have a plan for retrieving this car?"

"Ask me when we get there."

I groaned and gathered the trash, putting it in the nearest bin, then followed Fab back to the SUV.

Chapter Three

The upside to this job was that we didn't have to leave the Keys and it was just a few miles south of the Cove. Fab turned off the highway onto a sand-and-gravel road with a paved strip down the middle barely wide enough for one car. She slowed at the address, giving it a once-over before doing her usual trek up and down the block, turning around and parking across from the house on stilts. The navy SUV parked in plain sight under the house matched the picture that Gunz had texted, as did the license plate number. A pair of motorcycles were parked alongside it.

"If my son had the audacity to hold my car for ransom and I knew where it was, I'd have collected it already," I said.

"Then put a bullet in his butt?"

"I'm fairly certain that's not in the updated parenting handbook, but I'd be fine with it." I checked out the rest of the block, and there wasn't anyone hanging around.

"Everything looks quiet." Fab hung over the steering wheel, checking out the house.

"Since you always get the fun jobs, I vote that I

get this one." I opened the door, grabbing the keys for the SUV from the cup holder. "I'll follow you back to Pegleg's. Try not to leave me in your exhaust fumes so I don't get lost." I made a sad face. "You'd have a hard time explaining why I left the car in a field somewhere and hitched a ride home."

"You're not funny."

"Not even a little?" I laughed and closed the door, then crossed the street.

Fab gunned the engine.

As I was about to stick the key in the lock on the driver's side, two barely twenty-something guys burst out of the house. In a blink, they both brandished guns. "Step back or you're dead," one shouted as he made his way around the car.

I heard the squeal of tires and turned in time to see Fab fishtail the Hummer, managing to keep control of it and bring it a stop on the bumper of the SUV. The second guy shot out one of the Hummer's front tires and then the other. He moved to the passenger side and pointed his weapon through the windshield. "Get out," he yelled. The one who had his weapon trained on me lowered it and took out his phone.

Fab jumped out of the Hummer and yelled, "We're here to recover the SUV."

The man waved his gun around in response.

I noticed that, like me, Fab didn't reach for her weapon. She'd most likely come to the same conclusion I did—that it would set off an exchange of bullets.

"You might want to put that away before you hurt someone," I said, pocketing the keys before moving away from the car. "It won't go well for you."

The first one got off his phone and leveled his gun at me again. "Move and I'll shoot." He turned to his friend, his gun moving around erratically. "The cops are on their way."

Great, no firearms experience. "Nick Landry? Peg's son?" I asked. Thankfully, I'd read the text on the drive over and knew his name. From the look of surprise on his face, I'd guessed right. "Your mother hired us to pick up her SUV. She took your threat not to return it seriously."

"Don't believe us? Call her," Fab said. The woman was the picture of calm, but murder radiated from her blue orbs.

"You're an f-ing liar," Nick spit.

"It's easily cleared up with a phone call." I flicked my hand at his shirt pocket, where he'd stuffed his cell. "If I produce the keys, would that convince you?"

"We're not going to tell the two of you again. Don't move," the guy guarding Fab threatened.

"I'd like to check on my friend and make sure she's okay," Fab said.

"You can see from where you're standing that she's not dead. Yet."

My guess was that, in addition to shooting hate darts at the little bastard, Fab was arguing with herself about why she hadn't shot him already.

Apparently growing bored guarding me, Nick walked over to the driver's side of the Hummer and jerked on the handle. Locked. "Open the damn door," he screamed.

I bit my lip to keep from laughing, sharing my amusement with Fab. "Are you going to call your mother and get this straightened out?" I asked. I had a clear shot at his butt cheeks and was about to take it.

To my surprise, he pulled his phone out, turned his back, and made a call. I didn't have to hear the conversation to know that he was fighting with someone as his voice rose, and the madder he got, the more the expletives rolled off his tongue. He ended the call with another string of curse words and shoved his phone back in his pocket. "My mom doesn't know squat about your lies." Both guys reholstered their weapons as two cop cars blew up the street and interrupted the staredown we had going.

Kevin got out of the first car, and another officer I didn't recognize out of the second. The two deputies split up. Kevin sauntered over to Fab and motioned to me to join them. The other cop signaled the guys to meet him on the opposite side of the driveway.

"Not many people I know end up at two crime scenes in one day. Hope you're not planning on sneaking off again." Kevin smirked at the two of us. "You were caught boosting a car?"

Fab told him about the job. When she mentioned Gunz, Kevin looked like he'd stepped in something that smelled bad. I took the car keys out of my pocket and held them out to support our story.

"You two were hired by Theodore Gunzelman, a known criminal, for this job. And you took it?" Kevin snorted in disgust.

"People change," I said. "Gunz has reformed and is now an upstanding citizen."

"Pigs fly, too," Kevin said.

"All you have to do is ask the mother, Peg Landry; she can validate our story," Fab said.

Just then another car whizzed up the street and slammed on the brakes in front of the house. A woman got out and ran to Nick's side. It was a no-brainer that she was the mother in question, as she and her son clearly shared DNA. The second cop drew her away from the guys and questioned her. When he was done, he motioned Kevin over.

"Try not to run off." Kevin slowed, going by the SUV in question, inspecting the exterior and glancing briefly inside.

"You better be okay," I snapped at Fab and checked her over from head to toe.

"I'm fine. What about you?" Fab eyed me the same as I had her. "What do you suppose is going on? This should have been a simple job, with us already on our way."

"Okay… guessing… Nick and his friend must have seen us approach and thought they were stopping car thieves. Until mom coughs up her involvement, we need to at least show some patience."

"You don't know how badly I wanted to shoot them both," Fab growled. "My finger actually itched."

"One look at your face, and I knew that. If only there'd been someone I could've made a small wager with, I could have made some money." That got a small smile out of her.

"If you ever make money off me on one of your ridiculous bets, you owe me lunch."

"Some place really cool, I promise."

Fab groaned. "I hate to interrupt our bonding moment, but Kevin's headed back our way and he's wearing his arrogant dick face."

I stepped closer to Fab and turned to Kevin.

"You're both under arrest," Kevin barked. "Hands in the air. Using one hand, put your weapon on the ground."

Our expressions mirrored each other. He'd lost his mind.

"What's going on?" I asked.

"The mother didn't corroborate your story. You're being booked for grand theft auto. And before you go on about your innocence, it's the district attorney's job to sort it out."

"You know damn well that we're not car thieves," Fab snapped, struggling to control her frustration. "Why would we steal her SUV when any one of our cars is better than hers?"

"Did you call Gunz?" I asked.

"No one would take his word for anything," Kevin snapped. "Now turn around and do what you were told."

I laid my Glock on the ground and put my hands behind my back, making eye contact with Pegleg and yelling, "I'm going to prove that you lied to the cops and then sue those ugly shoes right off your feet."

Kevin cuffed us both, walked us over to his car, and put us in the back.

"This is a first. We get to ride together," Fab said.

"Except that when we get to the big house, we'll be separated."

"You'll be proud—I've worked up a plan," Fab said. "We both get a phone call. I'm calling Gunz. You use yours to call Tank and tell him that his big ass is needed pronto. He can double his fee if he keeps us out of jail."

Tank—AKA Patrick Cannon, but only in the courtroom—was a criminal defense lawyer that Fab had met behind bars on one of our visitation jaunts to the local jail. He'd said it was mistaken identity, and it turned out he wasn't full of it.

I didn't ask which of the men in question would have the honor of calling our husbands with the news. I turned when Fab did and watched as Kevin approached Peg again and talked to her before turning to her son. Minutes later, he returned and got behind the wheel.

"What about the Hummer?" I asked.

"Tow truck is on its way." Kevin turned and faced me. "Nothing personal. Just doing my job."

I didn't trust myself to say anything and instead turned away and looked out the side window, staring at the road as we headed to the station. We were booked and fingerprinted and, before being led to a cell, got to stand in line to make a phone call. There was only one person ahead of us. Tank accepted the collect call and assured me that he was on the way and not to worry. I asked him to call the husbands. I had no worries about Gunz—he wouldn't let Fab twist.

It seemed like forever, but it was only a couple of hours later when the door to my cell opened and a guard motioned me forward and escorted me to a conference room. It didn't surprise me to see Tank already seated, with Fab on the other side of the table. I sat down next to Fab and pulled her against my side in a quick hug.

"I want to hear both your versions of events, not that I expect them to be dramatically different. Then we'll sit here until we get kicked out," Tank said. "Bail was set at twenty-five thousand. Gunz didn't flinch at coming up with the fifty, and it's being posted now."

Fab imparted the facts of the job, starting with the morning meeting with Gunz. When she was done, I said, "I don't have anything to add.

Except that when this is behind us, I'm suing Peg Landry for lying."

"Be interesting to know why she refused to admit that she contacted Gunz for help," Tank said. "The man comes with a certain reputation. He's not one to screw; not if you want to live to talk about it. I do know that the days of someone disappearing are behind him, but still…"

"Gunz needs to hire a PR firm to get the word out," I said with a shake of my head.

"Did you get ahold of our husbands and spread the news?" Fab asked.

Tank hesitated. I wondered if Fab noticed. "They both know, and I promised I'd update them with any new information and let them know when you're released." More hesitation. "They were both relieved that neither of you were shot or suffered any other bodily harm."

There was a knock on the door as it opened; our stalling tactics were at an end, and we were led back to our cells.

The wait felt interminable, but the clock on the wall said that it had only been a few hours when we were both released right after shift change. When I walked into the reception area, Fab was sitting in one of the chairs next to Gunz. I pasted on a smile and hoped I didn't look deranged.

"Let's get out of here." Gunz stood and led us out to the parking lot, where Creole and Didier leaned against Didier's Mercedes. Didier closed the distance between him and Fab and put his arm around her, speaking to her in French.

Creole walked over and stood next to me but didn't say anything. I looked up at him, not sure what to say, and like him, couldn't come up with anything.

Gunz cleared his throat and said, "I wanted to ask you what the hell went down. But not inside the station."

Fab ran down the fourth or fifth retelling of events—could be more, but always the same account. I nodded in agreement.

"I'm not sure what went south." Gunz could barely contain his annoyance. "I don't know why Peg Landry lied, but I will get to the bottom of it and get all the charges against you dropped."

I believed him but wanted more. "Can you get the arrest expunged from our records?"

"I'll look into it, and if I can make it happen, I will," Gunz assured me. "I can't take back what you've already gone through, but I'll make the rest right, starting with having the Hummer returned in working order."

"It's in police impound. You'll need me to spring it, and I'm available anytime," I said.

"We'll talk tomorrow." Gunz waved and left.

"Today sucked," I said with a half-smile that no one responded to. "But that's the first of Fab's clients that gave a flip what happened to us, and we weren't left to fend for ourselves."

More silence. Fab gave me a weak smile.

The four of us climbed into the Mercedes, and

it was a quiet ride back to the compound. Didier dropped Creole and me off at our house, and before they sped off, Fab and I reassured each other that we'd talk in the morning.

It hadn't escaped my notice that Creole had barely said two words, and rather than get into a discussion I didn't care to have, I went inside and took a long shower. When I came out, he'd gone for a walk on the beach. I went to bed.

Chapter Four

Early the next morning, I sat across the island from Creole, frostbite in the air despite what was the start of a humid, sunshiny day. We hadn't said more than a handful of words since the night before. In our entire relationship, we'd never done the silent treatment thing, but we were making up for it now. My phone rang, and I glanced down at the screen before answering, "*Bonjour.* I hope you noticed I got it right this time." I consistently butchered the language for Fab's amusement.

Creole quirked his head in a silent question I didn't answer.

"Gunz called and wants to meet for coffee."

It surprised me that Didier was okay with this meeting after last night's debacle. I'd ask later.

"He's got an update for us," she continued. "I chose the Bakery Café and told him we'd meet him in a half-hour."

I brought my coffee cup to my lips and stared over the rim at Creole, not wanting to ask Fab my next question but needing to know. "Any word on when the Hummer will be sprung?"

"It already was and got towed for new tires.

Right after that, it's getting detailed; Gunz knows you're a stickler for a clean car."

I laughed at that one. It was Fab who couldn't drive anything with a speck of dust on it. "Without my signature?"

"Gunz knows everyone," Fab reminded me. "He expedited the release, paid the fines, and I told him no retreads."

I didn't tell her that I'd done that once back in the day. The tire exploded and never again. I'd have to thank Gunz, as I hated to deal with car repairs of any kind. "When you get here, call or lay on the horn." We hung up. I glanced down at my empty coffee mug and wished for something stronger. I looked up at Creole. "Do you want to come along so you can hear firsthand what Gunz has to say?"

"I've got a meeting," he said shortly.

I took a breath, fortifying myself to step into what felt like the lion's den. "And you're mad because…?"

"Aren't you tired of going on jobs where you get shot at? Chased?" His mouth drew into a tight line, his blue eyes thin slits. "Where generally everything that can go wrong does?"

"Yesterday was supposed to be a simple recovery job." That explanation didn't soften him a bit. "I certainly didn't expect the mother to lie when confronted by law enforcement."

"You always have one excuse or another for these cases going south." Creole stood, rinsed his cup, and put it in the dishwasher. "You're not going to enjoy prison life, and that's where you may end up this time."

"Will you at least come visit?"

My attempt at humor nose-dived. He rolled his eyes and walked into the living room, throwing a couple of files into his briefcase.

I lifted my empty cup to my lips and pretended to drink. Our relationship had changed, and I didn't like it and had no clue how to turn it around. Complaining would make me feel like the worst wife ever, and I'd had enough of those feelings of late.

"I'll see you later." He brushed past me and banged out the door.

Another thing that had changed: there were no more kisses when we parted company... or any other time.

A horn blared from out in front. I grabbed my purse and went out to meet Fab.

* * *

On the ride over to the Bakery Café, Fab said, "Tank called. He wants us to keep a low profile until the case is straightened out and we're no longer headed for a long stint in jail." She wrinkled her nose.

I shared her silent sentiment—jail was bad enough without going in for something you didn't do. Thankfully, coffee at the Bakery Café would qualify as a safe activity.

Fab found a parking space in front of our favorite table on the sidewalk—the perfect location for people watching should any drama break out. My hand was on the door handle when Fab nudged me and pointed to where Mother and Spoon were sitting on the patio. "We can't ignore them. I say we flip to see who tells them about being jailbirds." She flipped an imaginary coin in the air.

I slapped her hand down. "Let Gunz be the bearer of the news."

My father died when I was a pre-teen, and Mother raised me and my brother alone. I'm certain she thought she'd never survive, but she was tougher than she looked and never let her two kids boss her around, no matter how charming we could be... sometimes. Several years ago, she met her boy toy, Jimmy Spoon, who swept her off her feet. Okay, he was only ten years younger, but it was still fun to tease her about. They'd wed and were living happily ever after.

My brother, Brad, appeared from the back of the restaurant and snagged a chair, dragging it over. Before sitting, he leaned down and kissed Mother's cheek. She brushed his sun-bleached hair back from his face, and the two laughed.

Fab and I got out and crossed the sidewalk. Fab flagged down the busboy, and in a minute, two tables were pushed together and several more chairs added. She tipped the guy, who looked down and shot her a big grin. She turned toward where Mother sat and whistled... loudly. Heads turned, including those of Mother, Spoon, and Brad. "Over here," she yelled and waved.

"I don't even know you." I turned away and grabbed a chair, not making eye contact with anyone.

"Fabiana." Mother's tone held a note of censure but more humor.

I'd never get off so easy.

Everyone exchanged kisses and sat down.

"Here," I said to Brad and pointed to the chair next to me. "The one you're about to plunk your behind in is reserved."

"For who?" Brad raised his brows.

"Big surprise." I winked. "One hint: amigo of Fab's, so he needs to sit next to her."

The server came over and took our drink order. Coffee all around.

"Why aren't you at the office?" I asked Brad, remembering Creole's flight out of the house for a meeting.

Creole, Didier, and Brad were the managing partners of an extended-family-owned business and ran the day-to-day operations of the real estate holdings with little interference from anyone else.

"I dropped Mila at school and stopped by for coffee." Brad's eyes twinkled with amusement. "I'm glad I did."

Several years ago, to Brad's shock and surprise, he found out that he had a four-year-old daughter languishing in foster care. Her now-deceased mother was a nutcase. He'd hired a legal eagle who expedited the paperwork, got custody, and she came to live with him. He'd taken to fatherhood in an instant, and Mila came out of her shell thanks to all the love lavished on her.

The server came back with a tray of coffee. I licked my lips when I saw that he hadn't forgotten my extra whipped cream.

"This is a nice surprise," Mother cooed and smiled at each of us.

"Yes indeedy." I winked at her.

"Where are Creole and Didier?" Spoon asked, staring first at me, and then Fab.

I passed on the question and took a drink of coffee.

"Some people keep regular office hours." Fab eyed Brad, and when he frowned at her, she grinned.

Gunz trundled up and looked around in confusion. "Do you want to reschedule?"

"Have a seat," I said with a slight smile and flourished my hand towards the chair next to Fab. "Fab and I flipped… Well, not exactly, but the details aren't important. The gist is that it was decided that you can be the bearer of the fun news."

Gunz bent over my mother's hand and kissed

it, the sun shining off his bald head. "You look ravishing, Mrs. Spoon."

Spoon growled, and Gunz grinned. He winked at Fab and sat down.

"What about me?" I stuck my hand out.

He blew on it. "You're still growing on me."

Like fungus or something—I didn't ask. "So, loving family…" I said, and they groaned. "Fab and I agreed to do a job for…" I pointed to Gunz. "Your turn. You can take it from here."

"Cut to the chase," Fab told Gunz.

"Not sure what you want me to say." He shot me a shifty smile and leaned back, lacing his fingers against his massive chest, having caught on that I was attempting to hang him out to dry.

All eyes now turned to me.

Fab smirked.

"Things went… awry," I said. What an understatement. "Girlfriend and I got arrested for grand theft auto, booked, and bailed out. Gunz's presence at this soiree is because he's here with an update. How did I do?"

Mother squealed.

"Almost forgot the best part," I continued. "It's a client of Gunz's that set us up to do prison time. Now that I've started, take it away." I flourished my hand dramatically at Gunz, who, from the look on his face, wished he could make me disappear. The man could, but then things would get messy and he'd also disappear. I wasn't without friends.

Mother gasped. Spoon, who also had an intimidating presence, had smoke coming out his ears. Brad took it all in, leaning back in his chair, his mouth set in a grim line. It wasn't often my family was speechless.

Gunz gave them the backstory — succinctly and sucking out every bit of drama. "I met with Peg Landry early this morning and did most of the talking. Told her that she needed to clean up this mess and do it today."

"Is she still alive?" I asked.

"I really did want to wring her neck but managed to restrain myself." Gunz grinned. "Where was I?" He rubbed his chin, amusing himself as the rest of us stared.

"I can help you out," I said. "Is Peg going to recant her lies and fess up that she hired you to have the car picked up?"

"Peg's story is that she's protecting her son," Gunz said. "She didn't want the cops to find out that he stole the car to begin with and she paid to have it retrieved to teach him a lesson."

I noticed that he didn't answer the question. I wanted to take a quick poll as to how many of the others noticed the same thing.

"Peg did confess all to her son in the driveway. He guilted her into keeping quiet, convincing her that he'd be the one to end up in jail." Gunz sighed.

"To sum it up, Peg lies to the cops and files a bogus police report to protect her son, who stole the car to begin with, which I'm sure is a minor detail… to her anyway," Fab said.

"This could've been all straightened out with a simple explanation, and I highly doubt that the cops would have gotten involved in a family matter if she didn't press charges," I snapped.

"Did you point out to this Peg woman that she's now the one looking at jail time?" Spoon demanded.

"I gave Peg twenty-four hours to retract her story," Gunz reassured us.

"And if she doesn't? Then what?" Brad followed that up by mumbling what I was certain was an expletive.

"You and I both know that unless she admits that she lied, the district attorney could drag this case out for however long they feel inclined," I hissed at Gunz. "Especially if they think we're getting away with a crime."

"I agree with Madison," Spoon said. "Sounds to me like Peg needs a lawyer."

Fab turned to Gunz. "Peg needs to come clean. Don't just ship her off somewhere and think that will solve the problem—not showing up to testify banking on the case getting dismissed is weaselly. You have to know that we could still end up in jail."

"I give you my word that I'll straighten everything out." Gunz's phone rang. He looked relieved to have an excuse to beat it. "I'll be in touch." He stood. "Your Hummer will be delivered to your house in a couple of hours." He got up and practically ran back to his car. For a large man, he could hustle.

Once Gunz's Escalade roared away, Mother asked, "Are you two okay?" She gave us both a once-over. "This has been an eventful morning."

"Dude just hightailed it out of here without an update on the murder case," I said with a sneaky smile.

Mother shrieked.

Spoon groaned. "This ought to be good."

"He doesn't have one yet, but he's hoping to have something by tomorrow," Fab said.

"You're up." I smiled at Fab. "I expect you to put your flourish on the retelling."

"Your daughter is so mean." Fab faux pouted. "I'm assuming that you also want me to relay all the grisly details?" I nodded.

Brad laughed. "You're not serious."

"Sadly, it was an unfortunate incident and one that Fab can't wait to tell you about. If you ask nicely, she'll share her pictures of the corpse." I made a choking noise.

Mother's eyes flew to Fab. "Honey, that's so…"

"Ghoulish is the word you're looking for, Mother."

Fab relayed the events to her rapt audience.

"I vote that we get together for coffee more often." Brad reached out and picked up Fab's phone, flicking through her pictures.

It surprised me that she didn't stab him with a fork.

"Gross." Brad made a strangled noise. "Remind me that I don't need to see pictures of dead people in the future."

Chapter Five

It was late afternoon when the door banged open. Creole had gotten home early. He mumbled a greeting and hit the shower, changing into swim trunks.

"How was your day?" I asked as he passed me on his way to the kitchen, grabbing a beer out of the refrigerator.

He took so long to answer, I figured he planned to ignore me altogether. He paused going by the couch, where I was curled up, laptop on my lap, my cats, Jazz and Snow, asleep at my side. They didn't acknowledge his presence, especially since they didn't smell food.

"Got a headache." He headed out to the patio, pausing at the open door when my phone started to ring.

I glanced at the screen, hoping Fab didn't have some last-minute job.

"I thought the four of us could ride over to Jake's together tonight," Fab said when I answered.

"I've got no clue what you're talking about."

"The Chief invited us to dinner," Fab said, as though I already knew.

Chief Harder was Creole's old boss from back when they both worked for the Miami Police Department. He'd long ago become a friend, and we'd traded favors more than a few times. He'd only recently retired.

"That's swell, except I didn't get an invitation," I said. "By all means, have a good time at my bar—run a tab and sign my name."

"Hmm…" she said, followed by a long silence. "I told the Chief that I'd invite you, so you have to show up or it makes me look bad."

"Can't have that, now can we?" I imagined her annoyance and almost laughed. "I can call Jake's and give them a heads up if you know how many are on the invite list."

"The Chief has that covered, since he's friends with Cook. What I wouldn't give to eavesdrop on one of their conversations, see what those two have in common." Fab laughed. "The Chief mentioned that Cook has something special in mind."

I groaned. "Ever since he threatened goat burgers, I don't trust him. If I were you, I'd wait until everyone else has had a bite before taking one."

"So we're on?" Fab sounded pleased. "Didier and I will pick the two of you up."

"I can't give you a definitive answer since I haven't talked to Creole yet." I looked into Creole's frosty blue eyes; he raised his brows as he took a long pull on his beer. "I'm thinking it would be better if we meet you there." I hung up and told Creole, "We've been invited to dinner," and relayed the details of the call. His body language said it all: *no way*. Not that it surprised me. I felt a stab of guilt and let it go.

"Wonder what the Chief wants?" The suspicion in Creole's voice surprised me.

"It'll be fun to get together with friends."

"Maybe next time. My head's killing me." Creole turned and paused. "You go and have fun," he said over his shoulder. "No need to sit here and watch me sleep." He went out to the deck, stretching out on a chaise.

I got up and showered and changed into a short, red, spaghetti-strap sundress, pairing it with a pair of nude heels that I'd boosted from Mother. It was about time for her to come over and go through my closet to gather up her shoes. I shoved my wild red mane into a hair clip and gave myself a thumbs up in the mirror. Then I grabbed my purse and headed to the patio door. "Call if you need anything."

Creole responded with a grunt.

It was a short drive to Jake's. I'd inherited half the bar from my aunt and bought the other half from its namesake, who had thugs chasing him for money he owed. It was rumored that they planned to collect and then kill him, so he skipped town. Since I took over and made more than a few changes, Jake's had garnered a number of "best dive bar" awards, which had everything to do with serving the best Mexican food around.

The tiki-shaped building sat at the rear of the property on the short block I owned. I pulled into the parking lot and slowed. There was no action at Fab's lighthouse, which she'd acquired as payment for a job. I hadn't asked if cash had been one of the options when it appeared one day. Currently, Gunz was using it for office space but had informed her he'd be looking for a swankier address.

The old fifties gas station, which I loved, had been spit-shined and turned into an antiques garden store — Junker's. Another favorite of mine. The place was only jumping when a truck pulled up to offload or load up finds.

I cut around the back of the bar, parked at the kitchen entrance, and went through the door, almost smacking into Cook. The older man ran his domain with efficiency and hired mostly relatives. I waved at his two nephews, who were putting out orders.

"Come to sample the menu?" Cook asked in a deceptively polite tone. He didn't attempt to hide his ear-to-ear smirk.

I made a choking noise. "I'll wait until everyone else has had a bite. And then, if no one retches or dies, I'll consider it."

He unleashed a loud and hearty laugh. "I put together a platter, so there will be something for everyone."

"As long as there's leftovers for me to take home for breakfast." No one in the Westin family turned up their nose at leftovers.

"I've got you covered."

I waved and continued down the hall to the bar. The Chief was going to be happy—his favorite bartender was on tonight.

Kelpie, our pink-haired bartender, turned and caught sight of my approach. "Bossaroo," she yelled over the jukebox, waving. The barstools were filled with her regulars tonight, and they gave me a brief glance. A handful of people dotted the rest of the room, and one of the dart boards and the pool table were in use.

It was impolite to stare, but Kelpie made it darn difficult. Tonight, she wore a lime-green bathing suit top that barely corralled her enormous chest. "Double G's," she'd whispered once. If she could get one or both to take a tumble, her tips would go through the roof. Knowing her avaricious mind, she was working on how to make that happen and come off totally innocent. She'd finished off her outfit with a flirty black skirt that barely covered her lower cheeks, a pair of gossamer wings attached to her back, and a small star wand sticking out of the messy bun at the nape of her neck. The woman paired most of her outfits with boots, and I knelt on one of the stools and peered over the countertop to look—hot-pink motorcycle boots.

"I'll have a margarita." My inner voice said, *Sip slow. You're driving.*

"Margarita boy," Kelpie yelled.

Now what? Whatever it was, Kelpie was looking smirky-proud of herself. I was afraid to look around but sucked up the courage and turned.

Bouff, our closing bartender, came around the far side of the bar—shirtless. I did a double take at the plastic bra cups he'd strapped on. Plastic tubing hung from the nipple area, and he was wearing a backpack of green liquid.

I stared, open-mouthed. "What the hell?" It was my intention to close the space between me and him, but a woman barreled between us, shoving me out of the way, and affixed her mouth to his chest. With one hand, she waved money in his face, which he took and pocketed, shooting me a grin.

Kelpie reached up and yanked the rope on a large ship's bell.

"What?" I screeched.

She frowned.

When was the bell installed? And why? Questions I didn't ask, as I was too busy gawking at the six-foot, broad-chested man, who moved with confidence on his prosthetic leg.

Someone kissed me on the shoulder from behind. "Really, *cherie*, bad words?"

I turned and smiled at Didier. "Your wife catches you kissing women's shoulders, and she'll probably kill… me. That would be sad. You'd both miss me."

Didier laughed and looked around. "Where's Creole?"

"He's not feeling well."

Didier frowned. "I suggested that he change doctors, and he said he'd think about it. I passed along the names of two neurologists that came highly recommended, both expert at dealing with head injuries."

"That's sweet of you." I'd had the same conversation with Creole, who'd told me adamantly that he liked the doctor he had. "Where's your wife?"

"Fab headed to the kitchen."

"Margarita hour is over," Bouff yelled and rang the bell. He turned toward Kelpie and pointed to his backpack, which I assumed meant it was empty.

"What are you doing?" I'd seen plenty since I moved to the Keys and wasn't often shocked. At that moment, however, I had to keep my mouth from dropping open again. "You're a decorated war veteran—a real one, not pretend like some of the men in town—and you're prancing around like you've lost your mind."

"Calm your frizz." Bouff grinned. "Got that one from Kelpie."

"Never say that to a woman with humidity issues." I frowned at his sun-bleached mop and resisted the urge to brush at my own hair.

"Bossaroo doesn't like hair jokes," Kelpie yelled from behind the bar.

I was impressed with her eavesdropping skills.

"It was suggested that if I got a little giddy-up going, my tips would go up." Bouff ignored my eyeroll. "Why do I have to be the normal one? Besides, the proof is in the margaritas. The women are lining up for this new gig. You're the one who told me I should get a pair... well, here they are." He waved his hand across his chest.

"*Cherie?*" Didier scowled down at me, but he couldn't pull off the stern look with his lips quirking on the sides.

My cheeks burned. "It was a joke."

"One of the customers told me I was a flat-out bore." Bouff faux-frowned.

"You've been led down the path of..." I couldn't come up with anything. "If Kelpie is your competition, be prepared to up your game with even more outrageous antics."

Doodad — AKA the manager, Charles Wingate III — hustled around the end of the bar in the same getup that Bouff was now removing, leaving him bare-chested and the two women at the bar drooling.

"Dude, how did you run out before me?" Doodad sniffed and pointed to his plastic breasts. "I've got abs."

I squeezed my eyes shut and took a breath. Bouff ran marathons. Doodad had never once mentioned that he exercised, and I hadn't asked.

Doodad stabbed his finger in my direction. "I saw that."

"Happy you moseyed on in," Bouff cut in. "I was planning to call you; thought we could have a talk."

"Come out to the patio." I'd known this chat was coming — thanks for letting me work here, but I quit.

Bouff, short for Wilbur Bouffant, had taken the job to line up some street snitches on a big case he was working on with the Chief, but that was now over. Knowing there was time before the Chief showed up, I figured we might as well use those few minutes and get it over with.

I walked out onto the deck, flipped on the overhead lights and ceiling fans, and took a seat. "Is this a private conversation?"

"What's private in this joint?" Bouff chuckled.

I beckoned to Doodad, who stood in the doorway, Didier behind him.

"Sit your tuchus down and explain to me how you lost your mind since the last time I was here." I pointed to the empty chairs across from me. "Granted, I've been a bit lax of late, but you could've called and warned me that you left your common sense somewhere and forgot to go retrieve it."

Kelpie burst through the doorway. "Hey, hottie." All the men looked at her. She pointed to Didier and gave him a megawatt smile. "Drinks are ready." She set down the tray and served everyone. "I brought you guys water, since you're still on the clock." She banged the door closed on the way out.

"Before you get worked up and your hair stands on end, this new idea of ours is only one night a week," Doodad said, patting down his own hair, which was standing on end. "Every night and it would go stale."

"All I ask is that you make sure this stunt of yours is legal," I said. "Any other tricks up your sleeve?"

Doodad stuck his nose in his arm pit. "There's a couple. But I'm thinking we shouldn't spring them on you all at once. Besides, they're not my ideas, and I don't want to be getting the finger of blame."

"Maybe we should schedule a meeting, because you know how much I like those," I said.

Didier smirked.

"Not to be rude…" I said.

"But?" Doodad raised an eyebrow. "I already know that Bouff wants to speak to you, and I know what it's about. I'm thinking I should stick around to insert my two cents, since it's one of my better ideas."

"What's going on?" Fab said from the doorway, coming over to slip into a seat next to Didier. "I better not have missed anything."

"Fab and I are going to go inside and have our drinks." Didier started to stand, and Fab tugged him back down.

Fab humphed. "We can't eavesdrop from in there."

"Yeah, Didier," I teased. He wasn't amused.

"Besides, secondhand information is tedious." Bouff winked at Fab.

"Aren't you quitting?" Fab asked.

"Fabiana…" Didier said something in French that had her laughing up at him.

"I'm not quitting," Bouff said with an exasperated sigh. "I'd like to keep the job. Keeps me out and hobnobbing with the locals, and that's a good thing, if you get my drift. I know you only hired me as a favor to the Chief, but I was hoping you'd keep me on because I've done a decent job of keeping most of the locals happy."

"The Chief was how you got your foot in the door." I smiled at him. "You were hired because you assured me that you could kick ass with a prosthetic leg, and you're welcome to stay until you can't stand it another minute. Look at you— you've discouraged fight-pickers, the cops haven't shown up recently, and the women… 'drool-worthy' is what I've heard. I have a feeling that 'plastic boob night' is going to be standing room only until the aforementioned cops show up. Just know we've got a bail bondsman on speed dial."

"Phew." Doodad wiped his brow. "That saves me from interviewing new people, which is a total pain in the... you know." He pointed to his backside.

I laughed and was disgusted with myself. "Working here isn't going to interfere with investigating bad guys, is it?"

"So far, it's worked out good. I've already connected with a couple of good sources." Bouff grinned.

"Since I was supportive of hiring you, I'm assuming that when I need information, you'll fork it over without getting all sissy?" Fab asked.

I covered my mouth to keep from laughing. Sissy! If she were a man, she'd be airborne over the balcony and swimming in the murky water below.

Didier whispered furiously in her ear. Did it deter her? No.

Fab shot Bouff a sly smile.

"I got wind of this favor-doing scam you girls have going, and I want in on it," Bouff said.

"Cool, so you owe me one," Fab said.

I shook my head. Amongst our family and friends, we traded favors like currency... only in some cases, more valuable. "Just so you know, the favors come with terms. The biggest one: no whining when it's time to pay up."

Chapter Six

The Chief opened the patio door, drink in hand. If I hadn't been watching, I'd have missed the surprise that flickered across his face, rapidly replaced by a bland expression. He eyed everyone at the table. "Where's Creole?"

"He wasn't feeling well," I said casually.

"Needs a new doctor," the Chief grumped. "I thought he'd have his memory back by now." He took a seat on the other side of the table.

"Didier's got that covered." I smiled at the man.

Doodad stood. "We're having entertainment tonight. Be sure you stick around." He closed the door behind him.

"I'll be going," Bouff said.

"No need." The Chief waved him to sit back down. "You might as well get the details on the new case that came into the office and stay for dinner. The food is on its way out, and you know Cook makes plenty."

The door opened again, and Cook pulled out a cart. One of the guys from the kitchen set two big platters that appeared to hold everything on the menu and then some in the middle of the table.

I slipped out of my chair and grabbed plates and silverware, then opened the door and waved to Kelpie, mouthing *Refills.*

She shot me a thumbs up.

"You've outdone yourself," I said to Cook, who gave me a toothy grin and disappeared through the door.

All talking stopped while we loaded up our plates. Afterward, we engaged in small talk. I wanted to know what was on the agenda but managed to refrain from asking until the dishes were cleared away.

"As you all know, I was offered a partnership in a security business down in Marathon, and I recently bought out the other two partners," the Chief said.

The Chief had told me and Fab that the business had been grossly mismanaged, which they'd kept hidden with a second set of books. He'd delivered the "you or me" speech, and they left without an argument. He'd immediately begun looking for new people to fill key positions. I suspected that since the man was used to calling all the shots and not answering to anyone, total ownership would be more to his liking.

"You decide on a name?" Fab asked.

"Diligence Inc. Once word got out that I was the man in charge, the phones started ringing." The Chief grinned. "One of those calls was from a young woman who's requesting help in locating her missing sister. I came to the conclusion fairly quickly that I needed to add a few women to the team ASAP."

It didn't escape my notice that once he started talking about the new client, he made eye contact with Fab and spoke directly to her. Cool as a cucumber, Fab didn't react to his words one way or the other.

"I'm thinking this would be a good case to see how we work together," the Chief said to Fab. "If it goes well, I'd use you on other cases."

"I was never invited to this meeting," I said, surprising myself by blurting out what I was thinking.

"The invitation included you," Fab insisted.

"The Chief here wants to hire you, since you two get along so well," I said, eyeroll in my tone. "Get it in writing that he won't have you arrested when the two of you irritate each other's last nerve."

Bouff laughed. I flashed him a quick smile.

"I need a licensed private investigator, and to my knowledge, you never got your license," the Chief said, making it sound like it was just business.

"That's true." I gave him a tight smile.

"I might be interested on a case-by-case basis, but only with the understanding that I'd be free to turn you down without any hard feelings," Fab said. "I'm not giving up my business or my clients for any kind of exclusive relationship that wouldn't allow me to pick and choose."

"Everything is negotiable," the Chief said.

"I have my own hard limits on the cases that Fab takes," Didier interjected. "She's not allowed to take cases that endanger her life *in any way*. If that sounds overbearing, it's because I am when it comes to my wife's safety."

I winked at him.

"I also don't do jobs without backup, and that person would be of my own choosing. No offense," Fab said to Bouff.

"None taken." He'd leaned back in his chair at the beginning of the discussion and was all eyes as he watched the exchange.

"You even interested in hearing the details of the job?" the Chief asked, his tone suggesting that he was short on patience.

Fab nodded. "Then we'll know if I'm a good fit or not."

"As I said, my client's sister disappeared. So far, she hasn't been able to get any satisfactory answers from law enforcement, which is the reason she decided to hire a private company that would make it a priority." The Chief finished off his beer. "Before contacting me, she did some investigating of her own, but none of her attempts at locating her sister yielded any clues. As you can imagine, she's out of her mind with worry."

Why not get the news media involved and the

sister's picture circulated? The public had been found to be useful in missing persons cases. I kept that question to myself. "Is there any reason to believe that the woman wandered off of her own volition? Vacation from her life?" She wouldn't be the first to take off and worry loved ones. I hoped it was that, for her sake. Of those who disappeared due to foul play, only a small percentage returned safely.

"The woman described her sister as a free spirit who lives life to the fullest and added that she has enough money to do what she wants," the Chief said.

How much money? That was a red flag. For me, anyway.

"Does this woman have a track record of wandering off and leaving her family to worry about her?" Fab asked. The Chief shook his head. "What do you want me to do?"

"I want you to talk to her friends and associates," the Chief said. "Ask questions where she was last seen, which was partying it up at a casino resort in Ft. Lauderdale."

"Ft. Lauderdale?" Fab's nose went in the air, as though he'd suggested flying to the moon.

"Expenses are covered." The Chief gave her a stern stare.

"I'm honored that you'd think of me for the job. Any job, really," Fab said with a smile. "Maybe not so much if I knew you'd gone through a list of twenty ahead of me."

Bouff laughed.

"But I have to turn down the opportunity."

"You're not going to at least think about it?" the Chief asked indignantly.

"Regardless of what the woman across the table thinks—" Fab pointed to me, though I was certain that everyone at the table knew that since I was the only other woman. "—she's my backup, and I'm not doing a job without her. Since this gig doesn't include her, I decline. She's saved my life a couple of times. And recently. I trust her to always have my back."

"You're ahead of me on that life-saving score," I said.

"We should've kept a tally so one of us could lord it over the other." Fab gave me her most deranged smile.

The Chief turned to me. "I know you have a lot on your plate with Creole's health issues, which is another reason I didn't consider you."

Except I was never in consideration, according to his own words. I kept silent, pasting on a smile.

"You're a nitwit," Fab told the Chief.

Didier sucked in a breath.

"This team—" She flicked her finger between her and me. "—works well together. Sure, I can charm old men, but she can talk to crazy people. This is Florida, and they're on every corner, if you haven't noticed. So, discounting her because that dick Brick—friend of yours, by the way—

wouldn't sign off on her getting a license is short-sighted of you." Brick Famosa had been a long-time client of Fab's, but she got tired of dodging bullets on every case he sent her out on. Not to mention his complete disregard for her safety.

"Plus, here's a really big one that you're overlooking: you and me, we have zero affection for each other. You two actually like one another." She hissed out a sigh. "Thanks, but no thanks."

Suddenly, "Welcome to Jake's" came blaring through a speaker.

Tonight's entertainment had arrived, and just in the nick of time. I stood. "Excuse me." I disappeared back inside the bar before anyone could say anything. I knew everyone thought that I went to check on the band and would be back. They'd be wrong. I waved to Doodad and didn't break stride booking it out the back door.

Chapter Seven

Mid-morning the next day, my phone rang. I slid it out from under Jazz, who lay by my side on the couch, and glanced at the screen, then groaned, knowing it would be problematic news at best.

"You want a murder update?" Mac asked when I answered.

"I can't believe that you have news before Gunz, who has police connections." The woman never ceased to amaze me.

I could hear the sound of someone laying on a car horn, and it took me a minute to realize it was coming from right outside my house and not through Mac's phone. I didn't even have to open the door and stick my head out to know who was making the racket. It was a good thing Fab and I were the only ones who lived on this street. I told Mac, who laughed.

"Should we wait for her to break into your house?" Mac asked.

"I'm not inclined to interrupt her fun, since she's out there having a good time making a nuisance of herself."

"When Fab finds out that you didn't make an effort to share the news firsthand, I'll be finger-pointing your way." Mac chuckled. "The dead chick, Bonnie Maple, croaked from a gunshot that went through her back and out the front. She'd only been dead a few hours when Rude found her, but between the heat and humidity, she decomposed fast. Heard insects were looking for a new home, but I didn't see it for myself, and frankly, I would've passed on a look-see."

"There's something we agree on." The honking had stopped, so I knew the door would fly open any second. "What's her connection to Pastel? If any?"

"Rude's the one that thought Pastel was the one who bit it. Lookalike or some such. I saw a pic of Bonnie when she was still breathing and smiling at the camera, and they had similar features, but not a match by any stretch."

Just as I predicted, the door opened and Fab stormed in. "I know you heard me."

"You're so beyond annoying." I pointed to the chair across from me. "I'm sorry that we were so rudely interrupted," I said to Mac. "What were you saying?" Fab pointed at the phone. "I'm going to put you on speaker."

"I figured."

"Be nice to Mac," I said to Fab. "Okay, where were we?"

"Hold on a second, what did I miss?" Fab yelled.

Mac updated her in a sentence.

"You forgot the part where Bonnie was being

feasted on by bugs," I reminded her.

Fab made a barfing noise.

Mac ignored me and continued. "The cops went door to door, and Pastel was the only one who didn't answer. They were about to leave when she came out dressed for work. When questioned, she claimed not to know Bonnie, although one of the neighbors swore she saw them together. Just so you know, the woman didn't open her flap and report that to the cops." She slurped on something and made a smacking noise. "Another tidbit. Pastel has a boyfriend who's possessive and has a temper. They've had more than a few fights that scared the neighbors and were the reason no one wanted to talk."

"Since you're the Big Kahuna and Rude is new manager on the block, you might want to suggest to Pastel that she move her drama into someone else's building," I said. "I want to maintain the building's reputation as a quiet place to live."

"Why do I get the dirty jobs?" Mac grouched.

"Because you're the boss and you need to practice being bossy."

"I want a title."

"You make up whatever title makes you happy, and I'll get a plaque made for the door." I snapped my fingers at Fab, who was leaning back with her eyes closed, not fooling me for a second. Pretending to nod off was a new, and annoying, trick of hers. "Did Gunz have anything pertinent to add?" I asked, guessing an update from him was her reason for breaking into my house... this time.

"Mac already shared most of what he had — that the recently deceased had been gunned down, been dead for a few hours when found, and oh yeah, no arrests yet." Fab opened one eye, I assumed to make sure I was listening, and closed it again. "The one new tidbit is that the cops chatted with Pastel's beau and plan to have a formal sit-down, as he's been labeled a person of interest since he may have dated or just had sex with the dead chick."

"Where was Dodger while everything went down?" I asked Mac. He was the new security guard I'd hired to make his presence known in exchange for rent reduction. He wasn't on any kind of a schedule, but one could hope that he'd pop up at the first sign of trouble.

"Dodger had a family do to go to. He'll be back tonight. He's going to be annoyed to have missed the excitement."

"The Cottages are his first priority, but Dodger needs to keep an eye peeled for trouble at the apartments until someone is arrested," I said. "Maybe if he makes his burly presence known, that will calm down Pastel and the boyfriend. Does the boyfriend have a name?" Although many of the locals answered to *Hey you*.

"I'll find out and also check on whether he actually lives with Pastel or not," Mac said. "Better yet, farm it out to Rude."

"Before we hang up, is there anything else?" I asked.

"Everything is hunky-dory here," Mac said, and we disconnected.

"What brings you by?" I asked Fab.

"I'm here with the Gunz update I gave you. And it slipped my mind that I promised The Diggers we'd bodyguard for a funeral." Fab smirked.

I'd never get away with calling the funeral directors at Tropical Slumber Funeral Home that, but her, they'd smile at indulgently. Not fair. "I don't understand the need for a bodyguard at a funeral. Can't people be civilized, and if not, stay home?" Because the two had helped us more than a time or two in the past, we never said no to their requests.

"If you stop being surly and do this job, I'll take you to lunch."

"Only if you promise to take me someplace where we can sit outside and enjoy the water view." I stood, gave her skinny jeans and heels a once-over, and hoped we wouldn't be doing any running. I knew without asking that she had a firearm holstered to her back.

I went into the walk-in closet and grabbed my latest purchase, a hot-pink sleeveless t-shirt swing dress, and paired it with slide sandals. I grabbed a handful of jewelry, my Beretta and purse, and followed her outside.

On the way to the SUV, Fab said, "If you're

busy tomorrow, you need to change your plans." She got in the driver's side without further explanation.

Gunz job? More crazy relatives? "I'm busy," I said as I slid in on the passenger side. "Have you forgotten we're supposed to lie low for while?"

"Good news: the Chief is going to look into our case and put in a good word."

"That must mean you accepted his job." I strapped my Berretta to my thigh.

"I did. I also told him you'd be backing me up and if he didn't like it, he could find someone else." Fab flashed her sneaky smile. "Another thing: I printed off an application for a PI license. Fill it out, take care of the requirements, and Gunz will expedite it."

I'd think about it. Instead of getting into an argument, I changed the subject. "Today's job? Tomorrow's? A tidbit or two of information would be better than nothing."

Chapter Eight

Fab roared out of the compound and over to the funeral home. Tropical Slumber had once been a drive-thru hot dog stand that had undergone several renovations and was now your one-stop shop for all your final send-off needs. If you didn't have a clue, there was now a museum with vignettes to spur your imagination. The two men needed a sign: "If it seems weird, we'll pull it off anyway." My favorite was the pet cemetery, where Fido or Fidette could have their name etched into the brick.

"About the job, you know how our funeral friends are," Fab said evasively.

That kind of caginess had me on alert. "What I know is that the only reason we're being called in is because they're expecting trouble."

Fab pulled into the parking lot and parked opposite the front door, jumping out immediately and hurrying down the red carpet.

"Classy touch," both men had told me a time or two. I wondered how they kept it free of tire marks but never asked.

I got out and leaned against the bumper,

waiting for her to notice that I wasn't playing follow the leader.

Raul stood in the entry, beaming at her as she got closer. Dickie stuck his head over Raul's shoulder, both in black suits in the sweltering heat. The men couldn't be more different, Raul with a toned and ripped bodybuilder physique and Dickie a well-over-six-foot string bean, as pale as the dead he dressed.

Fab was almost to the doors, which were standing wide open, when she slowed and looked over her shoulder. I waved. She said a few words to the men, then turned and walked, or some would say stomped, back to me. When she was close enough that no one else would hear, she said, "No free lunch for you. Five minutes was all your non-snarky attitude lasted."

"You reneger." I bit back my laugh at the disgruntled look on her face. "If you want me to move, then you need to give me the deets for this job. It better be pronto, before I leave you here." I tapped my watch.

Fab hooked her arm around mine and tugged. I didn't make it easy; she had to put some oomph into her second attempt to get me to move forward. "Raul can tell us both at the same time."

"That's cowardly, making him cough up details that you already know." This one must be a doozy. I waved as we got closer. No handshaking for me. Dickie and I shared that quirk.

Raul stepped aside, and I slipped through the doorway and claimed my favorite plastic slipcovered chair next to the exit. With the door open, I could keep one eye on the parking lot, which was a short sprint away.

"Fab didn't pony up any information, so I can't wait to hear what you need," I announced.

Fab shot me a dirty look. I smiled back.

Raul smiled fondly at Fab. I swear, she could set his thick black hair on fire, and he'd still want to be besties. "Silas Wilfred died and... well... to put it nicely, nobody liked him."

Dickie groaned and squeezed his eyes shut, clearly uncomfortable with where the conversation was going.

"He didn't have a single friend," Raul continued. "His sister came up with the idea of having a grievance funeral. Associates, neighbors, and family could come and vent their feelings. Her rationale was that funerals are for the living. Her exact words were: 'Hell, the dead don't know from jack what's going on or being said.'"

"I insisted that Raul call back the sister and let her know that we could rent mourners for a nice turnout, but she laughed off that suggestion," Dickie said.

"So, the sister has invited family and non-friends to celebrate his death?" I asked.

"That sums it up," Dickie said drily.

"Let's hop along to the good part... Why are

we needed?" I asked.

"Really, Madison," Fab mimicked Mother. She'd finished making the rounds of the viewing rooms, opening the doors and sticking her head in, and came back to stand in the doorway of the main room.

"As you both know, it wouldn't be the first time a fight broke out." Raul grimaced. "You're here to make sure that doesn't happen and, if it does, put an end to it as quickly as possible."

"The quickest way to end the fisticuffs is a bullet or two in the ceiling." I aimed my finger upward and made popping noises. "You okay with that? Just know that one of the faux mourners will probably call the cops."

Dickie appeared faint as he leaned against the wall.

"I warned the sister that fistfights wouldn't be tolerated," Raul said, although he didn't sound confident that one wouldn't break out.

"In the future, after you've called Fab requesting our services, would you give me a jingle? Because she sucks at details." I flashed my growly dog smile at her.

Raul nodded absently. "It's my thought that if there aren't any problems here, then we won't need an escort to the cemetery."

Good thing.

"You know, it's never too early to think about your own final plans," Dickie said suddenly, clearly desperate to change the subject.

"I'm going to be composted, and Fab is going to be fertilizer for a young sapling so it grows big and strong." I'd done well not to laugh at their shocked expressions, and that included Fab's, for which I gave myself a figurative shoulder pat.

An RV pulled into the parking lot, interrupting the uncomfortable silence.

"Is that the Silas family arriving?" Fab crossed to the door and stuck her head out.

I peered out at the parking lot and counted as a dozen cars followed the RV into the lot. It appeared it would be a good turnout for someone no one liked.

"Madison owns a bus, and if you ever need to borrow it as an added service, call me," Fab informed the guys. "I know it's not in use all the time."

"Just know that you have to pay the driver," I said.

Raul went out to meet the guests while Dickie disappeared into the viewing room to make sure the deceased hadn't cut and run. Nothing would surprise me, based on prior send-offs.

I got up and went into the main room, intent on snagging a seat in the back row. I was an accurate shot, so I could shoot from anywhere and hit the target. The ceiling would be easy-peasy. Fab tried to shove me over, and when that didn't work, she huffed, stepped over me, and sat down.

"Silas is staring." I nodded toward the front.

"You might want to suggest to Raul that they snap the lid shut before the service gets started, in case anyone gets a wild hair to throw something."

"You seriously suck the fun out of everything," Fab said with a straight face.

I covered my face with my hands, looked down and laughed, then back at Fab. "Hopefully, no one will throw food like that one time." Ignoring her exaggerated eyeroll, I asked, "The plan is? Since you've had a ton of time to come up with one, spit it out." I made a blowing sound.

"Take a deep breath, and please exhale out some decorum," Fab admonished. I saluted. "We're going to sit back here, fingers crossed that everyone's on their best behavior. If not, we don't hesitate to blow up the ceiling."

"I say we make it a contest. Whoever gets off the first shot buys the first round of drinks."

"Can't wait to tell this story at the next family dinner," Fab said.

Talk about drama breaking out. Family dinners were always good for that. "Mother will be disappointed that she missed out on the action, even though she thinks this place is creepy. Imagine that." I almost laughed, and instead made a face.

A herd of people filed in, all casually dressed and joking with each other. They trooped by the casket single-file and paused to look their fill. A few had parting words, but they were hard to make out, although several laughed and not one had a teary eye.

"Party time," I whispered to Fab.

First up, a woman who appeared to be in her seventies, a contemporary of the deceased, took the mic off the podium and nodded to a man in the corner. Canned music filled the room, and the grey-haired woman belted out *Somewhere Over the Rainbow,* off-key and gravelly. Some in the audience lent their voices, also off-key, while others clapped.

"My ears hurt." Fab leaned her head on my shoulder.

A woman in the front row stood and gyrated in a circle, stripping down to a bathing suit, her tent dress landing in a heap on the floor. She twirled and shook to the rapt attention of the men, who all had stupid smiles on their faces.

When the song concluded, Raul approached the podium and tapped the side of the mic. "In lieu of a service, it's my understanding that a number of you would like to express your feelings about the deceased. We'll do it in an orderly fashion, one at a time, and start with the first row." He waved to Dickie, who motioned those who had stood forward.

A few ignored the "orderly fashion" request and pushed and shoved, forming a line to the side of the podium.

The first man bumbled up and shouted, "Silas

stole my girlfriend in high school. He knew I loved her."

Get over it. That happened a hundred years ago.

The next man up, who also appeared to be a contemporary of the deceased, said, "Silas stole the neighbor's lawn mower when we were kids and blamed me. Even though the old bastard got his mower back, I had to work at five cents an hour pulling weeds until I'd made up the replacement cost."

That sounded like something my mother would've made me and my brother do as penance for one of our petty crimes.

The next man, younger by half than the ones who'd spoken so far, stepped up. "Silas slept with my mom, and I walked in on them. How am I supposed to scrub that from my memory?"

"Silas slept with my sister," one of the men lined up yelled, then turned, stomped back to his seat, and threw himself down in a huff.

There were more grunts of agreement.

"Silas once ran short on cash and sold my dog," a seated man who hadn't shoved his way into the line yelled. "I thought it ran away until we got drunk one night and he confessed. Bastard wouldn't tell me where I could find it; instead, he laughed and called the cops when I threatened to beat his ass."

And on and on.

"I get it, the guy was a dick," I whispered to Fab. "Just leave him out for the birds to eat and get over it."

Fab giggled and pushed me away, shaking her head.

I watched as the line dwindled down to one person and wanted to cheer.

The last man held up a bottle of whiskey and toasted the guests, then sucked down the amber liquid and wiped his mouth on his shirt. "Silas wanted anyone two-faced enough to show up to get a memento of their colossal nerve." He motioned to a woman, who came up the aisle handing out small boxes. I tried to wave her off, but she shoved two at me. "Some are made from his own teeth, but the others had to be bought."

I opened the box. A ring was nestled inside, and instead of an oversized diamond or other gemstone, there was a tooth—a molar, to be exact.

"They can be resized," the man at the front said, sliding one on his own finger and holding it up, "or worn as a necklace."

I burst out laughing. I hung my head and tried to swallow it back, but it was too late. Several people heard me and turned to stare.

"Oh great, one person ruins the atmosphere we've got going by crying," a woman two rows up snapped. "I supposed you miss him."

All eyes turned to me and appeared to be waiting for an answer.

"I... I... don't know what to say," I choked out, trying to get myself under control before they figured out I wasn't crying.

"They were close," Fab announced.

"Oh…" the woman said knowingly. "Another one he slept with."

"He got all the good ones," a man yelled. "I asked him to share once. But noooo…"

A couple of the men jumped to their feet and started yelling at one another.

Raul shot to the microphone and yelled, "Can I have your attention?" his voice squealing through the speakers. He thumped the side of the microphone, which made more screeching noises. "There's food on the patio." He pointed to where Dickie had sprinted over and thrown open the side doors.

Everyone stood, the rows emptied out, and the guests moved towards the patio. Only half cleared to the outside. Two of the men still inside started arguing, a couple more stopped to throw a few angry words, and a fistfight broke out between two women, surprisingly not having anything to do with either of the two who were already in a war of words. It was unclear what started the flying fists, but the men stopped arguing and ran out the doors. The women danced in a circle, slapping wildly and pulling hair, and managed to maneuver the melee out to the patio.

"I don't do fights. I'm not getting hurt." I moved out of Fab's way so she could run to the rescue. "You better get moving."

"What am I supposed to do?" Fab grumped.

"You'll think of something."

Fab jumped over me and stomped up the aisle, removing her gun midway. She stopped inside the door and took a couple of shots. I'd ask later where she aimed. The chick fight was over just that fast. Fab moved into the middle of the group and yelled, "Knock it off." She went on in a lecturing tone, but I couldn't make out her words. The men standing around all grinned.

Dickie came over and sat down next to me. "If you two hadn't agreed to show up, I'd have never agreed to this funeral."

"You do know that once word gets out, more people are going to want a grievance funeral?"

He nodded glumly, then brightened. "The best part for me was that I got to dress Silas, and he came out pretty good — natural."

I nodded, unsure how to respond. "Out of curiosity, who had the idea for the rings?"

"Silas saw it online and thought it was gross but exactly what any person who would show up deserved. It surprised me that he paid for real silver for the settings," Dickie said. I nodded again. "It's the new thing to hand out parting gifts."

I was happy to see Fab coming up the aisle. I was ready to go home.

Chapter Nine

Fab called the next morning and told me that she needed to deliver an envelope locally for Gunz and if I came along, she'd treat me to lunch, for real this time and not a ruse. It wasn't until she turned on the highway going north that I got my first inkling that it had all been another con job.

"Where the Sam hell are we going?" I barked. I didn't contemplate jumping out, knowing that there was a chance that instead of landing on the side of the road, I might end up in the middle of traffic. Then do what? Walking was out of the question.

"Ft. Lauderdale," she said, with so much sweetness it made my teeth ache.

I followed through on my first inclination and clipped her on the side of the head.

"Ouch," she grouched and rubbed her head.

"If you don't start talking, I'm going to call 911 and report that I've been carjacked and am being held hostage."

Fab blew out a long, aggrieved sigh. "This is all your fault. If I'd been upfront, you'd have shut me down, insisting that you had menial tasks that needed your immediate attention.

After which, I'd drag you to the car. This was much quicker."

"911 it is." I pulled my phone out the pocket of my black dress.

Fab slapped at my hand. "I told the Chief that I wasn't doing this job without you." Da-da-da in her tone.

"You'd probably have more work than you could handle if you'd play nicely with Chiefy. One thing he's right about is that you need someone professional to back up your pert ass. We both know he doesn't want it to be me."

"When have you known me not to get what I want?"

"Never. Almost, anyway." I half-laughed. "And as proof, here I am."

Fab's phone rang, and since she started speaking French, I knew it was the husb. Sucked for eavesdropping if you weren't multilingual. I leaned back in my seat and closed my eyes.

Assuming the kissy noises meant they were about to hang up, I cracked an eye open, scanning for a road sign to determine our location. "I hope you're getting paid for mileage," I said as we exited the turnpike sooner than I'd thought, which meant that she hadn't disclosed the exact location.

"Of course. The Chief even offered to pay for lodging overnight, but I turned that down."

"Since I'm certain you've got a plan worked out, what's my role?" I asked.

"As you know, Seraphina Reynolds, AKA Sugar, hasn't been heard from in a couple of weeks. She's loaded and can do what she wants when she wants. She and her husband sold their software company for a lot of money, and he invested the proceeds, making them even more money; then, before he could enjoy the rewards, he dropped from a heart attack. Since then, her motto has been 'live life to the funnest.' According to her sister, she's always stayed in touch… until now."

"What else do you know about her?" I asked.

"Sugar owns a waterfront condo—a penthouse in Hollywood Beach. Xander sent over pictures he found online from when it was for sale, and it's impressive. Even has its own private pool on the thirty-eighth floor."

"You using your lockpick to get into the building?" I raised my brows. "Sounds like a swanky address, and we'll be arrested in a blink if caught." I pouted in an attempt to hide my grin, but she probably caught it, since she squinted at me.

"The sister sent over the code. And since you were about to ask the sister's name, it's Laurie Daily."

"Questioning the neighbors will be dicey. One of them might call the cops."

"You'll think of a way around any unfriendliness."

"My suggestion is that we go with some

version of the truth," I said. "Something along the lines of 'we haven't heard from our good friend Sugar, and we just stopped by to check on her and we're worried about not getting an answer.'"

"Told the Chief that I thought it was a long shot, but he wanted it checked out. Which makes sense, but I wasn't in the mood to agree to everything he proposed."

I didn't want to burst her bubble, but I'd bet that the Chief saw right through her antics and chose to ignore them.

Fab pulled into the parking lot of a multi-story glass-and-concrete high-rise that boasted a sweeping view of the Atlantic and grabbed one of the handful of visitor parking spaces.

"This place reeks of money and a lot of it." I joined Fab in the parking lot and looked up at the building, wondering if the thirty-eighth floor was at the very top. "If you pull out a lockpick, I'm leaving. I'd rather take a chance and hitch a ride home than land in jail."

We walked up the curved stairs, and true to her word, Fab opened the door using a code. Entering the lobby area, I nudged her. "They have an office."

The elevator door opened, and a maintenance man exited, holding it open.

Sugar's floor turned out to be the penthouse and required a key or code, and Fab again used the code. The car rose up. When the doors opened, we walked out and saw that Sugar had three neighbors.

"Before you use the code again, I suggest that you knock, and if you don't get an answer, then ring the bell and give them more than enough time to get to the door before barging inside."

Fab ignored my suggestion to knock and went straight to ringing the bell.

Rustling could be heard from behind the door and the peephole shadowed over, then the deadbolt turned and the door opened. An average-looking middle-aged man with a toupee that hung slightly askew stood in the doorway. "Ladies," he said with a big smile.

"Stopped by to say hello to Sugar," Fab said. She must have realized she didn't sound friendly and added a smile, which wasn't helpful. "Her calls are going to voicemail."

"Sugar. Sug." The man sighed. "Such an impetuous woman. That's one of the reasons I love her." He eyes ran up and down Fab. "My wife is off on another of her adventures. Give me your name, and I'll have her call as soon as she steps foot in the door."

"Congratulations," Fab said effusively. "Didn't know that Sugar got married. We really have been out of touch."

"Two weeks ago. Sug swept me off my feet, and we tied the knot by the pool at the Hard Rock where we met." The man sighed, a smile on his face. "We've been the best of friends for so long, and I've always encouraged her adventurous ways, never wanting to hold her back. She confided that she didn't want another woman snagging me, so we married."

"That's so romantic." Fab held out her hand. "I'm Fiona…" She stumbled with the last name, and I knew she didn't remember the phony one we'd made up. I know I didn't. "And you are…?"

"Bowman Reynolds." He clasped Fab's hand in his and held on longer than necessary. "I took Sug's last name."

They both seemed to have forgotten that I was standing there, which was fine with me. There was something not quite right with the man, as evidenced by his soulless eyes and fake smile. I looked over his shoulder, through the marble entry, and out to the patio, where doors stood open to take advantage of what I imagined was an amazing view. The patio would be the envy of any homeowner, with its outdoor kitchen, swimming pool, and hot tub.

"Do you know when Sugar will be back?" Fab asked.

"Soon, I'm certain, as she doesn't tend to stay away long." He exuded a friendliness that was at odds with the glint in his eye.

"That's good news." Fab turned to the elevator, and the doors opened.

"Tell me how you got up here," he demanded and, after several seconds, pasted on a smile.

I stepped into the elevator and held the door open.

"Sugar gave me the code a long time ago," Fab said casually.

"I'll be changing that today. I can't have people just showing up on the doorstep." Bowman's tone was bland, but it was belied by the darkness in his eyes.

"Nice meeting you." Fab waved breezily and stepped into the elevator.

Bowman watched until the doors closed.

"I decided that knocking on the neighbors' doors wasn't a good idea and would yield little but unwanted attention," Fab said.

"That condo has first-class finishes — marble flooring, top-quality furniture, and a patio that I'd sit on all day. Any idea on the price tag?"

"Eight million or so."

"Old Bowman gave me the creeps, and his wedding story seemed off to me," I said. "Although it's easy enough to check. Why get married and then go off on a trip without your spouse? You'd think they'd want a honeymoon." I didn't get a response, so I didn't know if she agreed or was even listening. "Do you have a budget for paying bribes? If so, I'd suggest tracking down that maintenance man or going to the office and seeing what information you can shake out of whoever you can find."

We walked out to the parking lot and over to the SUV, and Fab handed me the keys. "Since the car isn't starting, I'm going to go find the maintenance man."

"When you get back and the engine turns over?"

"You know how women are."

I shook my head, knowing a couple of women that single-handedly kept their cars in tiptop shape. Since we were supposed to have car trouble, I rolled down the windows. I wasn't in the mood to melt. I called Creole to give him an update, and after several rings, it went to voicemail. I sighed and threw my phone in the cup holder.

In my opinion, it was taking way too long for Fab to show back up, but since the cops hadn't flown into the parking lot, I talked myself out of storming the office and ruining whatever lie Fab had going. I kept my eyes glued to the side mirror and was happy when she came walking out the front door, the maintenance man by her side. He was doing the talking, so that was good. From his smile, it was an easy bet that Fab had flirted a little to brighten the man's day. They got to the rear bumper and finished up the conversation. Money changed hands, along with one of her business cards. He waved and, instead of going back the way the two came out, went around the side.

"You were gone for so long, it started to make me nervous," I said when Fab slid behind the wheel.

"I lucked out. The young woman in the business office was chatty. I appealed to her inner snob, dropping the names of a few trendy hotspots, and then had her feeling sorry for me about my car problems. She called the maintenance man, Gudin, giving me time to sneak in a few questions about Sugar while we waited for him to show. I flashed the cash, and he eagerly swore to do what he could for my car, and when he found out it was a ruse and that I had questions, he didn't skip a beat." Fab exited the parking lot after one last look at the building.

I bet he didn't.

"Gudin and the office assistant pretty much knew zero. Money well spent, though, as we won't have to make a second trip. I did find out that Sugar introduced Bowman to the maintenance man a couple of weeks ago when he went up to fix something, but said nothing about a marriage. They found out when Bowman announced it a few days ago when he went to the office to pick up a package. They both said that they seldom saw Sugar around and verified that she traveled a lot and kept to herself when in town. Sugar did boast that she liked to gamble, and since she won a lot, it kept her going back."

"I can't imagine that a trip to the casino would yield anything. They would know her as a high roller, but I highly doubt that their knowledge would extend to her personal life and travel plans. Even if it did, you showing up asking questions would, I'm certain, raise a red flag." I stared out the window, having no clue where we were headed now. "I'd order a background check on Bowman and see if that yields anything interesting. He didn't seem the least bit worried that his wife had jetted off, and he didn't answer when you asked when he expected her back."

Chapter Ten

Fab pulled back onto Ocean Drive and went north. "We have one more stop."

"I guess I missed where you told me about the detour."

"I just did," she said, a trace of a smile on her lips.

I paid attention as she made several turns through residential streets and ended up on the second block back from the water, just in case I needed to ditch her and get home. She pulled up in front of a colorfully painted retro art deco building—bright yellow with red awnings and a wall fashioned out of different sizes and shapes of ceramic.

"What is this place?" The exterior had a lot of charm, but it was hard to figure out if the house had been converted into units or was now a motel.

"According to Sugar's sister, this property is owned by Essie Newman, a longtime friend of Sugar's."

"Tell me again why the cops aren't involved?" I'd have called them if my brother went missing.

"If there's a possibility that you walked away from your life, I don't imagine the cops make you a high priority." Fab got out and stood on the sidewalk, scoping out the building.

I joined her. "Knock on Essie's door and then what?"

"If she's a good friend, which we should be able to figure out in a second, then I'd think she'd want to be helpful. I'm hoping she's got a way of contacting Sugar, and we can be done with this case."

We entered the inner courtyard through the wrought iron gates. It was filled with an assortment of patio furniture, and there was a banner advertising a beach café. According to the lopsided sign hanging in the window, the tiny restaurant was closed, and no hours were posted.

"Why couldn't Laurie play the sister card and get answers out of Essie herself?" I asked.

"She tried, and Essie hung up on her. Laurie's story is that she and Sugar had a falling out and only recently started speaking again. The kiss-and-make-up didn't extend to Essie."

The tenants had a common entrance off to one side. The glass door stood open, minimal lighting illuminated a long, dark hallway with doors off to each side and another exit at the back.

If I had my way, I'd sit outside. "Wonder if the food is any good." I glanced around at the front of the restaurant.

"You bet it is, dearie." An older white-haired

woman, her slipper-clad feet up in a lounge chair and a multi-colored caftan wrapped around her legs, had us in her sights.

I smiled at her and walked closer, reading the menu posted over her shoulder. My favorite, tacos, was the first item.

"Essie Newman?" Fab asked.

"Who wants to know?" She had a smoker's voice, low and raspy, and her fingers fidgeted on the pack of cigarettes resting in her lap.

"Fabiana." She stuck her hand out. The woman stared at it, then looked up and smiled. Fab didn't introduce me, which was hardly the first time that had happened. "I'm here about Seraphina Reynolds."

"You're the first person in a long time to call her by her given name." Essie eyed us both. "Not sure what you two want, but I'm certain Seraphina wouldn't want me spreading her personal business around." The staredown between Fab and Essie didn't last long. "It's my way of saying 'mind your own business,' but nicer. Good one, don't you think?" Essie said, amused with herself.

"I only need a few minutes of your time," Fab said.

Essie reached out and kicked a chair. "Have a seat." She looked at me, and I got the same once-over that Fab had. "You'll need to drag over your own chair."

I dropped onto a nearby bench that afforded

me a view of the two women, close enough that I could hear every word. "I realize I'm the odd woman out here, but why not cut to the chase, *Fabiana,* so we can go have the lunch you promised?"

Fab shot me the "behave" stare before turning her full attention to the woman in front of her. "Laurie Daily gave us your name as a good friend of Sugar's. She's been out of touch for two weeks, and we're trying to locate her and make sure she's okay. We're here to find out if you've heard from her."

Essie continued her assessing stare of Fab. "I'd been thinking that I was overdue for a call from Sugar. But I didn't think it was a big deal. Decided she must be winning big on one of her gambling jaunts." She pulled her phone out of her pocket and placed a call. "Voicemail," she mumbled. "Call me," she rasped into the phone, then hung up. "That's unusual. Sugar always keeps her phone turned on."

"Has Sugar ever disappeared for this long before?" Fab asked.

"Disappear isn't the right word." Essie humphed. "Sugar's a woman used to doing what she wants when she wants. Since the death of her husband, she likes to stay busy. When life slows, she takes a quick trip somewhere. But she always stays in touch." She paused. "Last time I saw her was three weeks ago, when she stopped by and we had lunch."

"What do you think of Sugar's new husband?" I asked. Essie stared back, clueless. "Bowman," I added.

"Bowman?" Essie said, more to herself than me. "There's no way Sugar would've gotten married without bringing the man over and introducing him first."

"Bowman told us that it was spur of the moment and they were married at a local casino," Fab told her.

"That may be true, but I'm telling you, Sugar would've brought him by first," Essie insisted. "I haven't met this Bowman person, and in fact, it's the first I'm hearing his name. If I were you, I'd ask to see the marriage certificate."

"What if I told you that he's living in her condo?" I asked.

"I'd say I didn't believe you, but then, why would you lie?" Essie's gaze locked on me, giving me a closer look.

"How did you meet Sugar?" Fab asked.

"It was years and years ago." Essie smiled fondly. "She and her mother moved into one of the apartments." She gestured over her shoulder. "I often looked after Sugar, since her mom held down two jobs. Although she was Seraphina then." She laughed at the reminiscence. "It wasn't long after her mom died that she met Malcolm, and he swept her off her feet. Those two were madly in love—the real deal. When he died, she swore she'd never remarry. Never figured she'd find a perfect husband twice."

"What do you know about her sister?" I asked.

Essie leaned her head back, looking up at the sky. "Half-sister, actually." After a few moments, she straightened and looked back at us. "They had a tumultuous relationship. Their parents divorced when the two were in grade school. They made an agreement that Laurie would live with her father and Sugar with her mother, and the two kids didn't really have a relationship until they got together as adults. Seemed to me they never meshed. Sugar felt guilty, and rather than give it a rest, she ignored the little voice that told her they'd never be best friends and tried harder. The final straw came when she got engaged to Malcolm and caught Laurie making a move on him. The woman wouldn't take no for an answer; she kept at it with innuendos and finally outright offers. Laurie swore she didn't mean anything by it but friendliness and that she was misunderstood. Neither Sugar nor Malcolm believed her. The three of them had a huge blowup, and Sugar and Malcolm distanced themselves from her. As far as I know, they never reconnected, even after he died."

"Any friends you can think of that we could contact?" Fab asked.

"The ones she made when she married Malcolm disappeared when he died. A single woman didn't fit into their group. That hurt her terribly. That's when she took up cards and found that she was good at it and didn't need a partner. It helped her work through her grief."

"Anything else you can think of that might help us find her?" I asked.

"I know she's mindful of her personal safety, as we've talked about it several times, and I know she wouldn't do anything reckless. There's no reason that she wouldn't stay in touch with me, and like I said, a call from her is overdue." Essie's voice trembled. "Sugar's a beautiful woman — her smile lights up a room. I pray nothing bad has happened."

"Thank you for your time." Fab pulled a business card out of her pocket and handed it to the woman. "If you think of anything, give me a call."

"As soon as you find Sugar, tell her to give me a call," Essie said.

"I'll keep you updated," Fab promised.

"If you need anything," I said, "you can call the number on the card anytime." I waved to the woman and followed Fab back to the car, turning to take a last look at the property. I got in and closed the door. "I'd be surprised if there was a happy ending to this case."

"I think we should talk to the sister."

"In addition to running a background check on Bowman, I'd add the sister to the list," I suggested. "It would be interesting to know more about those two. No need to for Essie because I genuinely believe the woman loves

Sugar and wouldn't hurt her." I breathed a sigh at seeing that Fab was headed back to the turnpike and hopefully home. "Is there a will?"

"I'm going to include all of your suggestions/questions in my report when I send it over to the Chief. I think he thought he'd send me out here, I'd knock on the door, and Sugar would answer—all a misunderstanding, end of case."

"And the Chief is going to send the file back and tell you to figure it out." I'd be surprised if it didn't turn out that way. "Isn't that an investigator's job?"

Fab ignored me. "Wonder what the Chief is going to report to the sister, since we didn't learn squat?"

"Please, the man's a pro; he'll dance Laurie around with something that sounds believable until you get something. You could tell him you're bored and be done with the case… and if you choose that option, don't expect to hear from him again."

Chapter Eleven

The offer of a nice lunch was a scam once again. Fab got a call from Didier, saying that he was headed home early, and she didn't even offer a quick slide through the hamburger stand.

Fab dropped me off at my front door, and I went inside, eager to shower. I used up at least half the hot water, got out and threw on a comfortable sundress, then took out a stack of to-go menus and settled on the couch to wait for Creole to come home.

The door flew open and hit the wall with a thud. Creole stormed across the threshold and kicked it closed with a resounding bang. "What the hell is wrong with you?" he bellowed, his eyes narrowed into two darkened slits.

I'd jumped up when the door crashed open and now side-stepped around the couch, never having seen him so out-of-control angry.

"Why would you go to our friends and complain about the state of our marriage?" His voice was hard and ugly.

"I didn't… I'd never. I did share my feelings with Fab—that I feel inadequate as a wife and struggle to know the right thing to do."

"Share your feelings." He snorted. "Oh brother. So, you were complaining."

I didn't know this rage-filled man and didn't want to. I stepped backwards. If he continued to prowl forward, I'd end up out on the deck.

He edged closer until he towered over me. "Keep. Your. Mouth. Shut. You want to be a good wifey, stop making me out to be an ass and the bad guy for having a head injury."

I flinched at his anger.

"How many times have you been told that it takes time to heal?" he demanded. "Were you even listening all the times I told you? Apparently not, because you hover and peck about, and it drives me crazy."

"I'm sorry—"

"Shut it with the excuses," he snapped. "You need something to gossip about, make it your own messed up life and those businesses you own. That ought to keep you talking for hours." His face puffed up with anger. "We better not have this discussion again."

His behavior intimidated me, never having witnessed an outburst of any kind from him. I tried for a conciliatory tone. "I'm certain that if I shared the entire conversation I had with Fab, you'd see that I never made any disparaging remarks about you or our marriage. And I wouldn't say anything to anyone else."

"Save it." He turned and strode into the closet,

grabbing a change of clothing and going into the bathroom.

I expected the door to come off the hinges from the violence with which he kicked it closed, the sound reverberating through the house. I sucked in a deep breath, shell-shocked. We'd never really had a fight before, and I was unsure how to calm the situation.

A fight takes two. This was more Creole unleashing his fury, and I didn't want to be on the receiving end ever again. Willing my feet to move, I went to the kitchen, grabbed a water, and went out to the deck. I sat in a chaise in the far corner where I could see inside the house. I hoped that when he came out of the bathroom, he'd come outside and we could have a quieter conversation.

It wasn't long before the door to the bathroom opened. He had changed into a t-shirt and loose shorts. He headed to the kitchen, grabbed a beer, and came out on the deck. He stopped mid-stride and stared at me briefly, the anger lines still etched in his face signaling he wasn't ready for a calm talk. "I'm going for a walk. Alone." He cut down the steps to the beach.

I missed my husband. Nothing had been the same since his injury. More than anything, I wanted the intimacy and the laughter back.

Something told me he wouldn't be back anytime soon. I got up and went inside, changing into a t-shirt dress that I often wore to bed. I grabbed my laptop and went back out to the deck, wrapping myself in an oversized beach towel and stretching out on the chaise.

I had no clue how much time had gone by when I heard the gate at the bottom of the stairs snick closed, but the sun had long since gone down. I snapped my laptop closed, shoved it under my leg, and turned onto my side. I looked out from under my lashes, not moving. It surprised me that the outside floodlight, which was on a sensor, hadn't gone on. Creole moved past me with barely a glance, quiet as a mouse. I took that to mean he still wasn't ready to talk. He moved stealthily around the house and went out the door without making any noise. In the quiet of the night, I heard the engine of what I assumed was the Mercedes turn over.

When his stolen truck was never recovered, he replaced it with a Mercedes sedan, which surprised me. I'd joked, "Fancy work truck," and got a dirty look. Okay then. That was one of the last times I teased him about anything.

I opened my laptop and checked the time. "Where's Creole going at midnight?" I mused out loud. Maybe Fab and Didier's, but since I was certain that was where he'd been all night, why not just stay down there?

I clicked on the app for the security feed inside and outside the house, backed up the video, and watched as he drove out of the compound. One question answered. He wasn't headed to Fab and

Didier's. Except that when I looked at the date stamp, it was from the night before, only he'd left earlier then. How did he manage to leave the house without me hearing a thing? I thought back and remembered that I'd gone to bed early. I'd tried to coax him to come with me, but he insisted he wasn't tired and had gone out to the deck, sitting where I was now and focusing on his phone. I closed the file and sat there for a moment, hesitating. Fab had set the system to save the footage for thirty days.

I started with the files for the exterior footage. I felt bad for snooping, hoping to catch my husband doing what? That was a good question, which wouldn't be answered by looking at security footage. It showed that Creole had a pattern. He left the house via the deck every night at approximately the same time, accessed the path that ran along the side of the house to the front, and took off in his car. Hours later, he came back the same way. I remembered once having woken up in the early hours to find him gone, and when I asked, he'd simply said, "I went for a walk on the beach." I'd offered that if he woke me, I'd walk with him if he wanted company, and he turned me down. Where was he going?

Can you say stalker… of sorts? I chided myself. The security files also showed that on several occasions, he'd tossed the house in the same furtive manner that Fab would and, like her, didn't leave any telltale signs that he'd done it. He'd gone through every drawer and cupboard and disappeared inside the closet long enough that he clearly wasn't changing clothes, which was verified when he came out with the same ones on. He'd opened the cabinet on one of the walls in the living room where I kept my files and flicked through those, but apparently hadn't found anything interesting, as he hadn't removed any of the paperwork. He'd apparently forgotten that we had a first-class security system, but then, why would he think I'd review the footage? What was he looking for? I could hardly ask or he'd know what I'd done.

More surprises came as I watched him going through my phone and laptop while I was in the shower. There was that one time I'd noticed him on my laptop and pointed out that he'd picked up the wrong one. He'd mumbled an apology, or so it seemed. If there was something specific he wanted, he could have just asked.

One thing for certain, I knew I wouldn't have another good night's sleep. I'd be listening for odd sounds — doors closing, engines firing up. Maybe Creole was doing something undercover for the Chief again. But there wasn't a single job I could think of that the Chief would ask him to do that would require him to snoop through my belongings. And it didn't seem likely as an explanation for his late-night trips either, since the Chief had expressed concern about Creole's health and commented that they hadn't had a conversation lasting more than a few minutes in a while. Asking questions of the Chief could blow up worse than my harmless conversation with Fab. I discounted the possibility of Creole having an affair, knowing that if he'd met someone, he'd leave me and not play us both. Besides, what woman would settle for a few hours in the middle of the night?

I stood and went into the house, crossing the room to where Creole's laptop sat on the island. I hit the power button, and it took me to a locked screen that required a password. I was surprised, remembering him saying that it was a pain in the butt to have to sign in every time. I shut it off, not wanting to alert him that I'd been snooping. I flipped on the television and turned to the screen with a view of the outside, so I'd have a warning if he returned. Then I crossed the room, moved the fake wall aside—easy since it was on a track—and opened the safe. Everything was there—papers, cash, passports, and some jewelry. Made sense, since none of the security footage showed him going near it. I looked around as Fab might and didn't see anything out of place. The only way to solve the mystery of what he was looking for would be to ask him, and based on tonight's yell-fest, that was out of the question.

After closing the safe and rolling the wall back, I checked that everything looked as it had when Creole left. Then I fell on the bed, wrapped the sheet around me and drifted off to sleep, despite the million questions on my mind. The sun streaming in the window woke me up the next morning. Creole was puttering in the kitchen, making coffee. I hadn't heard him come in. For the first time, I found his being quiet as a cat unnerving.

Chapter Twelve

It took Fab two days to set up an appointment with Laurie Daily, Sugar's sister. As predicted, the Chief had dumped the Sugar Reynolds file back on Fab and told her to tie up the loose ends of the case. Laurie hemmed and hawed and finally agreed to meet for coffee, insisting more than once in the course of the conversation that all business could be done by phone. She had not one iota of interest in meeting in person, despite her expressed anxiety over her missing sister, and considered it a complete waste of time. I'd warned Fab in advance that another trip to Ft. Lauderdale was out of the question for me, and she could take Mac or Rude as a sidekick. That didn't go over well. "You're going," she'd yelled.

As it turned out, Laurie didn't want a sit-down at her house in Miami and, to Fab's and my surprise, readily agreed to Fab's suggestion that they meet in Homestead. It was one of the few times I didn't gripe about Fab going over the speed limit as she cruised up the highway. As she pulled up in front of the coffee shop, we saw that no one had opted to sit outside on this sticky hot day. I licked my lips, planning what to drink—something ice cold and packed with caffeine.

We got out and trekked inside. Laurie was easy to spot, as she was the only woman sitting at a table by herself. Her ice-cold stare flickered over us, and she raised a hand to wave imperiously. She looked out of place in the casually clad crowd, with her blond hair pulled back in a chignon, impeccably overly made-up face, and black wrap dress with red-soled high heels. There was a diamond on her finger that could put your eye out.

All the thoughts that I'd had that this case might be about money were sidetracked by the woman appearing well-heeled; everything about her screamed money and a lot of it.

"Ms. Merceau?" Laurie pointed to a chair when Fab nodded.

"I'll get drinks. Would you like another?" I pointed to her cup.

"I'm fine," she answered, looking down her nose at me.

I was happy to run off, not even asking Fab what she wanted and only realizing it when I placed the order. Hope she was in the mood for her regular espresso. Since I was the only one in line, it didn't take long to retrieve the drinks and go back to the table. I interrupted Laurie telling Fab in a sad tone how much she missed her sister, how she had no clue where Sugar might have gone and hoped that nothing bad had happened.

"When was the last time you saw Sugar?" Fab asked.

"Last time…" Laurie paused. "I'd need my calendar. I'm so busy, it helps me keep track of appointments." She reached down and pulled her phone from her purse, looking through it for a moment. "Now I remember." She set it on the table. "We had lunch a month or so ago. But we talk constantly on the phone, so it doesn't seem that long."

Fab shot more questions at her about Sugar's life and friends. For most, she didn't have an answer, and several she danced around and was evasive, rather than admit she didn't know anything.

Fab took a drink of her coffee and nodded at me, then asked Laurie, "What do you know about Bowman?"

"I haven't met him. But my sister gushed over what a wonderful husband he was and how lucky she was to find happiness a second time. I was so happy for her," Laurie cooed, but her eyes were frigid and held no emotion.

Laurie was right about one thing: this get-together was turning out to be a waste of time, and she was making sure of it. Fab hadn't learned anything new about Sugar or even gotten a clue as to where to direct her investigation. It was evident that Laurie knew little to nothing about her sister. It surprised me that she even knew Sugar was missing.

I finally spoke up. "Did Sugar have any enemies?" Laurie did her best to appear shocked by the question, but it was a put-on and not a very good job. Not getting an answer, I asked, "Any business dealings you know about that could've gone awry?" A couple of long shots, but what the heck.

"Sugar didn't work," Laurie said. "She lived life to the fullest, as though any day could be her last."

We'd heard that said about the woman several times now. What hadn't been said was that she was reckless in any way.

"If you haven't already, it's my recommendation that you call the police and file a missing persons report," Fab told her, and she didn't respond one way or the other. "You can tell them you hired an investigator and that we were unable to come up with a single lead."

I knew Fab was thinking, like me, that there wasn't any reason for Sugar to up and disappear. It also wasn't something she'd done in the past. A few days out of town, but not two weeks.

"It saddens me to have to call in the authorities." Laurie sniffed and picked up her purse, getting out her keys. "I was certain that she'd be back by now and we'd be laughing over a drink."

"I know that you were expecting answers, but

honestly, it looks as though Sugar's taken off on one of her trips and will get in touch when she gets back." Fab handed her a business card. "If you think of anything else."

"Have you already filed a police report?" I asked.

The three of us stood and walked outside.

"I'll be giving the police a call," Laurie answered.

"I'm so sorry I couldn't give you something more definitive." Fab shook her hand.

Fab and I watched as Laurie managed to walk down the steps without a single stumble in her heels and slid gracefully behind the wheel of a white Lexus. Fab took her phone out of her pocket and snapped a discreet photo of the license plate.

"I was the under the impression that she'd talked to the cops. Now, I'm not sure of anything since she doesn't know how to answer a question directly," I said as we waited for Laurie to leave the parking lot before getting in the Hummer.

"It's easy enough to check out. I'd be interested in the answer."

"What was this meeting supposed to be about?"

"The Chief feels that the client is owed a face-to-face meeting." Fab sighed. "It's more professional." She mimicked his tone.

"You better not let him hear you do that."

"The Chief also thought I might get more out

of her than could be learned in a phone call. I agree in theory, but it didn't work today."

It caught my attention that Fab exited the parking lot via the same route as Laurie. "Please tell me we're not going to follow her to wherever."

"Case over." Fab brushed her hands together and looked happy. "Just wish I had more to report. What did you think of the client?"

"You showed more emotion during the conversation than Laurie, and you've never met Sugar. The woman made my spine tingle, and not in a good way. I might wonder about her motives if she didn't have an impressive amount of her net worth on her fingers and ears."

"According to the credit report Xander ran, Laurie and her husband are well-off but not in the same league as Sugar," Fab said. "I had him run a trace on Sugar's phone, and according to him, it's not emitting a signal and hasn't the whole time I've had this case."

"I feel like we've overlooked something." I turned from staring out the window. "You'd think the husband would be the one to report her missing, but he doesn't appear the least bit worried. Instead, it's the sister calling in an investigator, and they weren't even close, as evidenced by the evasive way she answered your questions."

"I don't have much to add to my original report, which won't please the Chief. I don't expect to hear from him again, since I didn't uncover anything, my only accomplishment running up billable hours."

"I got the impression that he'd like to add you to his roster of investigators. If he calls back, would you consider working for him on another case?"

"That would depend on whether you'd be backing me up." Fab flashed me a sneaky smile.

"I haven't done anything about getting my PI license." I grimaced at what Creole's reaction would be.

Fab knocked me in the shoulder. "If one of his stipulations is me finding another backup, it's not happening."

"You're lucky that didn't hurt very much."

Chapter Thirteen

It had been a quiet couple of days as I fell back into my usual routine, my unease fading when nothing else odd happened.

I was headed out to the patio with an iced coffee and my laptop when my phone rang. I debated answering, knowing that chances were good it wasn't going to be good news, but while I was deciding whether to answer or not, my thumb automatically hit the connect button.

"Hi," Tank's cheerful voice boomed through the phone.

"You don't sound very professional for a high-priced lawyer," I said, trying without a lot of effort to cover up that I was in a grumpy mood as I backed up and sat on a chaise.

"I've got good news and other things."

I groaned. "Let me guess, a good news-bad news call. I'm going to jail, but you'll come visit." Before he could confirm my fears, I cut him off. "Why aren't you calling Fab?" She wouldn't be a happy camperino to be the last to know, and I'd be hearing about it. "I know you're besties since your days in prison."

Tank laughed. "That's an outright fabrication of our alleged introduction."

I snorted.

"I'll have you know that I did call Fab, and she told me to ring you up and be the bearer of the news, that she was busy hoochieing it up with the husb."

"I don't believe you. Fab wouldn't answer the phone if that were the case."

"Are you suggesting that *I'm* now the one fabricating a story?" Tank didn't give me a chance to answer. "Well... what she did do was put me on speaker, and the husband laughed in the background as she ordered me to call you like I was her personal minion."

"That's Fab for you; she has that special way with folks." I sighed, hoping I wasn't going to regret asking. "The news?"

"I was in court this morning to enter a plea on your and Fab's behalf on the grand theft auto charges. To my surprise, the prosecutor stood up and withdrew her case. Apparently, when Peg Landry was asked to come in to prepare her testimony, it didn't go well. The prosecutor had barely gotten started when Peg jumped up and ran out of the office, saying she didn't want to press charges, then got sick in the hallway. The good news is that everything hit the trash." Tank sounded too pleased to be relaying the latter.

"It doesn't sound to me like she confessed to being a big fat liar." I tried to stay calm but was losing the battle and sucked in a big breath. "I'm still suing."

"I suggest that you rethink that course of action because it will cost you. Not that I think you won't win, but in the end, does Ms. Landry have any assets to go after?"

Silently conceding the point, I said, "The only upside is that I'm happy not to be going to trial. Being trapped in a courtroom for a couple of days isn't the way I want to spend my time."

"It's over now; no more charges hanging over your head," Tank said in a conciliatory tone. He paused slightly. "Another reason for my call is that I'd like to use one of my favors."

I thought briefly about hanging up and, if he ever spoke to me again, excusing my rudeness by saying, *Oops, we got disconnected and then my phone died.* "You should be hitting up your *friend…* Fab," I reminded him, in case he'd forgotten, "for any and all favors."

"Fab told me to jog your memory about the 'no whining' clause." He laughed, clearly amused with himself.

I groaned loudly into the phone.

"I have this divorce case," Tank said.

"That sounds fun."

Tank ignored my sarcasm and continued, "The couple fought over ownership of the family dog, and the judge awarded them joint custody until the final decree. Except that the missus wouldn't relinquish Poochy when it was the husband's time for visitation. So the judge changed the order, and the husband got full custody."

"Might I suggest that you tell the missus to go pick out a lookalike at the pound and bond with that lucky dog?"

"Where was I before being interrupted?" Tank asked, sounding more amused than irked. "Oh yes… his almost-ex-wife packed up the dog and split town. Next thing my client heard was from her attorney, informing him that the dog had died and sending pictures. Except that a mutual friend saw her walking Poochy on the beach. My client thinks she's here in the Keys and just wants the dog found."

Now I knew why Fab had foisted this call off on me. I'd be extracting a fistful of favors for myself. "Warning: I don't have dog rapport. Only puss rapport."

"You shouldn't talk dirty to your lawyer."

"You get extra points for making me laugh," I said. "Seriously, you need to get someone else. I hate to break it you, but Fab has zero rapport with animals, period." My cats were the only exception, but he didn't need to know that.

"Aren't animals all the same?"

"Spoken like a man who doesn't have any," I said. "Even if dognapping were legal, and it's not, I don't have the stomach to steal someone's pet if it's being taken care of. Do you have an exact address, or do you expect me to run up and down the beach with a picture in my hand?"

"Xander got me a couple of addresses. I'm only asking that you check them out and get back to me. I can take it from there. If this gets me points, I've already recommended Xander, and one of my colleagues used him and was happy with his services."

Xander was a hot commodity these days. He'd told me that his phone rang constantly with investigation jobs and he was loving it. I'd threatened him if he ever dumped me as a client, and he laughed.

Besides the whining clause being in the small print, how could I say no to our attorney? "What kind of dog?" I sighed.

"Great Dane."

If he were sitting in front of me, I'd give him an eyeroll, and then another to make sure he saw it. "Here's the thing about dogs: they're loyal to their owner and have a tendency to bark when a stranger comes around. Not like cats, who couldn't care less who shows up snooping around, especially if they have food. Out of curiosity, why aren't the cops beating the bushes for the missus if she's defying a court order? It's a jailable offense, isn't it?"

"He doesn't want her arrested."

"I'll check out the addresses, but I'm making it clear upfront that I'm not napping the dog. This is too reminiscent of the car job, and it makes me queasy." If the man had a court order, it might not be illegal, but no thanks, not taking the chance. "If I can locate it, I suggest that your client go get his own dog. That way, no one gets bitten. Or lands in jail."

"And I'll have him take the cops with him."

"Text me the addresses and a picture of the ex-wife and dog." I might as well appear somewhat agreeable. I was surprised that Fab hadn't just told him "done deal" and shoved it in my lap. In a way, she did just that. "Here's something to think about: you don't have any idea how the woman will react when faced with losing her dog. The husband better be careful. Can't you use your mediation skills and broker some kind of deal—happy ending for all?"

Tank sighed. "You know how much time I've spent on the custody of the dog already? Way too much. Neither wants to agree on anything, which is how we ended up here."

"I'll get on this and let you know what I find out." I managed to set my phone down and not throw it across the room.

Chapter Fourteen

My phone dinged with an incoming text message—Tank had sent the addresses. I stood and moved into the kitchen, slid onto a stool at the island, and opened my laptop to look them up. They were both down in Marathon. I called Fab, but she'd turned off her phone. If she thought I was going to go chasing around after a dog by myself, she was crazy.

I went into the closet and put on sweats and a t-shirt, then sat on the floor to tie my tennis shoes. I strapped on my gun—not expecting to shoot at anything, but it was good to be prepared—grabbed my purse, and slid out the door and behind the wheel of my SUV. I gunned the engine and headed to the other end of the compound, turning into Fab's driveway and parking at the front door. I got out, strode up to the door, and proceeded to kick the bottom and be as loud and obnoxious as I could without hurting my toes.

The door flew open, and Didier stuck his head out. "What the devil?" he barked and bent down to run his hand over the bottom of the door.

Phew. Fully dressed; that was good. I

squeezed by him. "Oh, calm down. I didn't wear the right shoes to kick a hole in it." I scooted into the kitchen. "Fabiana Merceau, get your butt out here. Pronto," I yelled. "Don't make me come looking for you." I opened the refrigerator and helped myself to a water.

"I feel compelled to apologize for my wife's behavior," Creole said, coming into the kitchen.

"I didn't see your car." I'd also missed that he'd been sitting in the living room.

"Would you have acted any different?"

There was humor in his question, which made me smile. "Probably not."

"Creole dropped his car off for service," Didier said. "I picked him up."

He could've called me, but I didn't say that and instead said, "That's nice."

"I'm ready." Fab leapt out from the hall, her tennis shoe-clad feet hitting the floor.

"Good thing, saves me from wrestling you out to the car." I flexed my muscles. "This shouldn't take long," I told Didier. "We're going to check out a couple of addresses, then turn the information over to Tank to act on."

Didier walked over to Fab and wrapped his arms around her. "Call on the way back, so I know that everything went okay."

Creole and I stared at one another. He didn't say a word. "We won't be gone long." I turned, walked out the door, and slid into the passenger side of the SUV.

Fab slid behind the wheel and roared out of the compound, turning onto the highway. "How's married life?" she asked. "Everything okay with you two?"

"It's good," I lied through my teeth, slapping on a phony smile. The last thing I wanted to do was color anyone else's opinion of my husband, hoping that we were going to get back to the way we were... or close anyway. Creole had barely said a word since his eruption. Another new, irritating element of our relationship, as we'd never done cold warfare before. "He took it well that I kicked in your door."

"He was probably remembering all the times I've done it at your house and thought it was about time for payback." Fab laughed. "I know Didier was amused."

"Since you're Tank's friend and it was your idea to dump this case in my lap, I've tweaked it a bit. I'll be sitting in the car while you determine if the dog is at either location."

"That's what you think."

It seemed like a shorter drive than usual down the Overseas. We exited the highway for the first address and cruised past a two-story house, then hung a u-turn and parked across the street. A woman was loading up the trunk of a small sedan, not a dog in sight.

"I'd need a closer look, but I think that might be the woman in the picture Tank sent me." I scrolled through my phone. "If so, she's changed her hair color."

"It's a wig."

"So you can sound friendly when you talk to her, her name is Dori Scott and the dog in question is named Max." I scanned the property—I could see most of it since the house was on stilts. "It would be hard to miss a Great Dane. Maybe it's in the house, except the door is open and you'd think it would run out and be sitting on the deck." I checked out the second story of the house.

The woman put the last box in the back of the car, then dragged a large plastic bag over to the trash can and struggled to get it inside. That done, she looked up and down the street but still hadn't noticed our arrival.

"That's Dori all right," I said.

"Let's go find out where the dog is," Fab said.

With one last look over her shoulder, the woman headed back towards the house and ran up the stairs.

"Not so fast." I grabbed Fab's arm before she could open the door. "When Dori turned, you must've missed the handgun tucked into the front of her jeans. I'd like it if we could avoid a shootout, and I'm betting that Didier would feel the same."

"So what do we do? Nothing?"

"This job is over. We found the address where she lives or lived, and we're turning it over to Tank. Let's go have something cold to drink."

"We can't let Dori get away without finding out anything." Fab got out of the car and shut the door on my screech.

I caught up to Fab and grabbed the back of her shirt. "If this goes to hell, I'm going to kick your butt."

"I'm going to pretend I don't know that she's the woman we're looking for and see if she fesses up, then talk her into making an amicable agreement with her ex-husband. Hopefully, she'll keep her word."

"I hate to be a killjoy…"

"No, you don't." Fab sniffed. "This idea just got retweaked, to use your words. You do the talking. I'm sure you remember my rapport is with old men." She tried to jump behind me.

I sidestepped her. "Let's just agree that if she's snooty, you do the talking, and if we get a whiff of crazy, I'll step up."

"What would I do without you?"

I almost laughed. "That sounds sweet and all to someone who doesn't know you, but we both know that if you could foist this case off on anyone else, you'd tell Tank to stuff it and he'd still be risking a bullet for having the nerve to ask to begin with."

We got to the bottom of the steps just as Dori came back out rolling a suitcase. Without looking below, she pitched it over the railing. If we hadn't been watching her every move, it would've hit one or both of us.

When she did notice, she asked, "Can I help you?" and beat it down the stairs. She skidded to a stop, out of breath, and checked us both out.

Fab pushed me in front of her.

I reached behind me to slap at her, knowing that had zero chance of success, and I was right. "We're here trying to locate a Great Dane named Max." I'd forgotten what plan we agreed on, as we probably hadn't, and decided on the direct approach.

"Max freakin' died," Dori exploded. "You can tell that damn ex-husband of mine and get off my property." She fingered the grip of her handgun.

"I'm so sorry for your loss," I said, and meant it. Having lost a pet or two, I knew it sucked.

Dori sneered at me, then ran about a foot, retrieved her suitcase, and beelined for the car.

Fab stepped in front of her. "How did Max die?" she asked in a sympathetic tone.

"Tell my ex to go screw himself. You're wasting your time, as I have no intention of answering any of your questions."

I tugged on Fab's arm.

Dori opened the back door of the car and pitched the suitcase inside, kicking the door shut. She ran back up the stairs and came back out, slamming the door, purse hooked over her shoulder. Before she jumped behind the wheel, she turned and shot us a manic grin, then squealed out of the driveway.

"I suppose it's not going to do any good to tell you not to follow her," I called after Fab as she ran across the street and jumped in the Hummer. I circled around and got in the passenger side. "She's going to notice."

"I'm curious to see how she reacts." Fab raced down the street after Dori's car. "My first choice would be to snoop around her house, but my luck, she'd turn around and catch me in the act."

Dori headed south on the Overseas, which surprised me. She must have another location in the Keys, and it wasn't the other address that Tank had sent over. Fab followed but hung back. Suddenly, Dori slammed on her brakes, hung an illegal and dangerous u-turn, and shot up the highway going north.

"That answers your question," I said snidely.

"She barely escaped being t-boned." Fab shook her head in disgust.

By the time Fab got turned around and was once again in hot pursuit, Dori had disappeared. I, for one, was happy.

Fab turned on the street to Dori's house and drove back by, parking in the same place as before. I didn't ask but assumed that she wanted to check to make sure Dori hadn't doubled back. That would've been a long shot.

"I'll be right back." Fab left the engine running and opened the door. "Before you start, I'm not picking the lock—a peek in the windows should tell me if she's coming back." She ran across the street and bounced up the stairs. She circled the deck and peered in the windows a couple of times, shaking her head. True to her word, she didn't even turn the doorknob to see if Dori had left it unlocked. On her way back to the car, she detoured by the trash and lifted the lid, then jumped back, slamming the lid back down.

"Gross," Fab said sliding behind the wheel. "Whatever she threw out smells really bad."

"It's not her dog, is it?" I asked in horror.

"The bag wasn't big enough. If I had to guess, maybe her refrigerator went out and the food went bad. You remember that smell?"

I grimaced. That had happened to me once, when the electricity went out during a hurricane and stayed off for several days.

"Another guess is that it's a rental house, because Dori trashed the inside." Fab shook her head. "What she didn't want, she threw on the floor." She hunched over the steering wheel, checking out the street. "Now what?"

"In the future, no more animal custody cases. Not liking this one at all," I said as she drove slowly down the street. I didn't know what she was looking for and didn't want to know. "The second address isn't that far." I programmed the GPS.

"Maybe that's where we'll find Dori."

It was less than a five-minute drive, and it turned out to be a quick stop, as it was an empty lot except for two contractor dumpsters filled with construction material.

"Wonder what used to be here?" I mused. "Judging by the neighborhood, it had to be residential."

Fab rolled down the window and snapped photos, getting close enough to snap a pic of the advertising on the side of the dumpsters.

"We're done here," I said. "Not getting any more involved in this case since the only way to get info would be to chat it up with Dori, and that's a bad idea. She appeared about ready to snap off the short tether that was holding her together." My phone rang, and I pulled it out of my pocket and groaned at Tank's name on the screen. I answered and put it on speaker. "I was just about to suggest that Fab call you."

Fab made a face at me.

"Were you able to locate Dori?" Tank asked.

Fab told him what happened.

"Wonder where she went," Tank said, more to himself than us. "I'd like to be able to tell the cops, as they have a few questions for her."

Fab and I exchanged "what the heck" stares.

"Dori's ex was crossing the street this morning and got struck by a hit-and-run driver. I'm headed to the hospital to check on his condition. A couple of witnesses said it was a small pickup with no plate and the driver had on a baseball cap."

"Are you suggesting that Dori might've been the one to run him over?" I asked. "You might want to give the cops a heads up that she carries." I told him that I'd spotted a gun in her waistband.

"Since the divorce was so contentious, the cops are going to want to know where Dori was at the time of the accident. She'd be my number one suspect," Tank said.

"Why would she run the man over?" I asked. "I know divorce cases can get nasty, but that's going a little far."

"Maybe Dori has the dog stashed somewhere and wants to make sure he doesn't find it," Fab said.

"Another favor?" Tank half-laughed.

Fab and I exchanged raised eyebrows.

"Would you go back and talk to one of the neighbors — see what you can find out? Maybe one of them will know where she went."

I looked at Fab and shook my head.

Fab spoke up. "I'll call you when I'm done. Shouldn't take long." She hit the disconnect button.

"Seriously?" I said. "You're as bad as me when it comes to saying no. I'm the nice one. You do it for the excitement."

Fab grinned and ignored me. "It's not going to take long." She drove back to the neighborhood and parked in the same place. "You coming?"

I shook my head.

Fab got out and stomped up the driveway of the only neighbor with cars in front of the house.

I texted Tank: "Ixnay on any more animal custody cases." I didn't get an answer.

Minutes later, Fab came back down the driveway with a hot-looking thirty-something in tow. He only had on a pair of board shorts, his muscled chest on display. They stood and talked, then shook hands... except he held on and attempted to pull her into him. She grabbed her hand back. He laughed and said something, and she shook her finger at him. He couldn't have missed the ginormous diamond and wedding band on her left hand. She left him smiling at her and came back to the car.

"Brent was friendly," Fab said, and turned and waved as she drove down the street.

"Looked like it."

"Be nice." She frowned, and I made an unsympathetic face. "Brent said Dori was weird and made his skin crawl. He felt sorry for her when the dog was run over by the neighbor two houses down and also said that he liked the dog better than her."

"So that's how the dog died. Horribly sad, but I'm happy to hear Dori didn't off the dog, which I thought was a possibility when you came back with the trash report."

"Here's the best part."

"I don't want to know." I covered my ears.

Fab slapped my hands down. "The neighbor is in the hospital recovering from a gunshot in the back. Happened two nights ago when she was out walking her dog a couple of blocks over."

"Coincidence? First the neighbor, now the husband. The cops will have plenty to talk to Dori about."

"If Tank calls back and wants us to track down Dori, he can forget it."

"Happy to hear that."

Chapter Fifteen

I got up early the next morning to make coffee, hoping to entice Creole into staying in bed and talking like we used to. I crossed the room with both mugs in hand and tried to hand him one, but he waved it off.

"I'm going to shower." He rolled off the side of the bed, and the bathroom door closed before I could say anything.

I went back to the kitchen, threw his coffee in the sink, and put the mug in the dishwasher. I sat at the island and checked my email, then sent a message to Xander that I'd be coming by the office later.

"I'll be here," he messaged back.

Creole came into the kitchen dressed in jeans and a t-shirt and busied himself making another cup of coffee. Another change he'd made was to throw his favorite blend in the trash, along with the coffee maker, and switched to the same sludge that Fab and Didier drank. I watched as he ground the beans and plugged in the espresso machine that I'd had to read the directions a couple of times to get it to work.

My phone rang, making me flinch; it was

never good news this early. I made a face when I saw Mac's face pop up, knowing that it could be any number of catastrophes.

"Dead body," she whispered when I answered.

"Another one?" I asked. "I'm afraid to ask where."

"Couple of blocks over. Another woman. I tried for pics, but the cops arrived before I could get there."

I groaned. "Do you think you can manage to stay out of trouble until I get there? Then you can fill me in on the details."

"Gotcha." She hung up.

Creole stared coldly the whole time I was on the phone, not thawing even a little. "Didier has plans for Fab, if you're planning on calling and interrupting them."

He'd know about their plans since he spent a lot of time hanging out with Didier. "I was planning on sharing a cup of coffee with you." I was annoyed that my cheeks turned red with embarrassment at getting no response. "How about we go away for the weekend and enjoy some good food and time on the beach?" And get back on track, but I didn't say as much since I didn't want to start a fight.

"I can't this weekend. I'll check my schedule, and we can talk about it."

That sounded like a stall to me. I bristled with hurt feelings and stood. "We both need to put some effort into this relationship. This coldness may work for you, but it doesn't for me."

"Don't overreact; we'll get back on track," he said blandly.

I went into the closet and changed into a jean skirt with a slit up the front and a t-shirt that covered the Glock holstered to the small of my back. I slipped into a pair of sandals, figuring if I needed to change into tennis shoes, I had a pair in the car. Then I went back to the kitchen and stuffed my laptop and phone into my leather tote, grabbed my purse, and flung both over my shoulder.

I looked up in time to see Creole's head disappear down the outside steps to the beach. "You have a nice day, too," I said to the empty room and went outside to my car.

The trip to The Cottages was a short one, thanks to very little traffic. I pulled into the driveway and parked in front of the office. Getting out, I noticed Rude barreling in my direction, yelling, "Oh good, I'm not late." She waved wildly, then tripped, only a jerking motion keeping her from landing on her face. She straightened and shook first one foot, then the other. "Damn shoes."

I looked down at her turquoise flipper-shaped sandals with matching knitted scarves tied around her ankles and suspected the reason she almost fell flat on her face was the fringe dragging on the ground. It was good to keep your ankles warm on a ninety-degree day. She and Mac must shoe shop together. I waited as she slapped to a stop in front of me. "Late for what?" I asked.

"You can't have a meeting without me. I was there, too." Rude huffed and bent over, hands on her knees, taking short breaths.

Once it appeared Rude wouldn't keel over, I headed to the office, opened the door, and nodded at Mac, who sat behind her desk. I claimed Fab's seat on the couch and propped my feet on the armrest. Rude threw herself in a chair.

"You need to show more interest in this case because the murders are going down in our beloved neighborhood," Mac said without me having to ask a question.

"That's laying it on thick."

Mac ignored me, which might have my hurt my feelings if I wasn't used to it. "The dead chick, Kay Little, has similar features to the other one. That's weird, if you ask me."

"How do you know all this?" I asked.

"You know how news travels around the neighborhood," Mac said evasively, her attention on something going on under her desk.

If it turned out to be a cockroach large enough to ride, I was out the door without a backwards glance. Pest control was Mac's job, and if not, it would be.

"We followed the sirens," Rude said proudly and followed up by mimicking the sound with an irritating noise of her own.

Mac leaned back in her chair and slammed her tennis shoes on top of her desk, beating her feet up and down and watching as the lights danced around the soles. At the same time, she blew a huge bubble and stuck her finger in it, the mess covering her mouth.

"I thought you gave up bubble gum." I watched as Mac, who wasn't listening, picked it off her face, rolled the ends up, and shoved them back in her mouth.

"I don't think my lights are in sync." She banged her shoes again. "What do you think?"

"I think…" I said in a frosty tone that got her attention, "I'm going to be buying a desk that's ten times nicer and spendier and you're going to pay for it." I'd been wanting for a while to upgrade from the standard business edition to something swankier, like the shiplap one Fab had had made for me at her office.

"You make my nerves hurt." Mac worked a large wad of gum between her fingers and shoved it in her mouth.

"The cure for that is to listen up, because when you miss something important, you'll be complaining," I said. "As for the shoes, I don't think the lights need to be matchy."

"I told her the same damn thing," Rude grouched. "Does she listen to me?" After a pause, she acknowledged, "Some of the time."

I'd long ago given up on the idea of hiring

someone normal, whatever that was; such a person wouldn't work here anyway. "Okay, ladies, can we get back to the latest murder and why you two are involved?"

Rude took a bag of M&M's out of her pocket, flipping them in the air one at a time and catching them in her mouth.

"You didn't want drug dealers in the neighborhood; I don't want a murderer." Mac blew another bubble almost large enough to cover her face and somehow sucked it back in without choking. She smirked at Rude, who hadn't let up on her antics either.

I kicked the back of Rude's chair. "Enough, you two. This is a business meeting, and we'll have some decorum." Both women stared at me like I'd lost my mind. "Last time I got involved in the illegal neighborhood goings-on, Creole and Didier were kidnapped. It's a good reminder to let the cops do their job." Judging by the scowls on the women's faces, they didn't like my idea. "Selfishly, who am I going to get to be manager extraordinaire if you end up face down in the bushes?" I asked Mac.

Rude snorted. "You're forever sticking your… whatever you want to call it… into stuff."

"You're lucky I don't have Fab tendencies, because if I did, I'd shoot you. If you don't believe me, try saying that to her and see what happens." I waved. "Nice knowing you."

Rude's cheeks burned red. "No need to open

that can of worms."

"There's something we agree on." I squinted at her and gave Mac the same look. "I want you to keep Dodger updated, and with any luck, he can fend off trouble before it gets started."

"It was my idea to get the men that live here at The Cottages to sign up for nightly patrol until the culprit is caught." Rude preened. "I thought to include those next door until Mac pointed out what an unsuitable bunch they are."

"That's a bad idea." I would've had to be deaf not to hear Rude's huff of annoyance. "It would be a good idea if all of the men that live here weren't half-crazy. You know that the ones that signed up only did it to strap on a gun. And I'd bet Dodger is the only one with a carry permit. The whole scenario I just concocted in my head makes me squeamish, so we're not doing it. Got it?" The women nodded reluctantly. I stuck my pinkie in the air. "Swear. Both of you."

"Yeah, okay," they said, almost in unison.

I'd regret this, but it was part of my job. "Anything else going on that I should know about?"

Mac, bored with her feet, put them back under the desk and waved to Rude, indicating it was her story to tell.

"Miss January and her boyfriend, whatever his name is—he stuttered when I asked and never answered," Rude said.

"Captain," I said. "And…"

"It occurred to me that he was probably on the run, with his skittishness, so I had Mac run a check on him. Came back squeaky clean, just weird as... Oops, sorry. That almost cost me a dollar. Me and Coots have a swear jar, and we're on our honor."

"That's nice," I mumbled.

Mac grinned.

"Anyway... where was I?" Rude scratched her chin. "The two got in a shouting match, about what I never figured out. It came to an end when they ran out of breath at almost the same time and started choking. When they recovered, Miss January jumped into his arms, wrapped her legs around his waist, and ground on him as he carried her into the house."

I grimaced. The woman was forty and looked eighty, drunk all the time and chain smoked, with a death warrant on her head that had long ago been signed off on by her doctors. Despite her issues, she could get a boyfriend with the snap of her fingers. "Did you think about offering assistance while they were choking?"

"Oh, hell no. That's a good way to get hurt and get my coif messed up." Rude flipped the ends of her grey scraggle.

"Rude assured me that if either of those two had turned blue, she would've called 911," Mac said.

"In the future, since you're reticent about interrupting smackdowns before they become a health issue, I suggest that you yell for help."

"Maybe," Rude mumbled.

"This isn't actually a problem..." Mac said, then shifted her focus to picking out a piece of gum that'd gotten tangled in her hair. Once it was free, she flicked it in the trash and looked up. "But Joseph is yammering on about wanting kids with his lady love."

I covered my face with my hands and laughed. I tried to recover, but the disgust of the other women started me laughing all over again. I sucked in a deep breath. "Does he have dementia?"

Rude shook her head and said in a sympathetic tone, "He gets drunk and goes off on these romantic tangents."

That's sweet. "Do I need to flip a coin to see which of you informs him that his rubber girlfriend can't conceive?"

Rude pointed to Mac. "That's her problem, since he's her tenant. I've got my own problems next door. Besides, Mac and Joseph have a copasetic relationship; she can have the sex talk with the old goat."

"What problems?" I demanded.

"Just kicked out two non-payers." Rude grinned. "Cootie is in the process of spit-shining the units, and then I'll be on the hunt for new tenants."

"That was fast," I said. "You served notice and did it all legal-like?"

"Hell to the no." Rude smirked. "And let these people take advantage? I sent a message, which is faster and cheaper. They packed their bags and were gone in two days, which is all the time I gave them."

I quirked my head and glared at Mac.

Mac held up her hands. "I've done my best to train her, but she doesn't always listen. Besides, I like having someone on speed dial that will kick non-payers to the curb. They ignore the warning, and it's their a— on the line. Cuts down on me running back and forth to court and them thumbing their noses in my face."

"When was the last time you had a date with the judge? The court clerk, even?" I asked.

"Exactly." Mac grinned.

I'd had enough of the news. I stood and pointed to my watch. Neither needed to know I never set the time or that my excuse for running out the door was a ruse. "I've got an appointment."

"One more thing." Mac danced her finger around in the air. "Crum has a surprise to show me, so you might want to stop back by and pee on his parade after he's unveiled it."

"I object." I pasted on a faux-frown. "Just because I'm the one who promotes common sense once in a while doesn't make me the bad guy."

"Don't show back up too late and pee on our other plans," Rude said, laughing at her humor.

"We've got a sunset dinner bus tour going out tonight. I'll be the hostess with the mostest, pointing out the highlights of the Cove. I've got us dinner reservations at the Fish Stand."

"Reservations? That metal drive-up building with picnic benches?" I snorted and made a barfing noise, and both women glared. "Direct your guests to sit by the dumpster, where they'll have the best view of a strip of murky swamp water." More glares. "I'd prefer that you do the tour first and then eat. That way, if anyone needs to puke, hopefully you'll be back here by then and it can be hosed off the concrete easier than out of the bus."

"You're a killer of joy," Mac said.

I crossed the room and turned back with my hand on the doorknob. "One more thing, when you get called out for making up BS stuff for one of these little tours of yours—you know, this and that that never happened in the Cove or anywhere else—don't come whining to me. Offer a refund before fists fly." I held my hand up to cut off more spoilsport responses. "One more thing before I leave. Neither of you..." I pointed back and forth between the two women, so they couldn't say they didn't know it was them I was referring to; didn't matter that there wasn't anyone else in the room. "...is to stick your neck out to get it chopped off." I made a choking noise. "I'm rather fond of you both." I headed out the door, closed it on any further comments, and race-walked to my SUV.

"Caffeine," I moaned to myself.

Chapter Sixteen

After hitting the drive-thru of my favorite coffee stand, ordering an extra-large iced coffee and downing half, I got back on the road and took one of Fab's infamous shortcuts down an alley, then cut over to the street that led to her offices. In retribution for her cozying up to Didier all morning, she could call Mac to get caught up on the latest. I smiled, knowing that Mac would drag it out and make it painful, at least until Fab threatened to shoot her if she didn't hurry up; then she'd be quick to spit it out.

I pulled up to the security gate, entered the code, then veered left and parked in front of the building opposite Fab's. I hadn't been inside since a couple of owners ago. The garage underneath was full, with an assortment of Toady's cars and Xander's truck. I got out and climbed the fifty outside steps. The door was open when I got to the top, and Xander ushered me inside.

"Like the old days," I said, and we knuckle-bumped.

The inside was as I remembered—a large open space that had been completely renovated into ultra-modern living quarters with glass, chrome, and a leather couch that had been left behind. The large island that separated the kitchen from the rest of the space now doubled as a desk, as evidenced by the paperwork spread out.

I waved to Toady, who reached in the refrigerator and held up a bottle of water. I nodded. "I hung out and waited for you; got an update or two," he said.

I opened my bag, handed my laptop to Xander, and slid onto a stool. "Can you give me a list of the files that have been accessed in the last month?"

"No worries there." Xander sat next to me. "I monitor your computer and have firewalls in place to stop any hacking attempts. A couple of months ago, you had a rash of attempts from a couple of foreign countries, but they were kept out." He opened the lid and powered it up.

"I need a tracker for a car," I said. "A couple, in fact. A girl should be prepared. That's something Fab would usually take care of, but I don't want to have to answer any questions. At least, not yet."

Toady opened a drawer on the other side of the island. "Two enough?" I nodded, and he handed them to me. "Xander can add the app to your phone. They can be attached easily inside the wheel well. If you need me to do it, let me know."

"It's for Creole's Mercedes. I think it would be

better if I do it, as it would attract less attention and I could come up with some excuse if I got caught." I'd wait until he was in the shower if they were that easy to attach.

Neither man said anything, but they were clearly surprised.

I wasn't up to discussing Creole's middle of the night jaunts.

"Just know I'm here for you, no matter the job," Toady said.

"I appreciate that and sincerely thank you for all the jobs you've already done for me." I smiled at him, and he smiled back with his only tooth—a gold one—front and center.

"I've got a warehouse update for you," Toady said. "The exterior renovation is done, as you know, and it's not the dump it once was—makes those other three down the road look like they're in need of a bulldozer. The interior is close enough to being done that you can start thinking about who you want as tenants. Anyone in your inner circle know that you bought the place?"

I shook my head. "As you know, it was meant as a surprise for Creole, but with all that's happened, there hasn't been a good time to tell him. Especially since I'm certain that he wouldn't agree with the decision to acquire the building." Would he even remember that he was the one to suggest it?

The original owner, Hank Michaels, had been a piece of work who set me up to be implicated when he faked his own murder. When his machinations came to light, Creole told him it would be healthier for him if he left town. Little did he know that I was the buyer, and I planned to keep it that way. His brother owned the other three look-alikes and had left them to rot.

"The businesses nearby think I'm the owner and haven't had any objections so far. They're just happy that the place is finally getting cleaned up. It's their hope that the code department will stop cruising the streets, looking for reasons to write citations," Toady related.

I'd had to put more money than I'd originally planned into the old warehouse. It turned out that the electrical, HVAC, and plumbing all needed updating. I'd also had the interior and exterior painted and security fencing installed. Since parking was an issue, I'd decided to rent the floors to companies with under five employees, which suited me, as I didn't think the neighborhood needed the added traffic.

"I plan to be very picky about who I rent to, so I won't be hanging out a 'for rent' sign," I told Toady. "My main goal is to *not* invite trouble. So whoever I decide on has to be running a legal, verifiable business."

"I've got someone for you to mull over," Toady said. "He's an investment advisor and currently has two employees, with the potential for two more, and he's wanting a bigger space. No worries about him paying. If I go out on a limb and refer someone, it's in their best interest not to renege on any part of the agreement," he growled.

Xander and I traded raised eyebrows at the hair-raising sound.

"Even though I don't have a financial interest in the building," Toady continued, "I've done enough work on it that I want you to succeed and make money. It's already good for property values—one less blight on the landscape."

"I have an artist friend from college that's looking for space and might be a good choice," Xander said. "No worries about him paying; he's a trust fund kid and rolling in the dough."

"As soon as I get the occupancy permit, I'll set up a meeting with the interested parties. They can walk the property, and we can go over the details," I said. "I'll give anyone that comes with a recommendation first consideration."

"Heads up: there's a new honcho in the Code Department—Mr. Russell, Russ to his employees," Toady said. "He expects businesses and residences to follow the rules, and when they don't, he'll be issuing citations, which he's already proven in his short tenure."

"Long overdue," I said. "What does that mean for the three warehouses owned by the other Michaels brother?" Eyesores was too kind a word. I'd never understood why someone would let a big investment deteriorate in the manner these two brothers had.

"When Russ took over the job, the first order to his staff was to write clean-up notices. Those that thought it was business as usual and ignored them got a surprise when they were hit hard with citations and started racking up fines. Most didn't need to be told twice. Ted Michaels, thinking none of it applied to him, found out that was a costly mistake when he got a notice to appear in court."

"Good. Now he's going to be forced to clean them up or risk having them sold out from under him," I said.

"Win for you," Toady said. "Ted was livid and mouthing off to anyone who'd listen that he should be exempt from paying. But he's finally realized that that faulty line of thought isn't going to work for him anymore and is ready to entertain an offer, as long as it includes the stipulation that the buyer pays the fines."

"How did you find out all this?" I asked in awe.

"Everyone talks to me." Toady grinned. "If they don't, then their friends do. That's how I know that Ted has zero interest in the property; his only concern is that it might go to auction and he won't be able to control who gets it."

I was afraid to ask but did anyway. "How much are the fines?"

Toady chuckled. "Now, *there's* some good news; even though they're substantial, there's a loophole. Just so you know I'm not full of it, I got the info from Russ himself. I did the man a favor, so he bought me a beer and I learned a few tricks."

"That was fast," I murmured.

"Wait until you hear the favor." Xander grimaced.

"Somebody with a grudge on for Russ dumped a baby alligator on his doorstep and scared the daylights out of him." Toady took out his phone and showed me a picture.

Baby, huh? I didn't want to admit my ignorance by telling the man they all looked dangerous to me, no matter the size.

"That sheriff's deputy friend of yours knows that I have animal rapport and gave Russ my number," Toady said.

Kevin? Friend was a stretch, but okay.

Toady flexed his muscles, which were impressive. "I rounded up the gator and took him to a friend's farm up north, had him checked over before he got released into a marshy habitat. I didn't share this with Russ because I don't have proof, but I'd bet that Ted Michaels cretin had something to do with the surprise. Not that he'd do it himself because he's too much of a… never mind that, but he paid someone else."

"You'd think an alligator of any size would be hard to buy, rent, or snatch up, from where I'm not sure," I said, and Xander nodded in agreement.

"You know, sister, that if you've got the cash,

you can buy anything," Toady said.

"That alligator was lucky that you got the call to round him up; it's not your first reptile, and none have turned up dead."

"Toady and I agreed on a 'no pets' policy here," Xander joked.

"Back to the fines," Toady said. "Got some good news there. I might've asked Russ a question or two when he stopped by your warehouse a couple of times while I was there overseeing the updates, thinking you'd ask and wanting to show how smart I was by knowing the answer."

I laughed.

"If you were to acquire the other three, as the new owner, you go in and fix up the property and the city will work with you and oftentimes wipe out the fines. You've got a good track record, in that with this current property you bought, you jumped right in and had it cleaned up and didn't have to be hounded to get on it."

"What happens when Russ finds out you're not the owner?" I asked.

"He already knows." Toady stared, trying to judge my reaction. "I put a bug in his ear about what a couple of turds the Michaels brothers were and told him I got hired to oversee the renovations as the owner didn't want any problems. He's happy that the property got cleaned up, and if it stays that way, it makes him look good."

"I want the other three." I almost laughed at the fierceness of my statement. "Once I've got them all rented, I won't care who knows that I own them."

"I approached Ted, and he worked me, thinking he had me on a string, enjoying his own game. I listened and let him think he was dealing with a dimwit. I'll give him a call and apply some pressure, tell him it's time to make up his mind, as I've got another deal on my plate and if he's not selling, I'm moving on."

"If Ted accepts the offer, I'll buy it in the same corporate name as before and have my CPA handle the deal."

"I'm on it," Toady assured me.

Xander set my laptop in front of me. "Looks good. I saved the list you asked for on the desktop."

The door flew open and Fab walked in, pocketing her lockpick.

"The door was locked," Xander said, amusement in his tone.

"There's no such thing with Fab," I said.

"Why do I have to look all over town for you?" Fab grouched as she stormed inside, letting the door bang closed.

"If you hadn't been burning up the sheets with your husband…"

The guys laughed.

"What are you talking about?" Fab demanded as she slid onto a stool at the end of the island, her cheeks pink.

I'd say she looked embarrassed. "Creole told me—"

"He must've misunderstood," Fab snapped. "Since when does that stop you from interrupting? You've done it in the past."

"Good friends and all. I thought you needed the exercise," I teased. I got the 'you've lost your mind' look.

The guys broke into another fit of laughter.

"Who's going to tell me what's going on?" Fab demanded.

"You should offer her a water; maybe it will cool her off," I said to Toady.

He whirled around, retrieved a bottle from the fridge, and set it down in front of her.

"As for the first part of the morning, I had a meeting with Mac and Rude, and I won't deprive Mac of the opportunity to rehash the agenda." I smiled at her annoyance. "Once was enough. And so you know, I need to stop by the property again, so you can ask the details then… or not. I'm here checking on the guys, making sure they're staying out of trouble. Xander went over my laptop and updated and backed up files, or whatever he does." I winked at him.

"The reason I'm here is to pitch an opportunity to Toady," Fab said.

So much for her searching all over town for me; she was coming here anyway.

"I picked up a new client, a repo account…

maybe, since it's dependent on you agreeing to do the dirty work. If I even attempt to run the idea of me doing any of these jobs past Didier, he'll flip."

"What a suck account. Let me guess—one of Gunz's comrades?" I asked. "You need to think three times before jumping on that rotten opportunity," I said to Toady.

"Count me in." Toady air-boxed, and the muscles in his arms rippled. "I can't be only taking the soft jobs; I'll lose my edge."

I made a zero with my thumb and forefinger. "That's the odds of you losing your edge."

"Are you done?" Fab asked me, sounding a bit snappish.

"I reserve the right to complain some more later."

Xander grinned at me behind Fab's back.

"I don't need to explain the job to you and outline the pluses and minuses," Fab said to Toady.

"Mostly minuses," I said. "And don't minimize the danger."

"You know I'm your man, Frenchie," Toady said. "I got a partner who'll go along on these jobs. He's got a tow truck, which will make them easier."

Not you, I mouthed to Xander, even though I knew he wasn't the truck owner. I didn't want him volunteering his muscle.

Xander laughed and shook his head, letting me know there was no way he'd be getting involved.

Chapter Seventeen

Fab pointed to the door, which I translated as 'time to go.'

The guys laughed, not one bit put off by what could be construed as rudeness.

I followed her down the stairs, and we bypassed the Porsche and got into the Hummer. We hadn't been on the road two minutes before she headed the wrong way. I should've known something was up when she slid into the driver's seat without so much as a snarky comment about going to The Cottages, since I knew it wasn't her favorite place. I jabbed my finger at the window. "You missed the turn."

"We're going to take a slight detour." Fab flashed me a sneaky smile and took the back road to the main highway.

"You know I need to go by the property; you couldn't at least ask if it was an emergency?"

"If it was, you would've said so. I shouldn't have to ask over every little thing when you and I both know you'll say yes."

Oh brother. "Next time, ask, and I mean ahead of time, or I might not go just to be mean. You might also want to smooth my 'tudiness by plying me with caffeine." I glared at the empty cup holder. "You need to tell me where we're going and why." I breathed a silent sigh when she turned south; at least we weren't headed to Miami. "If you hurry it up, I'll know if I need to get ready to jump out at the upcoming light."

"I got a new client." Fab handed me a slip of paper and pointed to the GPS. "Referral from Gunz."

"Another crazy relative that can't get their life to work?" I programmed in the address and realized it wasn't far.

"A friend of Gunz's whose had a couple of break-ins at his business and wants to upgrade the security system. I'm going to meet the client, walk the perimeter, take some pictures, and shoot the guy a report." Fab exited the highway on the outskirts of the Cove.

"That sounds fun."

At least, the road was paved. Industrial buildings lined the short block on both sides, advertising an assortment of businesses. And of course, we pulled up to the only one without a sign. One would think the eight-foot metal fencing would be a deterrent to thieves, and if not, then the rolled barbed wire, even if chunks of it were missing.

"I'll do what I do best on these jobs of yours that I have no skills for — look pretty."

Fab laughed and got out of the SUV. She

pounded on a metal door off to one side, then stepped back, took her phone out, and snapped pictures, continuing along the front.

A forty-something man with short dark hair standing on end poked his head out the door. He whistled, and when Fab turned, his hard eyes bored into her. She responded by ignoring his lack of friendless and waved. The man stepped out, tall and broad with a muscular build; anyone who would mess with him wasn't thinking how badly the situation could end.

If it weren't a referral from Gunz, I'd have my Glock out, ready to back her up, but none of his associates would dare to screw with Fab and live to tell about it. I sat back and watched as the two walked the perimeter, Fab firing one question after another. They disappeared around one side of the building.

I glanced in the side mirror and caught sight of a Jeep pulling up behind the Hummer, a young guy leaning out of the passenger side to snap a picture of the back of my SUV. The baseball hat and aviator sunglasses covering his face made it difficult to get a good look at him. The window rolled back up, and the Jeep rolled out to the street and disappeared towards the dead end. A minute later, it reappeared and parked a half-block down on the other side of the street.

What were the occupants of that vehicle up to? I hated that they had a picture of what I was certain was my license plate, which had me wondering why he took it and what he planned to do with it.

Fab and her soon-to-be client came back and stood in front of the Hummer, but it was a good fifteen minutes before they finished up their conversation.

I kept an eye on the Jeep, which hadn't moved. When Fab slid behind the wheel, I said, "Before you blow out of here, take notice of the Jeep across the street." I told her what happened.

Fab backed out of the parking lot and headed to the corner in a more sedate fashion than usual.

"What kind of business?" I asked.

"Smith tricks out cars." She kept one eye glued to the rearview mirror.

I almost snorted at the name. "Is that a pseudonym?" She didn't answer. "Stolen ones?"

"You're so suspicious," Fab said with a shake of her head. "The Jeep is tailing us and not doing a very good job. I vote that we get some answers, retrieve the phone, and crush it under our tires. I'm going to pull into the grocery store, park and approach them, and see what they do next."

"I don't have the energy to list all the ways your idea could go bad, but I'm in." I unholstered my Glock and stuck it in the back of my waistband.

"Isn't this where you remind me I can't shoot them just because they snapped a picture?"

"Just make sure it's self-defense so one or both

of us don't end up in jail."

Fab pulled into the parking lot, pulled down a row about halfway back from the entrance, and chose a space with no other cars around. Right behind us, the Jeep pulled in and parked next to us, straddling two spaces. "This ought to be interesting."

Fab got out, and I followed.

It was hard to make out the faces of the men in the Jeep, thanks to the tinted windows.

"You disappoint me," I said to Fab as she headed inside the store. "I thought you'd march over, jerk the door open, and toss at least one of the occupants to the ground."

"That's Plan B."

"What are those two up to?" I said as we stood out of sight by the front window as two young guys got out of the Jeep and cautiously approached the Hummer, looking around as they did so. One headed to the driver's side, while the other leaned against the rear bumper.

"Car theft? I don't think so," I said. "I'm not standing here while they mutilate my SUV so they can make a buck or two." I ran back out the door and didn't need to check to see if Fab followed, as she showed up at my side a moment later, and the two of us ran down the aisle.

"They're not going to get a chance to damage anything," Fab said.

The young man at the bumper saw us coming and yelled something before stepping around the driver's side. The two men reappeared, both with weapons in hand and pointed at us.

Fab's hiss confirmed that she recognized them, as did I. These were the two from the car recovery case that landed us in jail. "Nick Landry, isn't it?" I asked in disdain.

Nick stepped forward. "Hand over the keys. Now."

"Have you lost your mind?" I asked in exasperation. "What you're doing is a felony; you'll go to jail."

"You didn't," Nick spat as he stepped forward.

Fab and I stepped back out of arm's reach.

"You have a short memory. We were hauled off in cuffs, and the only reason the case got dismissed was your mother wasn't willing to get caught lying and go to jail." I refrained from telling him how stupid I thought he and his friend were. "You had so much fun stealing mommy's car that you thought you'd take it up as a profession?"

"Want the keys?" Fab twirled them on her finger. "Tell me what you're up to and maybe I'll hand them over."

"You two were going to jack mine, and now I'm returning the favor," Nick gloated, as though he already had possession of the keys. "Except I'm smarter than you. I've got a buyer lined up for yours. Wave good-bye because you'll never see it again."

"You're willing to go to prison for years and be on the hook for damages, just so he can get his revenge?" I asked the friend.

He looked scared but didn't say anything. He'd kept his gun at his side, not waving it around like Nick, who had his finger on the trigger.

Fab's leg shot out and kicked Nick's arm. The gun discharged, a bullet flying through the back window and out the windshield of the Hummer, and the gun hit the pavement. Her leg shot out a second time, making contact with the middle of his chest, and he ended up in a heap on the asphalt.

The friend dropped his gun and took off running.

Nick reached out and grabbed Fab's ankle, jerking hard enough that she tipped sideways and almost fell. He jumped to his feet, scrambled back, and kicked out. She evaded him and kicked back, and he ended up on his butt again.

I pulled my Glock and pointed it at Nick. "Move and I'll shoot you."

"If she doesn't, I will. You're not going anywhere, except to the police station," Fab assured him. "Call 911."

"I suspect it won't be the first call." I pointed to several people who'd taken out their phones when the shot rang out and also noted that no one offered help. I took my phone out of my pocket and made the call.

Minutes later, two cop cars skidded into the parking lot and came to a stop. An officer hopped out of each car, and of course, one would be Kevin.

"Put your weapons on the ground and hands in the air," Kevin barked at the two of us. "Step back."

I followed his instructions. Fab hadn't drawn her weapon.

"Before you take a side, the security footage will back our version of events," I said.

The second cop, whose nametag said Ryan, motioned me over. "What happened?"

I told him what went down in the parking lot, then filled him in on the previous incident. He asked a few questions, which I answered shortly and succinctly, just like any good lawyer would advise. I gave him a description of the other guy and told him that the runner's name and information should be in the previous report, and if not, Nick's mother would know. I also told him that Fab and I had carry permits, in case it slipped Kevin's mind, and that neither of us had discharged our weapon.

"Wait here," Ryan told me and moved to Fab, questioning her where she leaned up against the side of the Hummer while Kevin spent his time questioning Nick.

It unnerved me that when Kevin cuffed Nick and put him in the back of his patrol car, he turned and gave me a smirk that said, 'this isn't over.' I really hoped he wasn't going to skate on this.

Ryan finished questioning Fab, and she came over and stood next to me. "The Hummer needs to be towed and a truck is on the way. I'll call Didier and have him pick us up."

I sighed. "No thanks. I'll get a ride, since I'm going to need one until the glass is replaced."

"Ryan told me the Jeep was stolen, so Nick and his friend are racking up the felonies. Hello to jail for the both of them for a long time."

First-name basis with the other cop had me almost rolling my eyes. He'd get an earful from Kevin. If it hadn't been for several witnesses corroborating our story, we might have found ourselves in the back of a cop car. When the tow truck showed up, I gave the driver the address for Spoon's Auto Body.

"Nick's pretty cocky; we need to keep tabs on him." I took my phone out of my pocket and called Spoon. "It's your favorite step-daughter," I said when he answered.

"How much trouble are you in?" he grouched.

I gave him a quick version of the events of the afternoon and a heads up that the Hummer was en route. "I need a ride to pick up my beater truck." One of my better buys had been the small pickup, which had come in handy a few times. It didn't look great, which added to its appeal, but ran like a charm.

"Ride is on the way," Spoon assured me, and

we hung up.

Fab joined me. "Called Didier, who wasn't happy. I told him I was riding with you back to the office to pick up my car, since I figured you were getting your truck, and I'd see him at home. You call Creole?"

Before I could answer, Fab's phone rang, and it was Mother. I leaned in and heard Mother, after complaining I hadn't answered my phone, invite us to dinner. I didn't want to go and shook my head furiously. When I heard Fab say, "We'll be there," I stalked away and headed toward the exit.

Billy Keith must've pushed the speed limit, as it wasn't long before he was pulling into the parking lot and coasting to a stop next to me. I opened the door and climbed in the back seat of the truck. Before lying down, I pointed. "Fab's over there." I closed my eyes and exhaled a quiet sigh. "Thanks for never grumbling when Spoon sends you out to help us yet again."

Billy turned in his seat and growled out a laugh, his sun-bleached hair windblown. The man minded his own business and kept to himself, but take him on and you'd have your backside handed to you in short order. "I get to hear a good story and get off work early. I'd be annoyed if he asked someone else."

The door flew open, and Fab jumped in the front seat.

Billy asked what happened and added, "Don't

skimp on the details."

Fab should've been an actress, the way she juiced up the story. "What worries me is that when Nick gets bailed out, he'll be back." She cast a sympathetic eye in my direction. "Little snot feels entitled and thinks he can do whatever he wants, and if all he gets is a short stay in the clink, it won't disabuse him of the notion."

"You need to get hot on the phone with your bestie, Gunz, and he needs to talk some sense into Nick, the mother, or both. Whichever works," I said.

"Another option..." Billy grinned. "I'll pay him a visit and have a little chat, and that's the last you'll see of him."

Chapter Eighteen

Billy pulled up to the security gates at the office, and Fab and I hopped out. "You need anything, call," he yelled, and drove away with a wave.

Fab stayed at the office, having made plans to meet Didier and go to Mother's together in his car. I got in my beater truck and headed straight home. On the way, I called Mother and begged off dinner, complaining of a migraine. She was sympathetic and told me that Brad wouldn't be there either, as Mila's school was having parent night, so I didn't feel so bad.

When I drove up to the house, it didn't surprise me that Creole's car was nowhere in sight. I went inside and showered. Digging around in the refrigerator, I scored with a piece of leftover pizza. After I curled up on the bed with the cats and before falling asleep, I texted Creole and didn't get a response. Somehow, in a short period, I'd trained myself to respond to the slightest noise, and checked the clock with one eye when Creole showed up in the early morning hours.

I got up early, having planned a thank you for Billy, and wasn't particularly quiet moving around and getting dressed. It wasn't terribly rude, as Creole was awake, but he kept his back turned until I was ready to go out the door.

Then he sat up and propped a pillow under his head. "Whose truck?"

"Mine," I barely stopped myself from snapping. That's all he had to say? All he wanted to know? "I'm surprised you don't remember it, since you've driven it a number of times."

He responded by adjusting the sheet over his shoulder.

I shut the door with a bang and was about to jump behind the wheel when I had a thought. I dug through my tote, pulled out a tracker and hurriedly affixed it to the wheel well on the back passenger side of the Mercedes. It only took a minute, and the whole time, I kept an eye peeled, in case the gate should open, and my fingers crossed that he didn't have a reason to access the security system. Then I got into the truck and headed over to the Bakery Café. This early, I knew the cases would be filled with fresh pastries and breakfast items. I made enough choices to fill up three large pink boxes and ordered myself a large caramel coffee, my favorite of their choices by far. One of the busboys helped me get everything in the truck. I went out the back and took a shortcut that, at first glance, appeared to be someone's driveway, but I knew it was a cut through to the street I wanted to be on. I pulled into the parking lot of

JS Auto and parked in front, and before I could get out, Spoon stood in the doorway. He had a monitor on his desk that showed the coming and goings on his property. I got out and motioned him over, grabbed my coffee, and walked around to the passenger side.

"What's all this?" he asked, peering in the window and spotting the signature pink boxes.

I unlocked the door and held it open. "A thank you to you, Billy, and the guys. Mother would be horrified if I didn't show up with enough food to feed a small army of hungry men."

"Madeline has my guys pretty well spoiled, dropping off her homemade goods fairly often." Spoon laughed and grabbed the boxes. "They definitely like her better than me."

"Do they know Mother's idea of homemade is to buy it already made?" I followed him into his office, a wide open space, unlike any other car repair place I'd been in. For one thing, no car smells. In addition to his office furniture, he had a leather couch, chairs, and an arcade game. I claimed a chair in front of his desk.

"Madeline's got them fooled into thinking she slaves in the kitchen, and I know it pleases her that they're not onto her." Spoon dropped the boxes on the counter in the strip kitchen along one wall, then opened the door to the bays, whistled, and waved. He took out a stack of paper plates and dropped them on the counter, taking one. He helped himself to a couple of pastries and sat behind his desk.

Billy came through the door, eyebrows arched. He saw me and waved.

Spoon pointed to the boxes.

I waved back. "My way of saying thank you. If there's anything left, take something home to Xander." He and Xander had been roommates since the latter came to town.

"All of us out in the shop love food." Billy flicked one of the lids open. "You know I don't mind helping you out. You've got my number; call anytime." He picked up the boxes and plates and disappeared back out the door.

"Sorry about missing dinner," I said, then picked up my coffee and took a long drink.

"Probably our smallest turnout but still fun. As it turned out, Creole was the life of the party and kept us all entertained."

I managed to keep from spitting out my coffee. "That's great," I said lamely, wanting to ask if there was video tape, as that was a side of my husband I hadn't seen in a while.

"Your mother and I were happy to hear all about his physical therapy and that his hard work is paying off and the doctor is happy with the improvement he's showing."

"Great news, isn't it?" Another thing I didn't know, as he was loath to talk about any of his appointments and I'd stopped asking when he grouched at me to do just that.

"Fab also took center stage with her retelling

of the carjacking." Spoon's humor rapidly changed to annoyance. "Those two hoodlums are headed for time behind bars, where they won't find life cushy. If they make bail, Gunz needs to have a sit-down with them and explain how they could easily become fish food if they so much as look in your direction again."

"Not sure the one kid, Nick Landry, is going to be scared off that easily. I'm going to get on Fab to call Gunz today and also tell him to keep us updated on what happens with the court case."

"Not sure if you heard, but Fab got a text last night after dinner that the cops had Landry's friend in custody."

One less person to be on the lookout for. "That's good news." I pasted on a smile.

"We should have the Hummer ready in a couple of days. The glass has been ordered."

"If you've got someone that specializes in glass cleanup, that would be swell." I sucked down the last of my coffee and looked mournfully at the empty cup.

"No worries, I've got it handled. If I didn't, I'd have farmed it out to someone reliable."

"I'm going to run out on you." I stood and leaned on the arm of the chair. "I blew Mac off yesterday when she had a surprise for me, and I need to hop on over and put on my smiley face."

"It probably involves one of your whack-job tenants." Spoon chuckled. "You should've told her you'd pass."

I laughed. "One more thing before I run out the door. I know you like to be in the know ahead of time, and so... drumroll... I'm planning a girl party, and I'd like to pull it off as a surprise to the invitees. We haven't been to the Crab Shack in a while, and I thought it would be fun to chow down on good food and get our drunk on."

Spoon raised his hand. "I volunteer to be your designated driver. Depending on the number, I can pick you up in the bus or my Escalade."

"The bus is a fun idea for at least one way. I'll lure the ladies on board and not give them a clue as to where we're going." I laughed, knowing one woman that would have a fit about not getting any upfront details. "That way, we won't have to leave our cars in the parking lot overnight."

"Madeline will love being included, and she'll be fine with me keeping the secret. It'll make it even more fun for her. I'm all in for anything that makes your mother happy."

"She's also going to be happy that you're involved." I went around his desk and hugged him. He walked me outside and stood in the doorway until I backed out.

Chapter Nineteen

I drove to The Cottages and took the space in front of the office. Mac's truck wasn't parked in her driveway, so I decided to walk around and make sure all was well. It would've been hard not to notice Miss January, who was slouched in a chair on her porch singing off-key. On the rare occasions that I'd seen her sitting outside, she'd been passed out most of the time. I sucked in a deep breath and crossed the driveway.

Miss January peered over the top of her newspaper and watched as I approached. I wondered where she'd gotten it, since she didn't subscribe, and hoped that it was delivered with her liquor order and not boosted off one of the neighbors.

"Anything good in the news?" I refrained from turning the paper around so she wouldn't have to read upside down.

"I only read the obituaries." She gave me a toothy smile.

"Hopefully you don't see a name you recognize." I tugged her gently into an upright position, thinking I should've asked first, but she

171

didn't seem to mind. "You doing okay?" I brushed her cheek, which was paler than usual.

The door of her cottage flew open, and Captain stared at me like he didn't know who I was. He stepped out and swept Miss January into his arms, walked down the stairs, and set her on her feet, hooking his arm around her shoulders. "Promised my girl that I'd treat her to a hot dog."

"He's the sweetest," Miss January cooed up at him.

"He's something all right." I folded up the newspaper and set it on her chair.

Captain squinted at me.

I pasted on a smile and hoped I didn't look deranged. "You have a phone?"

Captain pulled a burner out of his pocket and held it out.

"If you need a ride, call Mac," I told him. "You have the number?"

"Yeah, yeah," Captain grunted. "Mac-y already gave me the 'no drinking and walking or driving, even on the beach' speech. I'll tell you what I told her—we don't drink out. Cheaper to do it at home."

"You two have fun," I said, and watched as they walked out to the street and turned the corner.

Miss January looked twice her age, helped along by illness, cigarettes, and alcohol, but none of that impeded her when it came to picking up men. Captain had been around for a while and hadn't died or been carted off to jail like his predecessors. I considered that a good sign.

I did a slow turn and checked out all the porches, then made a second check of the bushes, and all was quiet. I cut back across the driveway and headed to the pool, rounded the corner, and jerked to a halt when I saw that Crum's shed was gone. I'd let him put one in his parking space, and he parked his latest ride on the street. Was this the surprise? I squirmed, wondering where he'd store his trash finds now. I knew he'd never give up his hobby, which he insisted made him money.

I turned my head at the sound of coughing and wheezing and saw Joseph leaning against his unit. He struggled to catch his breath and hocked spit into the flowers, then reached out and dragged a chair across the pavement, plopping down with a loud groan.

I crept up behind him and kicked the chair.

He clutched his chest. "You shouldn't be scaring an old man like that."

I ignored him because he had color in his cheeks, not his usual sallow look. If you didn't know better, you'd think the man was maybe on his way to decent health, even with a doctor-signed death warrant hanging over his head. "Be sure you hose your spit away."

"No peeing, no spitting, what next?" Joseph laughed and slapped his knee.

"I've got an easy question for you, since you claim to know everything that goes on in the Cove — where did the shed go?"

Joseph pointed to the other side of his cottage. Since he had an end unit, his parking space was partially hidden from view. "Crum and I thought it would be a better location."

"Did you ask anyone?" Not me, I thought.

Crum cut off Joseph's stuttering response by stepping out of the shed and rolling out a hot-pink Barbie Jeep. "This is one of my better finds," he yelled when he saw me eyeing it.

I walked over and inspected the vehicle, which was a replica of a real Jeep, only waist high. It appeared to have been modified with extra leg room and had one pedal on the floorboard that I'd bet didn't work.

Noting my interest, Crum said, "It's battery operated and runs great. Tops out at five miles an hour. Got it fully charged and took it for a ride myself."

If Crum could squeeze his over-six-foot frame behind the wheel, then... I climbed inside.

Crum leaned over, gave me a brief demonstration of how it worked, and hit the button that started it up. "Fasten your seatbelt."

I made a wide turn and headed toward the street. I wouldn't be breaking any speed limits, but it was still fun.

"You wreck it, you buy it," he shouted after me.

I was almost to the end of the driveway when Fab's Porsche blew in. She blared the horn and parked next to my truck.

Safety issue. I'd need to talk to Mac.

Fab jumped out, rounded the car, and descended on me. "Move over; I want to drive. Then you can explain why, once again, you couldn't be bothered to call and I had to track you down."

I pointed to the passenger seat. "Maybe you can drive on the way back, if your attitude improves." Surprisingly, she didn't argue and squeezed in next to me. I pulled into the street and headed in the opposite direction from how I usually came and went, slowing for a quick peek at the apartment building. All was quiet. Yay! Once I passed it, I pulled onto the sidewalk, since it was all clear to the corner.

"You buy this?" Fab checked out the dashboard and rest of the interior.

"This is a Crum find. I'd be tempted if he could put an engine under the hood."

Fab hung her head over the windshield and knocked on the hood. "All the parts are plastic, so it would catch fire."

"Before you start complaining, slow is the only speed. It's so kids with a need for speed won't drag race in the street." I gave her a rundown of the morning, letting her know that she didn't miss anything, except maybe a trip for hotdogs with the romantic couple.

Fab gagged.

I stayed on the sidewalk until it ran out at the end of the block. My only option was to weave around the parked cars, and I decided that was a bad idea and u-turned. I was about to change places with Fab when a cop car rounded the corner and turned on its lights.

"What the…?" I said.

"I bet your joyride is illegal," Fab said with a big grin.

"Quick, fasten your seatbelt," I said, and turned in my seat (no mirrors), groaning when I saw Kevin step out of the police cruiser.

Kevin stalked up, wearing a big smirk. "License and insurance."

"I left my purse in my other ride." I sucked it up and managed to maintain a bland expression.

Kevin tsked, which set my teeth on edge. "The laws you're breaking by having this kid's toy on the street…"

"If I were five years old and out for a spin with mommy, would you have pulled me over?" I turned slightly and winked at Fab.

"You really need to have a better attitude toward the rule of law." He smiled, clearly enjoying himself. "You'll need to push your new wheels back to the property."

Fab and I got out and, with one hand each on the roll bar, pushed it up the street. Kevin got back in his car and followed.

"At least, he didn't arrest us," Fab said. "Probably you, since you were the driver. I'd plead ignorance, claiming you duped me, assuring me it was a legal ride."

"Duped? Good one. Regardless of how our jaunt ended, it was fun. You're going to have to take a turn around the driveway." It didn't take long for us to get back in sight of the property.

Crum stood at the end of the driveway, arms crossed, a militant glare on his face. "You break it already?" he yelled, stomping towards us.

"Hold your shorts," I barked.

"I had that problem earlier… Never mind." Crum looked down and patted his makeshift skirt.

Whatever was going on under the towel held on with a safety pin, I didn't want to know and hoped Fab didn't ask.

Mac, who'd gotten back, strolled out of the office. "You spoiled my surprise. Isn't it cool?"

I jerked my head over my shoulder. "Don't take it out of the driveway, or killjoy will pull you over."

"I did some research," Mac said, proud of herself. "The sidewalk is okay but not the street."

Crum took it from me and started to push it back toward his shed, but Fab stopped him with a shake of her head.

Kevin pulled into the driveway, parked in front of his cottage, and headed back toward me with his ticket book in hand and a huge grin on his face. He looked down, and when he looked back up, he had no expression.

Mac groaned. "Try to be nice."

"Me?" I hissed.

"He can't possibly be going to…" Fab said.

I stepped forward when he got close enough and said, "Did you know that as a landlord, I'm not legally obligated to provide air conditioning?" as though the question made sense in the situation. If he planned to write me a ticket, then game on.

"I think I did know that. Didn't you use it to get someone to move out, in hopes of avoiding going to court?"

"They lasted three days. Heard that they almost expired from the sweat." I pasted on what I hoped was a friendly smile. Since Fab laughed, I knew it failed.

"I thought you had a sense of humor," Kevin griped.

"It comes and goes."

"This is a quiet street, but it only takes one drunk or someone speeding or coming around the corner too fast for you to be toast." Kevin turned. "I've got to get back to work."

Fab waited until he was out of hearing to say, "Probably the only thing that saved you from getting a ticket is that he lives here and doesn't want to move." She got behind the wheel of the Jeep and took off down the driveway toward the pool.

"You in the mood to listen to my great idea?" Mac asked.

Not really, since I was never sure where the conversation would go. I nodded.

"We acquire a couple of fun rides, starting with the Jeep, and let the guests use them on the beach. I checked with the insurance company, and as long as we restrict use to the property and the sand, it won't be a problem."

"Maybe post a sign with the rules. Rule number one: no drunk driving, or privileges will be revoked." I eyed Crum out of the corner of my eye. He'd stopped pursuing Fab when Mac made her pitch and moved into eavesdropping range. "Get a good deal."

"You know it." Mac winked.

Fab rolled up in the Jeep and stopped at Crum's feet. "This needs to be charged."

I laughed. "It's fun, isn't it?"

Fab climbed out, ignoring my question. "I hate to be the bearer of bad news, but playtime is over."

Mac snorted. "Sure you do."

"You're the second one this morning to insinuate I enjoy 'stirring stuff,' as Kelpie put it in my brief conversation with her." Fab faux huffed, enjoying creating more drama.

I closed my eyes for a second and took a fortifying breath. "Jake's burned down, and you're just now getting around to telling me?" I grumbled. "Whatever the problem is, why would she call you and not me?"

"Kelpie claims she couldn't reach you. She also doesn't like to disappoint you in any way and decided her next best option was to shove the job off on me. Before I could tell her off, she hung up and didn't answer when I called back."

I pulled my phone out of my pocket and checked the screen. "I missed Kelpie's call. So what did she want?"

"There was a bar fight last night. Good news: no casualties," Fab reported.

"It was Carnival night. The place was packed, and a little fracas broke out. Bouff kicked butt." Mac air-boxed. "He threw the first two rabble-rousers out the door—and I mean threw—and when he shouted, 'Who's next?' the place quieted down."

I stared at her, not sure if I believed her, but then, she never lied.

"You're doing good with the theme stuff," Mac added.

"You're both full of information." The sarcasm rolled out. "Neither one of you works there, and I'd be willing to bet that you weren't even in attendance last night, and yet you both know more than me—the owner. I'll be calling an employee meeting and, at the top of the agenda, reminding everyone who's boss and that I should be on speed dial."

Rude came barreling down the sidewalk and flew into the driveway. "Did you ask her yet?"

she yelled at the top of her lungs.

"Her" probably meant me, and I wondered what else I was about to be the last to find out about.

"Let's go into the office." Mac didn't wait for an answer, instead turning and heading in that direction.

"Is Fab invited?" I yelled.

"It saves you from repeating everything," Fab said.

"We need both of your input." Mac held the door open and motioned us inside.

The four of us trooped into the office. Fab sat on the couch, Rude and I in the chairs in front of the desk.

Mac settled behind her desk. "Rude and I have been asking around about the two women who were found murdered."

"The murderer finds out, and you'll be next on the list." I made a choking noise.

Mac slammed her hand down on her desk. "You want to know what we found out or not?"

"It better be good," Fab said, making it sound like a threat.

"Both of the dead women were banging Pastel's boyfriend, Canton Long," Mac said, pleased with her revelation. "Canton has a reputation as a player—doesn't do relationships, has sex and moves on."

"Are the cops investigating him?" Fab asked.

"We tried to get Kevin interested in

investigating Canton, sharing what we found out," Rude said. "He flipped his top and told us to let law enforcement do their job and if we ended up dead, it would be our own fault."

"Kind of like what I said, and you ignored." I got up and opened the refrigerator, pulling out a bottle of water and holding it up. Fab was the only other taker. I handed her one and sat back down.

"If you compare Pastel and the other two women, looks wise, he has a type," Mac continued, as though I hadn't said anything.

"It's creepy that the women look alike," Fab said. "I take it Canton lives in the neighborhood?"

"Canton lives with Pastel, though he says he doesn't," Rude said. "He's there all the time, and I find it hard to believe that he's paying rent somewhere else. Per your instructions, I made everyone fill out a rental application—told them the previous owner kept crap records, which was true, and the new one was a stickler. I also got the ones that didn't get kicked to the curb to sign a month-to-month agreement so there wouldn't be an issue about the amount of the rent and any deposits we're holding. When I talked to Canton, he refused to fill out the application, saying he was Pastel's friend and nothing more."

"Tell Madison the rest," Mac prodded.

"I only told Mac this next part in case I got hurt or anything else happened." Rude shuddered. "Canton told me he'd knock my teeth out if I brought trouble to the door."

"Short fuse is another good reason to make our suspect list," Mac said. "Rude forgot the part about how Canton and Pastel fight like cats and she's always sporting a bruise or two. What's mind-boggling is that when you see the two together, she's hanging all over him, all smiles. I asked her once who beat the smack out of her, and she lied through her teeth and said she fell, all with a big smile."

"Anyone else on your suspect list?" Fab asked.

"Canton is the only one we could find that knew both women," Mac answered.

"These relationships with Canton, were they recent?" Fab asked.

"Canton was banging both of them at the same time and both relationships ended a month ago," Rude said without hesitation.

"And Pastel puts up with his philandering?" Fab asked.

I shook my head at her, telegraphing that we weren't getting involved either.

"Canton and Pastel have been together about a year, and it's rumored that they have an open relationship," Rude answered.

"We weren't able to find out anything about either of the dead women," Mac said. "I wanted to know about their relationship with Canton and if they thought they were exclusive, but couldn't find anyone to ask. We didn't find any close friends, only casual acquaintances."

I reached out and slapped my hand on the desk. "Enough with the questions. It's not often I agree with Kevin, but in this case, I do."

"Wait. One more." Fab laughed at my disgust. "Other than Pastel, is Canton seeing anyone right now?"

"Rude and I found out in short order that when you start asking questions about Canton, folks clam up," Mac said. "I even asked a couple of know-it-alls at Custer's and got nothing." The rathole bar was good for neighborhood information, especially regarding lowlifes.

"Would you stop investigating if I set up a meeting so you can share your suspicions with someone with connections?" I already knew who I'd ask. "Then you promise to sit back and let law enforcement do their job. I can guarantee that your accusations will be looked at carefully."

Excited, Mac nodded. "That would be great."

"Then you're going to pinkie swear not to ask another question regarding the murders or Canton." I looked at Mac, then Rude. "No more confronting Canton until he's been checked out. Either way, he's not on the rental agreement, so he needs to move. Domestic abuse won't be tolerated. If need be, he'll be banned from the property and it will be made clear that if he wants to continue breathing, he better not show his face in the neighborhood."

Rude beamed. "You know the coolest people."

"So you both swear?" I asked.
They agreed.

Chapter Twenty

Fab stood and waved me toward the door, making it official that the meeting was over. "Let's take my car," she said once we were outside. She glanced over at my truck, nose in the air. "It's hot, and the thought of riding around with the windows down makes me crabby."

"Can't have the princess feeling less than her usual self." I turned so she couldn't see my smirk and climbed into her Porsche. "For a spendy ride, it feels like my butt is dragging on the pavement."

Fab responded by hitting the gas and roaring out of the driveway. "We missed you last night. Creole's head injury has affected you both differently. He's gotten more outgoing, which was evident last night, and you've gotten quieter."

"No reason for both of us to stay home just because I had a headache." I leaned back against the seat and skipped telling her that Creole and I hadn't communicated about who would be where last night—or any of our other communication problems—lest I burst into tears because I'd begun to wonder if our relationship would ever be the same again.

A truck barreled down the highway behind us, rolled up on the bumper, and came within an inch of making contact before cutting around. The driver briefly hit his brakes and turned into the parking lot of Jake's at such a high rate of speed that he came up on two tires. Still not bothering to slow, he hit the gas and headed for the only other car in the parking lot, hitting it dead on and sending it flying forward, where it came to rest against the fencing that separated the property from the side street.

Fab had slowed and hung back at the entrance to the parking lot, and we both watched as he smashed into the back end of the SUV again. The driver backed up and did it again, its steel grille appearing to protect it. The SUV was a crunched-up mess, while the truck didn't appear to have a scratch.

"What the heck is going on?" I squealed.

"An accident can't be the excuse, since it was deliberate." Fab pulled over in front of the lighthouse and parked. We both jumped out.

"You run down and check on the drivers." I winced at the sight of the damage. "Let's hope no one was in the SUV. If the driver of the truck is all right, you can get answers out of him and then beat him up."

"I guess I need to remind you that I'm not the

owner, and therefore, it's not my job." Fab brushed her hands together and pulled out her phone.

"Bad attitude," I mumbled.

The truck squealed into reverse and made a turn to head in our direction. Fab dropped her phone and pulled her firearm. The driver made a wide swerve, rolling down his window and unleashing a litany of foul language before taking out one of the poles holding up the corner of Junker's and rumbling out of the parking lot.

"You owe me for this." Fab ran to the SUV.

"No, I don't. This is your area of expertise," I yelled, and collected her phone. To my surprise, it looked intact. "Thumbs down, and I know to tell the 911 operator to send the coroner," I yelled again.

Fab ran up to the driver's window and looked in, then stepped back and shot me a thumbs up. "No one inside."

"I'm over here." Bouff waved from the entrance to Jake's, then walked over and joined Fab in inspecting the damage to what turned out to be his ride.

After reporting the incident to the 911 operator, I walked up to the two in time to hear Bouff tell Fab, "Disgruntled customer from last night. He thought I was hitting on his woman when I suggested that she call a friend to get a ride home. She stumbled out drunk without a word to him, and he got enraged, thinking I was hiding her under the bar or… where I'm not sure, since I stood in the same place almost the entire shift."

Kelpie and Cook ran around the side of the building at the same time that Doodad came out the front. Kelpie, phone in hand, slowed to take pictures.

I sidled over to Doodad and asked, "You ever go home?"

"Lucky me—liquor delivery. Or I'd have missed the fun and had to listen to someone yammer on, retelling the story third- or fourth-hand." He turned slowly, inspecting the exterior of all the buildings that shared the parking lot. "Could have been worse."

"You want to be the one to tell Junker he's got to stay out of the building until we make sure it's safe?" I followed the abrupt turn of Fab's head and saw the two cop cars that'd pulled into the parking lot.

Doodad snorted. "I'll bet you five that it's repaired and looking like new by tomorrow. No, make it the following day."

Kevin and another officer got out of their cars, and Bouff waved them over.

"Sucker's bet." I glared at his grin, which only made it bigger. I wondered if Kevin had flipped a coin with the other officer and lost, as he was now questioning Fab. "If you can wave your magic wand and get it taken care of without us getting into a paperwork nightmare, I'd extend one of those favors you're eager to amass."

"Hello *again*." Kevin sauntered over. "You got anything to add different from your friend, as you two seem to always have the same story?"

"Probably not." I gave a concise version of what went down.

"Based on the description we got of the truck's grille, I've got a good idea who we're looking for," Kevin said as his partner rejoined him. The two of them turned and walked over to inspect the damage.

"Cold drinks before you go," I yelled.

Kevin waved over his head.

Cook had been standing a foot away, surveying the damage, and then he wasn't. Disappeared. I'd bet one of his relatives would soon be on the way over to fix the damage.

Kelpie skipped over. "You're going to love my idea," she said in a bubbly tone. "Huge, and I mean huge." She threw out her arms. "Grand reopening. It'll be a blowout."

"Except that to reopen, we have to close, and that's not happening," I said.

"Killjoy," Doodad mumbled.

"Don't you worry; I'll handle it. It's all in how you present it. We'll have the patrons believing the building was demolished and rebuilt overnight." Kelpie's hands waved wildly.

Drunks might believe the story, but no one sober. "You hit me, and I'll shoot you." I backed up.

"Overreaction much?" Kelpie crossed her arms and tapped her foot.

"I'm hungry." I felt mildly confident that if I didn't give her idea a thumbs up or down, she might forget about it. If not, I'd sic Doodad on her.

Fab strode over. "SUV's probably totaled. Told Bouff that you could hook him up with a tow job and a loaner. I offered to squeeze the money for repairs out of the driver, but he said he'd rather his insurance take care of it and they can go after him."

"Does what just happened here have anything to do with the fight you didn't bother to call me about?" I asked Kelpie.

"Not exactly. Maybe." Kelpie rolled her head around. "I called. Check your phone."

I squinted at her until she looked away.

"I do my best," Kelpie said emphatically. "Some dude was yelling at Bouff about him stealing his girlfriend, and I asked, 'The one that slunk out the back, hanging on some other guy?'" He went running for the exit. At the same time, two guys started pushing and shoving, then fists got thrown."

"And?" I asked, not sure why she stopped suddenly.

"Bouff rounded the bar and separated the two guys, and words were exchanged that I couldn't hear. He signaled for me to toss him the shotgun, which he cocked, and that's all it took to clear a few tables. So smoking hot," Kelpie gushed. "Told him so."

I caught Fab smirking at Kelpie and frowned. "Did you or Bouff by chance call the cops?" I asked Kelpie.

Her pink strands of hair flew from one side to the other, which I interrupted as an emphatic no.

"If Kevin hasn't heard, he will, and then he'll be all over me with questions and I'll plead complete ignorance, which I'm sure he'll believe."

"Here he comes, and he doesn't appear happy." Doodad nodded. "If you need me, I'll be locked in the office. Don't forget the secret knock." He went back through the front door before anyone could blink.

"A little shot of sugar, and Kev lightens right up," Kelpie whispered.

"Once again, excitement last night and no 911 calls. What do you give the patrons for such cooperation?" Kevin asked.

"I plead ignorance, since I wasn't here," I said. "After our employee meeting, I'll have someone call you. How's that?" His lips quirked, so I knew he wasn't totally irked. "Is it okay to have the SUV towed, or are the cops doing it?"

"After we're done here, you can have it hauled off," Kevin said.

Following through on Kelpie's idea, I said. "You or your partner want food or drink, Kelpie will put in the order." I didn't feel the least bit bad about siccing Kelpie on Kevin. He tolerated her more than the rest of us, as evidenced by his smile as she gyrated around. I waved and headed around the side of the building, Fab by my side.

"Kevin was in a good mood. For him," Fab said as we entered Jake's through the kitchen door.

Cook was on the phone in his office. We walked down the hall to the bar area and slid onto stools. I did a one-eighty. The interior looked like a bomb of confetti and streamers had gone off, covering the floor.

"Theme night got a tad messy." Doodad, who was behind the bar, waved his arm. "Don't worry, we'll have everything cleaned and ready to open on time."

I found that hard to believe, since opening was in an hour. A locked door wouldn't detour anyone; they'd go through the kitchen and kick through the mess.

"As for the fight, if you can call it that, a few punches were traded and it was over." Doodad sounded disappointed. "Can you believe we had another surge after the fight? Good news travels fast." He brightened up at relaying the last part.

"Don't go all Kelpie on me," I said. "Two of you would be too much for me."

Fab slapped her hand down. "We'll take our non-alkie usuals. You know which of us wants extra cherries." She pointed to me.

"Where did Bouff disappear to?" I asked.

"Right here." He came through the deck doors dragging a trash can, a push broom in the other hand. "After Kevin got done grilling me, I went around the back and up the stairs."

Doodad set down our drinks.

"Where's Kelpie?" I asked.

"Out in the parking lot. Young, old, half-dead—as long as they're still breathing, she's flirting." Bouff laughed.

"I need to talk you," I said to Bouff. "I'll be out on the deck making a few phone calls." I walked outside, flipped on the overhead ceiling fans, and sat down. "You can leave me here," I said to Fab as she sat down across from me. "I can catch a ride."

"I'm hungry, what about you? I bet I can talk Cook into making something we like."

"While you're charming him, can you find out why python was listed on the chalkboard as a special last night?" I about fainted when I saw it listed prominently on the top as we passed it leaning up against the wall in the hallway. "You're to tell him in explicit terms that he's never to sell it or any of its family members again. Poor snake," I muttered under my breath.

"I need extra favors for these dirty jobs." Fab gave me the stink eye, and I laughed.

"Righty-o. I'll be sure and keep track for you."

Fab did her best to maintain her annoyance, but who knew her better than me? I winked at her. She turned and stomped back inside. Bouff crossed paths with her as he came out and slipped into a seat across from me.

"I'm going to call about your car," I told him.

"No need. Got it taken care of. I'm not without a few connections."

"You've probably heard about the two women that were recently found dead."

Bouff appeared surprised that I knew. "Also know there's no suspects yet."

"I've got two Nancy Drew wannabes that have a theory or two and a suspect. I'd like you to hear them out, as it could turn out to be good info, and then discourage them from any more investigation."

"They going to listen?" He raised his brows.

"If you assure them that they're being taken seriously, then hopefully. I'd like you to make it clear that they're to butt out. I don't want either woman getting hurt… or worse." I told him that it was Mac and Rude.

"Since they know the neighborhood, it could very well turn out to be a good lead."

Fab came through the door and said, "I ordered a lunch platter. Plenty for everyone. I did your dirty work and ixnayed any future snake choices on the menu. I pointed the finger of blame at you, and Cook laughed. So that went well."

Doodad came through the door behind Fab and sniffed. "Terrible seller. It doesn't taste like chicken as advertised, more like shoe leather."

Chapter Twenty-One

The sun had barely made an appearance the next morning when I rolled over in time to see Creole's backside going through the door. I stuck my hand out from the under the sheet and waved. "Good excuse to get up early," I grumbled to myself as I rolled out of bed and hit the shower.

I spent about a second giving thought to my appearance, then put on a jean skirt, tucked in a white button-down shirt, and slid into sandals that could be easily swapped out for tennis shoes if needed. The day needed a jump start of a double dose of caffeine, and I slid through the drive-thru on the short drive across the Cove to the office. I pulled in through the security gate, squinted over at Toady's side and, not seeing any activity, parked on Fab's side and hiked up the stairs.

As I unlocked the door, I realized it was the first time I'd been in the office alone. I curved around the corner and into my space and set my tote down, then opened the sliding door and took a seat at my desk. If I could make one change, it would be to add rippling water sounds

197

coming up from below, but not much chance of that since it was used for boat parking. I pulled my laptop out and started the process of updating files.

The door opened and slammed shut. I didn't have to wonder who was making all the noise for very long.

"Why is it that I'm always chasing you around town?" Fab bellowed.

"Can you bring me a water?" I yelled, and laughed to myself. It's always a good day when you can annoy your best friend.

Fab slammed around, and I listened as her footsteps went from her desk to the kitchen and stomped into my office. She set two waters down and slipped into a chair.

"Good news," I said. "Spoon assured me that the Hummer would be as good as new and ready for pickup tomorrow. I'll be happy to ditch the beater truck until the next emergency."

"You couldn't call that you were coming in early?" She sniffed and stared around my small space as though I'd moved something.

"Next time, okay? We both know there will be one." I smiled cheekily.

"Almost forgot. Gunz called. He's got a job, and he'll be here in a few with the details."

I didn't believe for a second that she hadn't asked for the particulars. If I had to venture a guess, the odds on favorite was that it had to do with another relative of his. "Here's a suggestion:

why don't you have Gunz get to the point in an email or over the phone, like the rest of your clients? Unless you like these in-person sit downs and enjoy that he drools all over you."

Fab scrunched up her nose. "Eww."

The door slammed open again. "Fabiana, my dear," Gunz hollered, his heavy footsteps barreling down the hallway.

I made a barfing noise. "Let's take this party out to your desk."

Before we could move, he rounded the corner, settled his bulk in one of my chairs, and threw his briefcase on the desk. I made a face when he turned to Fab and got a stink-eye response from her.

"Nick Landry bailed out," Gunz announced.

"So much for 'Hello, how are you?'" Okay, that came out snarkier than I planned.

Gunz ignored me, his attention centered on Fab. "Kid disappeared. So keep an eye out. Though he's got bigger problems than the two of you shooting him on sight." He chuckled.

"You promised to make this problem go away," I snapped. "A warning to watch our backs falls short of keeping your word."

Gunz continued to ignore me. "The Jeep the two were joyriding around in was stolen from the daughter of a drug dealer. She claims Nick boosted her keys while they were making out and took off, leaving her stranded."

"Isn't he clever," Fab said sarcastically.

"When the girl's old man finds him, Nick won't have to worry about any future court dates," Gunz continued.

"Nick's barely eighteen, and at the rate he's going, he's going to be found dead in an alley somewhere," I said.

"I used Nick's current problems to your advantage," he told Fab. "Had a chat with Peg and offered to help Sonny Boy when she recanted her story against the two of you. Promised to fix her up with a good lawyer."

"You're too late. The case has been closed," I snapped. "No good lawyer is going to have her recant now and risk the ire of the prosecutor after she left them hanging the first time."

"Tank called with the update," Fab told Gunz in a more conciliatory tone.

"I don't understand why Peg gets to walk for filing a fake police report. If one of us did that, we'd be behind bars." I ignored Fab shaking her head for me to tone it down. "Let's not forget the woman impugned our reputation."

Gunz whirled around and finally made eye contact. "Since the case is closed, we can just move on and I'll owe you one."

"And our arrest record?"

"It will show that the charges were dropped."

"Swell." I amped up my glare to equal his. Not quite but close enough.

Gunz turned his attention to his briefcase, snapping it open and taking out a single sheet of paper that he slapped down in front of Fab. "I need you to serve this eviction notice and strongly suggest to the tenant that he hit the road before the three days are up." He'd removed the bite from his tone that he'd used with me. "My patience is at an end."

Fab glanced at it and slid it across the desk to me.

"If anyone could put the fear of death into someone, it would be you, so why send us?" I asked.

"That was Plan A." Gunz's eyes filled with anger. "Paid the little bastard a visit, knocked politely on the door, and the coward wouldn't answer, even though I knew he was home."

I'd bet he took his meaty fist and beat on the door until the hinges rattled.

"Next thing I know, the cops showed up. Told them I scared him." Gunz grinned. "Fortunately for me and him, one of the officers was an acquaintance, who pulled me aside and stressed that I needed to boot his ass to the curb all legal-like. So here's where you two lovely ladies come in."

I managed to stop myself from retching.

"I want to make it clear up front that we won't be doing anything to prompt your tenant into making another call to the cops," Fab told him. "If I get arrested doing another job for you, I'll be forced to choose between you and Didier, and I'll be sad to end our relationship."

I grinned.

"You know…" Gunz turned to me as though he was about to say something, then changed his mind and turned his full attention back to Fab.

I made a brooming motion behind his back, which Fab ignored.

Gunz turned slightly, and I feigned interest in my laptop screen.

"I have this lawyer friend that's in need of an investigator. Before I recommend you, I thought I'd run it by you first." Gunz continued when Fab nodded noncommittally. "Primarily divorce cases, which would require you to serve papers and, on occasion, tail cheating spouses."

I was about to answer for her— "Not interested." —when she spoke up.

"Based on past jobs, divorce cases come with a fair bit of drama, especially if it's a surprise to the one being served. I'm going to refer you to Toady, as he never complains if anything goes south."

Gunz grunted in annoyance but didn't say anything one way or the other. He once again inched the eviction notice towards Fab. "Will you give me a call once the job is completed?" He didn't wait for a response, but stood and grabbed his briefcase.

The two walked out together, and I waved at his back. I heard Fab's promise to get right on serving the notice, and the door closed.

I shoved my laptop and a couple of folders

into my leather tote. When she came back to my desk, I asked, "Can I drive?" knowing it would be a cold day in hell before she let me behind the wheel of the Porsche.

"We're taking the pickup, and the answer is still no."

I followed her downstairs, and we got in the truck. Once out on the highway, she stopped without asking and got us both an iced tea.

Headed down the Overseas, Fab said, "Didier and I were talking, and we've both noticed a few changes in you." She peered at me out of the corner of her eye. "You're quieter, more introspective. I don't know what's going on with Creole's recovery, but if there's anything either of us can do, all you have to do is ask."

No way was I having this conversation with her or anyone else. And the one I wanted to open up to—Creole—did everything he could to avoid anything emotional. "We're getting along great; it's almost like the injury never happened," I lied. "You're turning at the next block," I added in an attempt to change the subject. Thankfully, it was a short drive, since Gunz always bought his investment property in and around the Cove.

For once, Fab didn't bother with a sweep of the block, but pulled up in front of the duplex and parked. "We're dropping this and leaving."

We got out and walked up to the door. The drapes were open, which afforded a view of the empty living and dining room.

"We lucked out," I said. "Legally, we tack it to the door, mail a copy, and job complete."

Fab turned the knob, and of course, it opened. She walked in and went down the hall, poking her head into one of the two open doors and then the other.

I stayed in the doorway.

She came back and went through the small dining room and into the kitchen. Suddenly, she screamed and hustled backward, then turned and hightailed it back across the room and pushed me out the door, slamming it behind her.

"What?" It couldn't be a body or Fab would be too busy taking pictures to rush out the door.

"Alligator."

"A real one?" Recovering from the shock, I said, "I suppose it's alive?"

"Oh yeah. It moved." Fab grimaced. "The apartment is empty, except for one large exception; the tenant left his alligator behind." She peered into the front window. "Look." She tugged on my sleeve.

Sure enough, an alligator poked its head out of the kitchen and turned in our direction.

"You're on your own." I backed up toward the truck. "Just a reminder: it's illegal to shoot them." I turned and hustled to the curb. I'd had enough of this day, and it was barely afternoon.

Fab ran after me. "Where do you think you're going?" She jerked on the back of my top, and I wiggled out of her hold.

"Not my job. Not even close." I held up my hands. "Free advice: get Gunz on the phone and see if he'll get down off his snooty high horse regarding Toady and have him relocate one of his friends. Before you start, I saw Gunz's face when you mentioned Toady, and he thinks he's better than him. Well, he needs him now, doesn't he?" I pulled my phone out of my pocket.

"Who are you calling?" Fab demanded.

"Toady. I'm giving him a heads up to expect a call from Gunz and that he's to charge double — no, make that triple — his usual roundup fee. If the man gives him the slightest attitude, he's to boost his fee even more."

Fab pulled her phone out and backed away. I'd be reminding her of what she just did the next time she wanted to listen in. I called Toady and left a detailed message. Fab moving her phone from one ear to the other, and I guessed that Gunz was having a hissy fit. It was another few minutes before she hung up.

"I thought he'd never calm down," Fad said. "Gunz wants me to take care of rodent removal. His word, not mine," she clarified when I rolled my eyes. "Get the locks changed and send him the invoices."

"You're in luck because Toady can be your one call for getting everything taken care of — the *rodent* and the locks." My phone rang and Toady's name popped up, so I handed it to Fab, who took my suggestion and foisted the entire job off on the man.

"Do you think the tenant was keeping it as a pet?" Fab asked.

"This is Florida. It's probably a support animal and comes with only a slight chance of eating you for dinner."

Chapter Twenty-Two

It took me a couple of days to set everything up for the girl lunch. I could have been straightforward and just extended invitations, but where was the fun in that?

Creole left early to go to the office and had no clue what I was planning, which was fine with me, since the fewer people that knew, the better.

My first call was to Mother. I knew she had nothing planned, as I'd checked with Spoon. "You up for a surprise?" I asked when she answered. I caught her off guard with the question and didn't get the phone manners speech.

Mother hesitated. "What kind?"

"One that you're going to have to trust me on," I said, detecting a small groan. "Pick you up in two hours. Wear your new black sleeveless sundress and some cute sandals."

"It's not that I don't trust you—"

"That's good to know," I interrupted, knowing where she was headed. "Love you." I hung up.

Next on my list was Fab, and there was already a checkmark next to her name. I'd booked her for the day on a bogus case of my own. When she shot questions at me, I told her I had another call coming in. "I'll be at your house in a half-hour. Dress cute." I hung up without giving her a chance to respond.

Spoon called from the gate, and I buzzed him in. I grabbed my purse and a shopping bag and was outside when the short bus that Mac had purchased to take guests at The Cottages on excursions around town pulled up in front. Thus far, there had been rave reviews about the impromptu sightseeing trips. I could have squeezed everyone into the Hummer, which had been returned with new glass and no telltale signs that it had been shot at, but this was more fun.

I waved as he opened the door, then grabbed the bar, climbed the steps, and took a seat.

"Where's your friend?" Spoon asked.

"Slight detour." I felt my cheeks turn pink, as I was about to make a nervy request. "We're picking her up at her house. If you could pull up in front of her door and lay on the horn and generally be obnoxious, that would be fun. Don't you think?" I said in response to his raised brows.

After a minute of thought, he laughed. "Be my pleasure. Your mother will be annoyed that I didn't pick her up first." He put the bus in gear, rolled down the street, and pulled into the driveway. I stood, waiting for him to open the doors, and retrieved the bullhorn from a shopping bag. It made the rounds of whoever could lay their hands on it, and right now, that was me. The whole time, he non-stop honked.

Fab stuck her head out the door, mean-girl glare on her face, and didn't move or say a word.

"All aboard," I yelled into the bullhorn. I'd have to come up with a really good hiding place for the horn, or Fab would break in and steal it.

Spoon laughed.

"One minute is all the time you've got to make up your mind," I yelled again, then lowered my voice, which was loud enough. "If you don't speed it up and take a seat, you're going to miss out on the fun."

Fab slammed her door.

"That didn't go well," Spoon said. "At least, she didn't shoot us."

"Patience," I said with a big grin.

The door opened again, and Fab came out, banging the door closed behind her. In stiletto heels, her bag over her shoulder, she stomped over, managing to stay upright, but didn't get on. "I'll take my own car," she said in her snootiest tone to date.

"The hell," I yelled into the horn.

"Put that damn thing down." Fab's arm shot out, but she was too far away to get possession.

"Ladies, as much fun as it would be to break up a chick fight, we're going to be late," Spoon said.

"Last chance — your butt on the bus or see ya."

I waved like a lunatic.

Spoon turned and looked out the side window, his shoulders shaking."You be quiet," Fab snapped at him, "or I'll be driving and you'll walk." She came up the steps and sat across the aisle from me, staring straight ahead.

I'd given Spoon the addresses ahead of time and which order for pickup.

We pulled into the complex where Mother and Spoon lived, and he parked. "I'm going to go get your mother. No fighting while I'm gone. Wouldn't want to miss anything." He laughed and jumped down the steps of the bus.

"You can't go the whole day without talking to me." I stood and crossed the aisle to sit next to Fab, but she wouldn't scoot over. "You're mean."

"Your job? New client? All a ruse?"

I went back to my seat, ignoring her irritated tone. "If this excursion totally blows, I'll owe you one. How about that?"

"Deal." The corners of her mouth turned up.

Spoon came back downstairs, his arm hooked through Mother's, and she was laughing up at him. He helped her on board, and I stood and hugged and kissed her cheek before she sat next to Fab, who moved over. Spoon winked at me.

Last stop: The Cottages.

I'd called a staff meeting, and only Mac, Rude, and Kelpie were invited. My only edict was "wear something cute." None were happy that I hadn't answered a single question, but not a one confronted me or told me they wouldn't be showing up, even after I told them attendance wasn't mandatory. I did tell them that if they weren't at The Cottages at the appointed time, I would know that they weren't interested in having their questions answered. My ending comment with each one before hanging up was, "See you or not."

The three women were laughing it up in the barbecue area, and when the bus slowed into the driveway, they waved and cat-called. As soon as Spoon had the doors open, they lined up and trooped aboard. They took seats, and Spoon roared off to our final destination.

It was a quick ride to the Crab Shack, where I'd made reservations for a window table. The restaurant was a favorite of everyone in the family. He pulled up to the front door and helped each of us down the steps.

"Are you coming in with us?" Mother asked Spoon.

In response, he laid a big kiss on her that inspired a shrill wolf whistle from Kelpie. He whispered in Mother's ear, and she giggled. Spoon climbed back on the bus and honked.

"Don't worry, ladies," I said as Spoon pulled out. "He'll be back to get us all home safely, so we can all get our drunk on." I led the way, pausing briefly at the hostess stand. We were led around the bar and seated at a table on the deck overlooking the water.

When the drinks were served and my pitcher of margaritas was set in front of me, I stood. "I want to thank you all for coming." I tipped my glass. "Some of you were more gracious than others." I pinned Fab with a stare, and her nose went in the air. "This is my way of saying thank you for all that you do to make my life less interesting."

"I'm not sure that's a compliment, honey," Mother said, and raised her glass of Jack whiskey.

"Please..." I grinned. "Without these women, the you-know-what would continue to hit the fan, but it would fly everywhere instead of being contained... somewhat." I toasted again.

Everyone laughed.

"Anything new on your murder investigation?" I directed the question to Mac and Rude. Both blushed and fidgeted, so I knew they were still snooping around. So far, the body count was still two and there were no new persons of interest, at least not that the two women had been able to ferret out. Bouff was sufficiently impressed and took the information to a friend on the force, assuring me that Canton would get a closer look.

"Now what?" Mother groaned.

"I share your sentiment, Mother, and since they're not listening to me telling them to leave it to the cops on this one, maybe you can talk some sense into them."

I'd pre-ordered an appetizer platter, which arrived and was set in the middle of the table. The talk was light and funny as we enjoyed the food and our drinks.

Kelpie kept us entertained with stories about the regulars that came into Jake's. She'd had six proposals of marriage and a dozen to shack-up. She wasn't interested in doing either. She also had an update on Bouff's car. The driver of the truck had tested positive for drugs. He'd at least had insurance, and Bouff got a loaner while his was being fixed. A restraining order had been issued against the driver—the man had to stay away from both Bouff and Jake's.

"My turn." Fab held up her glass. "Since Madison has set a precedent..." She paused to take a healthy sip of her martini.

I eyed her as if she were a roach that I was about to step on, which only widened her grin.

"Now is the time to air anything inappropriate," Fab continued. "Just blurt it out. If you can embarrass anyone else at the table, all the better."

"Madison's not that bad." Mother smiled.

If I'd been sitting closer, I felt certain she would've patted me on the head. "Mother, since you're sitting next to Fab—smack her one."

All eyes shot to Mother and Fab, waiting to see what happened. They exchanged a look and laughed.

I pointed at Fab. "You're lucky that I don't

have some petty crime to out you on, or I'd be jumping to my feet and announcing it with gusto."

The laughter and talk continued, nothing scandalous.

A pale forty-something woman, her stringy brown hair in disarray, approached the table. She jerked Mother's chair back, leaning down into her face. "Stay away from my man," she spit out.

The table went silent, as did the one next to us. Kelpie and Fab, the first to react, jumped to their feet. A step ahead of Fab, Kelpie grabbed the woman by her shirt and flung her off the deck, where she bumped her butt down four wooden steps to a small strip of sand. She immediately jumped to her feet, screeching.

I got up and took Fab's empty chair, sitting next to Mother.

Fab scowled at me when she turned. "What's she talking about?" she asked Mother.

The woman started back up the steps, and Rude, now on her feet, advanced on her and pushed her back into the sand.

I motioned to Mac. "Get a picture of her."

"Spoon is mine and always has been," the woman screeched.

I laughed. "And to think the guys are missing this."

That earned me a glare from Mother and Fab.

"You're delusional," Fab growled at the woman. "Where have you been, if he's your supposed man?"

"Suppose nothing." The woman unleashed a slew of four-letter words.

Mother leaned toward me. "I've never seen her before. Shouldn't you be the one defending me? Beating the heck out of her? I am your mother, in case you forgot."

The only reason I didn't roll my eyes was because she'd forbidden it when I was a kid and was staring right at me, and some things stuck. "I'm not getting in a fistfight. If whoever that is gets close to you, I'll shoot her. But the chances of her getting past your bodyguards are nil."

The manager flew out the door, and Kelpie told her that the woman had shown up ready to brawl. The manager had a few words with the woman, who responded by nodding and was quietly escorted out.

"The manager threatened to call the cops, and that's what shut her up," Kelpie, who'd been hanging over the railing listening, reported. "Makes you think she's wanted."

"Where's Rude going?" Mother asked.

Rude had disappeared into the restaurant and followed the other woman.

"Knowing Rude, she's questioning the woman, getting her life story," Mac said, and stared at me. "Like someone else we know."

"So you stole the chick's boyfriend and then got him to marry you?" Kelpie beamed at Mother. "Impressive."

Mother, not the least bit insulted, grinned back. "I'm not jumping to any conclusions until I talk to my husband."

Rude came back to the table, her eyes leaping with excitement as she slid into her chair. "That was Sharl Wells. She and Spoon used to bang, but that came to a halt when she went to prison for attempted murder. Sharl claims that thoughts of Spoon were the only thing that got her through ten hellish years behind bars. She got early parole because she was a model prisoner and hightailed it back here. Personally, I thought she got off easy but kept it to myself."

"How did she find Mother?" I asked.

"Luck. Sharl came to the Cove looking for Spoon, but wanted to find a job and a place to live before making contact," Rude said. "She knew he had someone new and even spotted the two of you having coffee at the Bakery Café — twice. Today, she came in to apply for a job, spotted you out here, and without thinking, she said, came out to stake her claim."

"You're telling us that Mother has to look over her shoulder?" That wasn't happening. I'd run the woman out of town myself.

"I told her that Spoon was very happily married and she needed to move on," Rude said. "Felt bad when she got teary-eyed, but she needed to hear the truth. Reminded her that if she'd been hauled off by the cops, she'd be on her way back to the pokey for violating her probation, and that put the fear into her." She looked at Mother. "I told her that your daughter just got out of the nuthouse and wasn't entirely cured, and she wouldn't be the first person your daughter fed to wildlife." Rude was clearly enjoying her description of me.

I shook my head. "You could've told Sharl that Fab would use her for target practice."

"That's a good one. If there's a next time, I'll use it." Rude grinned at Fab, who growled at her.

I banged my spoon on the table and held up my glass, which I'd refilled. "I want to thank you for jumping to Mother's defense; you're an impressive lot."

When we stumbled out of the Crab Shack hours later, pleasantly tipsy, I was disappointed to see that Spoon had sent Billy in the Escalade to drive us all home. I'd hoped for the man himself, so we could each have a turn grilling him.

I got out of the car and hugged Mother. "Call me and tell me, word for word, what Spoon says or, better yet, have a family dinner. It's not like anything is private in this family."

Chapter Twenty-Three

It had been a quiet day. I spent it at home on the deck, working on my laptop, updating files. Finally done, I snapped the lid shut and went into the house, crossing to the kitchen for something cold to drink.

The door flew open and hit the wall with a thud. Startled, I slipped behind the island.

Creole stormed inside in the suit pants he wore to work, the sleeves of his dress shirt rolled up and his jacket slung over his shoulder. He tossed it on the counter, crossed his arms over his chest, and stared at me, his eyes on fire. His shoulders shook with barely contained rage.

It was the second time I was truly scared of him. This time seemed worse than the first, when he'd yelled his head off. There was a time when I could easily have said that he'd never hurt me. At least, not the man I married. This new version... all bets were off, and right now, I wasn't sure.

I waited for him to speak, but he just glared. I didn't know whether to run or close the distance between us. I stayed rooted to where I stood. "How was your day?"

He lunged at me with lightning speed and grabbed me by the neck, sinking his fingers into my throat before he slapped me so hard that I stumbled backward.

One hand went to my throat, the other to my cheek, and I stared at him in shock.

With uncontrolled fury rippling through his body, he came after me again, grabbing me by the back of the hair and yanking my head back, forcing me to look into his icy-hard eyes. He pulled on my hair so hard that I yelped. The ferocity in his eyes only grew as he breathed hard, directly into my face. "What the fuck were you thinking?" His face turned red as spit flew from his mouth.

"I don't know what—"

"Shut. Up." He tightened his hold on my hair. "You disrespected me and our marriage by blabbing my health issues all over town. Who else besides Didier and Fab?"

He'd told me not to speak, but I couldn't stay silent. "I haven't talked to anyone about you. When asked, I say that you're doing fine and nothing more."

He released his hold and pushed me back. I stumbled against a stool and managed to stay upright. "How could you do this to me? You don't think I've been through enough?"

He stalked forward, and I backed up until I ended up in the living room, intent on putting the couch between us. The cats, who'd been fast asleep, had disappeared.

"You think I'm not haunted by the events of the past?" A vein throbbed on the side of his head. "You. Betrayed. Me."

"I didn't. If you'd give me a chance—"

"I'll never forgive you." He shoved his finger in my face, shaking it. "You know I've been working closely with my doctor to get back to a hundred percent. I asked you to keep my personal business private. You pushed me too far this time. Too fucking far," he ranted.

I fought the tears that burned in the back of my eyes. They weren't from the pain of my cheek burning where he struck me. They were from the heartbreak of watching our marriage crumble.

His features still contorted in anger, he growled, "I don't want to speak of this again."

Enraged, Creole was clearly unwilling to listen and showing no signs of calming down, so I kept my mouth shut and brushed at the tears that leaked from the corners of my eyes.

He turned and walked into the closet, came out with a change of clothes, and went into the bathroom, then turned again. "I hate this place, always stepping over one another." His shoulders rigid, he looked ready to destroy everything in his path. He kicked the door shut, and the noise reverberated through the house.

I collapsed into a chair, fingering my cheek gently, still fighting the tears but losing as they streamed down my cheeks. I hoped that once he calmed down, we could speak rationally. I'd at least try. That didn't happen.

Creole opened the bathroom door and stood in the doorway, continuing to glare. He'd changed into shorts and a t-shirt. "Since you can't keep from running your mouth, stay away from our friends."

I stood and moved behind the chair. "If you'd hear me out—"

He sneered. "Save it." He slammed out of the house.

My attempt to brush away more tears failed as I stared at the door.

* * *

After a long night of little sleep, tossing and turning and staring at the clock, I got out of bed at first light, made a cup of coffee, and took it out to the patio. I chose a chair with a view of the beach below, where I could also keep the door in my peripheral vision. My hope was that after a night apart, Creole and I would be able to talk. I didn't know the man he'd become and frankly didn't like him. Worse, he scared me.

The door opened, and he barreled through. His eyes darkened noticeably when he saw me staring back at him. He looked at me with indifference, devoid of any affection.

I stood and moved to the open pocket door. Now that we were together again, I didn't know where to begin. I'd hoped for an apology, some kind of explanation for his abhorrent behavior, and promises that it would never happen again. It didn't appear that I'd be getting any of those things.

He didn't say a word and instead walked into the closet, grabbed a change of clothes, and disappeared into the bathroom to take a shower like he did every morning.

I thought about breaking the cold silence but realized I was afraid of his reaction. It wouldn't be the first time of late that I'd been afraid. I didn't know how women who lived with fear every day did it. I went back to my chair and turned it slightly to give me a clear view of the inside of the house, picked up my coffee mug, and stared down at the remnants, having lost interest in downing the rest. I refused to be intimidated by him, but it took everything I had to sit there, be silent, and see how things played out.

Creole came out of the bathroom dressed in jeans and a shirt. He glanced my way, and his jaw clenched. His eyes narrowed in a fierce frightening glare. "In case you've forgotten, keep your mouth shut about anything having to do with me. Got it?" I nodded. This time when he left, he closed the door softly, and if I hadn't been watching, I wouldn't have known he was gone. But then, he'd had plenty of practice sneaking in and out with all the nights he'd slipped away.

Hearing his car start up, I stood, crossed to the kitchen, and placed my cup in the dishwasher. I grabbed the remote and flipped on the TV, catching sight of his car as it cleared the compound. I watched as the security gates closed behind him. Not sure how much time I had, I ran to the closet and lifted my suitcase and the cat carrier down off the shelf. I emptied the drawers into the suitcase and threw my clothes on hangers in a garment bag; shoes went into a shopping bag. My personal items in the bathroom went into another bag, my electronics into my briefcase.

"Come on, kitties." I unzipped the cat carrier and put a fleece throw in the bottom. Neither cat bothered to open their eyes. I picked them up and put them inside, and they both meowed their displeasure. "I know you hate riding in the car." I filled another tote with all their food and tossed in a couple of toys for them to ignore.

I knew where I wanted to go, but it didn't have a stick of furniture. The last thing I wanted to do was involve my family, and for now, I'd keep it secret that I'd moved out. No one would notice a night or two at The Cottages, but beyond that, someone would spot my SUV and ask questions.

Chapter Twenty-Four

It didn't take long to pack up the Hummer. Anything I forgot, I'd buy. I put the cats on the passenger seat and talked to them as I drove, which they ignored, but at least they stopped meowing. Thankfully, Fab and Didier had plans for the day, and I didn't have to come up with any excuses that my friend would be able to see through. I wasn't ready to tell the truth.

I'd already checked cottage availability with Mac, only to find out that we were booked. I headed there anyway and set the cats up in the office. They gave the place a sniff over, then jumped up on the couch and stretched out. Mac and Rude were gone for the day, off on a sightseeing trip, taking the latest guests out for a spin on the bus.

I called Xander. "I've got a top secret project."

"I'm in," he said, excitement in his voice.

I gave him a list of instructions, and we hung up. I drove around the side of the property and parked in front of the garage, which was used for storage. Hoping to escape everyone's attention, I cut through the bushes and entered through the door at the back of the laundry room. I checked over the few pieces of furniture there and mentally tagged a couple, already trying to figure out how I'd get everything moved with no one asking questions. I loaded a few essentials into a plastic bin, carted it out to the Hummer, and shoved it into the back seat.

Climbing back behind the wheel, I cut through the back streets to my new warehouse acquisition, opened the security gates with the keypad that Xander had programmed, and drove around the back. Once I hit the Overseas after leaving the compound, I knew that I wouldn't be going back to the beach house, maybe not ever. I fingered my cheek and winced. I'd avoided the bathroom mirror this morning after a quick glance—the bruise on my cheek showed, as well as a faint one on my neck.

For now, the third floor of the warehouse would be my temporary home. Only a handful of people knew that I'd purchased the property, and not a one of them concerned themselves with my personal business.

Xander had already arrived and was sitting on the bumper of his truck. He'd unloaded several boxes, a ladder, and a toolbox and stacked them in the elevator. "You need furniture," he yelled as I got out of my SUV, having parked next to him.

"I'm going to snag a few pieces from The Cottages. Any clue how I can get them here with no questions asked?"

"You going to tell me what's going on?" he asked expectantly.

"You can't tell anyone. Pinkie swear and all that?" I asked. Xander nodded, and we held our fingers up in a symbolic gesture. I gave him a bare-bones version of what had happened the night before, which he saw right through.

Xander's face clouded over. "What a dick," he snapped. "I get that head injuries are serious, but to go from easygoing to a dick-weasel? Is he ever going to be his old self, or are you stuck with the new version? Know that if there's anything I can do for you—call. You don't need to worry about me telling anyone anything."

"I'm hoping… I don't know what I want. I do know that I need time to think." Except that wasn't the whole truth. I wanted my old husband back, and as time went by, it didn't appear that that was going to happen.

"Toady's at the office." Xander pulled his phone out of his pocket. "You know he can be trusted not to talk. I'll have him bring his truck and meet us at The Cottages, and we can get everything moved."

"I should probably be the one to ask."

"I got this." Xander made the call and, with minimal explanation, got the man to agree to meet us in half an hour.

The two of us rode up to the third floor and unloaded everything. Once finished, he looked the place over, and we left. I followed him back to The Cottages and pointed out the pieces of furniture I wanted—a rollaway double bed, kitchen table, two chairs, television, and a standing lamp. The men had the truck loaded in short order. While they did that, I put the cats in the Hummer and, once back at the warehouse, got them situated. They were happy once they sniffed out their food and water.

The men unloaded everything and placed it facing the windows. So the place wouldn't feel like a tomb, I'd opened the metal louvers, where they'd stay.

I told Toady what had happened and asked that he not say anything to anyone.

He came over and patted me on the back. "You need anything…" He shook his phone.

"I appreciate you."

He grinned and roared out of the driveway.

Before he left, Xander hung the television on the wall so I could see it from the table or bed and made sure that my electronics were up and running.

* * *

My first night on the top floor of an otherwise empty warehouse was creepy. I'd left the television on all night, the sound down low, to drown out any noises, and thankfully didn't hear anything. The quiet of the night also held a certain eeriness, knowing that there weren't any neighbors close by and wouldn't be until the businesses opened in the morning. After giving the space a once-over, the cats jumped up on the bed, having identified it as the only comfortable place to sleep, and sacked out. They didn't venture from my side except for food and water.

Sleep had been fitful, so I was awake when the sun came up and shone through the slats on the windows, reminding me to call someone to clean the glass before the floors were leased. When I first opened my eyes, it took me a minute to adjust to where I was. Then the memories of why I wasn't home in my cushy bed came crashing back. To be honest, I'd expected a phone call, but my phone hadn't rung once. I stared at the ceiling and mulled over my choices, wondering if I should've made different ones. Except that I honestly hadn't done the things Creole accused me of.

My phone rang, making me jump. I reached out and grabbed it off the chair I'd dragged over next to the bed. Creole's face popped up on the screen, and I hesitated to answer. "Hello?" I said hesitantly. It was an early hour for us both.

"Do you intend on ambushing me and turning family and friends against me?" Creole's barely controlled anger radiated through the phone.

Swallowing back hurt and anger, I said, "No one needs to know that we're living separately, and they won't be hearing it from me."

"Let's hope you can keep your word. This time." He hung up.

I stared at the phone, unable to believe that he'd hung up, but sure enough. Interesting that he thought more of other peoples' opinions than mine. It was never that way before, but that was then and this was now. A lot of things had changed. Not one word about working out our problems, and not talking wasn't a good way to figure out our relationship.

The phone rang again. I groaned and flipped the screen up. This time, it was Fab. I hadn't even had my coffee.

"Where are you?" Fab grouched as soon as I answered.

"I had an early morning errand," I said evasively.

"Doing what?"

"Fabiana," Didier admonished in the background.

"Isn't it a little early for you to be out and about?" I asked — more evasion, which I knew had no chance of derailing the woman.

"When Didier and I came home last night, the Hummer wasn't parked at your house. In case you've forgotten, I have security cameras and checked them this morning and still no SUV."

"That's a total invasion of my privacy," I said with as much sarcasm as I could muster. "I'll be at The Cottages in about an hour."

Chapter Twenty-Five

In a mood to be obnoxious, I snagged the parking spot in front of the office door at The Cottages and laid on the horn. The door flew open, Mac poked her head out, and I waved her over. I cast a quick glance over my shoulder, making sure I hadn't woken the drunks. Then I got out, went around to the back, and opened the liftgate, handing a tray of coffee to Mac. I grabbed my tote and retrieved two pink bakery boxes, having stopped at the Bakery Café, and followed her into the office.

Before we could get the door closed, a pricey sports car squealed up and parked next to my SUV. I knew who the driver was without having to look. After setting everything on the desktop, I picked up the coffee with Mac's name scribbled on the side and handed it to her. "Not knowing your favorite, I took a guess." Mac grinned at me. "If you don't like it, you can pour it in the bushes."

"Love coffee, no matter the flavor." Mac took the lid off and licked her lips, taking a long drink.

Fab threw the door open and flounced inside. "This better be the last time I have to hunt you down."

"Or what?" I didn't wait for an answer and pointed out the obvious: "You found me, didn't you?" I handed her a cup of what I knew to be her favorite brew — she'd be calmer after a super jolt of caffeine.

Fab took the cup but eyed it suspiciously. She took off the lid and sniffed, then took a long swig. "Didier and I are worried about you." She turned doubting eyes on me. "What happened to your face?" she demanded in a huff.

"There's a mark on her neck too," Mac said, as though that should've been obvious.

"I fell," I said lamely. I guess I didn't do a good job covering the marks.

Fab set her coffee down, got in my face, and stared. "It's not that I don't believe your explanation, but I don't. I could be persuaded if you were to expand on the details."

I put my hand on her biceps and gave her a slight shove. "I'm claustrophobic."

Fab backed up and sat next to me.

When no one said anything, I guessed that Fab was waiting for me to break the silence. I didn't have the energy to hide the drama surrounding me anymore and knew that Fab would be relentless in ferreting it out. "Can you swear that what I'm about to tell you, you won't share with anyone else, and that includes Didier?"

Mac opened one of the pink boxes and smiled while choosing a breakfast pastry.

Fab looked surprised. "I don't hide things from Didier."

"I understand, and normally I wouldn't ask, but this situation is personal, and therefore, I need the non-disclosure pact." I'd never given it much thought, but I hadn't expected her to ever repeat our private conversations unless it was some funny tidbit or about our personal safety. It was hard to know what was said to Creole or by whom or how much he'd overreacted. I attempted to change the subject. "Why were you looking for me? You in need of backup?"

"Nice try. You're not changing the subject," Fab said. "I'm your best friend, and knowing you as well as I do, I know there's something going on with you. I want to know what it is." She held up her right hand. "I won't say a word to Didier. If he suspects something and asks me, I'll tell him you took me into your confidence and I promised not to repeat anything."

"I just don't want to cause a problem between you and your husband."

"No worries."

"Do you want me to leave?" Mac brushed crumbs off her lips. "But know that I'm a good secret-keeper." She locked her lips.

"You're good." I took a long drink of my coffee, not sure where to begin. "To backtrack a bit…" I told them about the first argument that

Creole and I had.

"That was my fault." Fab frowned. "I was worried about the changes in you and how you seemed on edge, so I discussed it with Didier." She blew out a long sigh. "I'm so sorry. I should've known that Didier would go to Creole and offer to do whatever he could, and as it turned out, he offered to help him find a new doctor. I found out after the fact, but Didier assured me that Creole took it well and appreciated the offer, and I didn't think anything more about it."

"Neither of you could've known that Creole would flip out. I sure as heck didn't." I cut off my memories of that first night. "I agreed not to speak of our marriage to anyone, and anytime someone asked, I gave a noncommittal response." I downed the rest of my coffee. "Night before last, Creole came home livid. I didn't know what he was talking about, as I'd been careful not to mention our life or his health to anyone, but he didn't give me a chance to tell him any of that, to defend myself. The anger poured off him, and he got so enraged, he grabbed me by the throat and slapped me, almost knocking me off my feet." I fingered the sore spot on my neck.

"He wouldn't. He hit you?" Fab sat forward and stared again. "The bruise on your cheek is faint, but that's because you've tried to cover it with something." I nodded. "I thought you were joking when you said you fell and that there'd be a better explanation, but not this."

"Creole's changed all right," Mac said. "Saw him a few days back at the gas station, and he didn't acknowledge me when I said hello. I made an excuse for him at the time, like maybe he hadn't heard me, even though he made eye contact. He was never like that before... well, you know."

I knew Fab believed me, but I didn't want there to be any doubt that I was exaggerating. I pulled my laptop out of my tote and set it on the desktop, opening the lid and waiting for it to start up.

"The reason you didn't come home last night is because you left him?" Fab asked. "Not seeing the Hummer yesterday was weird enough, and then it was still gone this morning."

While waiting for him to come home that night, I'd set up a file and stored copies of all the exterior and interior footage. I'd made a separate file for what went down the other night. Pressing play, I turned it around for Fab and Mac to see. They both watched in silence.

Mac sucked in a breath.

"What the hell's gotten into that man?" Fab demanded. "I've never seen him so out of control. Creole practically lives at our house, comes over almost every night, and Didier and he walk the beach. Whenever we're out with him, he's the life of the party. He slapped you!"

"It's come to my attention that my husband has a social life that doesn't include me. A few times now, I've found out after the fact that invitations were issued to both of us to come to dinner at your house or Mother's, and he never said a word. A couple of times, you asked why I was a no-show, and I came up with some excuse, probably a headache." I grimaced. "He must have heard me, because one time, he gave Mother the same excuse for my not showing up."

"I was about to suggest that you see a doctor about those headaches." Fab's face tightened with annoyance. "It never occurred to me that he didn't share the invitation."

"I'm not giving Creole a pass for slapping you, but what about the rest of your relationship?" Mac asked. "I'm asking because it might be something you two could work through, as long as that never happened again."

"Since the kidnapping, we're two people who share the same space, roommates and nothing else." I looked at Fab. "When we got arrested for that carjacking, he didn't say a word to me, didn't even ask if I was okay. It was a long ride home. You probably haven't noticed, but he never calls and checks on me anymore."

"Why in the heck didn't you tell me what was going on?" Fab practically shouted, then took in a deep breath, sighed it right back out, and flipped her hair over her shoulder. "So you packed up, and you're staying here?"

"No vacancies. Which is good," I said.

"We have one starting tomorrow," Mac said.

"I've got accommodations at another place." I reached over, closed my laptop, and shoved it back in my bag. "It was a surprise for Creole that he never got to unwrap." My phone rang, and I took it out of my pocket. Casio's face popped up. "I thought about you for a second the other day," I said when I answered.

"Nice to know I haven't been forgotten." Casio thundered a laugh. "Calling to cash in one of my favors."

"No and no, and I don't owe you squat." Both Fab and Mac were all eyes. Fab motioned for me to put the call on speaker, and I shook my head and mouthed *Casio*. She kicked me, but not very hard. I swiveled my legs away, in case she decided to do it again.

"Don't hang up," Casio ordered. "You do, and I'll show up on your doorstep."

That was the last thing I wanted. "Get to your request and be quick."

"I have a job interview down in your neck of the woods and need you to look after my kids for a couple of hours. I won't make a good impression showing up with my brood, even though they're well-behaved."

"Hang on." I looked up and asked Mac. "Crum home?" She nodded. "Can you fetch him? Make sure he has clothes on." I said to Casio, "As long as we're agreed that when you come to pick up the kids, you'll make time for a chat and not split and say, 'I forgot.'"

"Deal."

"I'm in the office at The Cottages."

"I'll be there in five."

I could hear the humor in Casio's voice and snarked, "You were sure of yourself."

"It's part of my charm." He hung up.

"I'll be right back." Mac jumped up and rounded her desk.

"Mention cash up front and he'll probably beat you back here," I said before Mac blew out the door. Seeing that Fab was about to grill me, I cut her off and repeated the conversation. "Wonder what kind of job he's interviewing for down here."

Casio recently retired from the Miami Police Department to be a full-time dad to his children, who'd lost their mom to cancer. His last case was the drug bust of Trigger and his million-dollar operation—the same man who'd kidnapped Creole and Didier when I bested him on a real estate deal. It was unclear to me whether Trigger'd planned on releasing the men when he got what he wanted. We'd never know, as he died during the takedown.

"Casio's not short on nerve," Fab said, as though I needed reminding. "What do you want to talk to him about? You do know that if you want something, he'll use it to extract more favors. He's forgotten that he still owes you big for taking care of his kids the last time he asked. On the 'who owes who' list, you're way ahead."

Crum saved me from all the other questions that Fab wanted to ask by opening the door and ushering Mac inside. "You snap your fingers, and here I am." He curtsied awkwardly, looking like a frog. He'd donned a towel, which he'd fashioned into a skirt, and a stained dress shirt which only had one button.

"I need you to corral four of your favorite students and keep them entertained for a couple of hours." I held my hand two feet off the ground as a clue. "It's your job to make sure they don't drown and have a good time. Name your price. You screw me, and it's the last time I hire you for squat."

"Include food, and I'll toss you a freebie." Crum's smile had me doing a double-take.

"Not so fast. I'll need you for the rest of the day, and I'm sure you'll want some cash in addition to all the food you can eat."

He opened the door and stuck his head out. "They're here. I'm going to go out the back and put some pants on; some folks just don't get my fashion sense." He closed the door, rounded Mac's desk, and went out the back door.

Fab made a choking noise.

I got up and went outside as the kids piled out of the SUV, retrieving their backpacks and screaming their hellos.

I gave them a frantic wave, and the oldest

FRAUD IN PARADISE

rolled his eyes. "Let's see if I can remember your names. The youngest and prettiest, Lili." I smiled at the little girl, who launched herself at me for a big hug. "Number one and number two." I pointed to the identical twins, still not knowing which was which. "And Alex."

"We're moving down here," Lila announced, a huge smile on her face.

Alex and Fab engaged in a convoluted secret handshake.

Casio lumbered out from behind the wheel and clapped hands with his kids. "Behave, and that includes you, Alex." He turned to me. "Headed down to Marathon. Shouldn't be more than a couple of hours. Then I'm all yours." Before I could ask any questions, he jumped back in his SUV and roared off.

Crum came around the corner, dressed in board shorts and the same dress shirt. He hadn't bothered with the button, and his chest, white hairs here and there, was on display. "Hey kids," he yelled.

They screamed hellos and ran to meet him.

"I'm taking them to my place so they can put their stuff down and get some towels," Crum said to me.

"Got that covered. I'll meet you at the pool," Mac said, and disappeared back into the office.

"This is just what I need—a few hours by the pool, kids laughing and having fun," I said, and meant it. I followed Mac into the office, got a tub

239

out of the cupboard, and filled it with cold drinks
from the refrigerator.

Chapter Twenty-Six

Behind schedule and running late to pick up his kids, Casio texted that he was on his way and would bring pizza. I read it to the kids, and a round of cheers went up. We'd spent the day hanging around the pool. Crum had kept the kids entertained, jumping in and out of the water and playing games.

"You should go home and be with your husband," I said to Fab, who sat next to me. I'd asked her if we could talk about something other than Creole, to which she'd reluctantly agreed.

"Not a chance." Fab got up, taking out her phone, and walked over to the tiki bar. She talked and laughed for several minutes, then came back and sat down. "Cleared it with Didier."

I stood. "I could use some extra muscle." I flexed my own, which got a laugh out of Fab.

We pushed several tables together so there'd be room for everyone. Joseph, who'd been hanging out by the pool, got invited with the understanding that he bring Svetlana. The kids liked her more than they did him, since he had a tendency to grumble under his breath while Svet, his rubber girlfriend, always had a smile for everyone. The old guy had acted half-pleasant all day, which probably had to do with the fact that he'd been drinking out of a paper cup most of the time and was half-snockered.

True to his word, Casio showed up with several boxes in hand and a shopping bag of cold drinks. He'd met Mac in the driveway, and she held the gate open for him. He set everything down on the table, then waved to his kids and pointed to the pizza.

I finished setting the table and Casio set up the chairs. The adults sat down while the kids continued splashing in the pool. Mac refilled the enamel bucket with ice, restocked the soda, water, and beer, and sat down.

"The Chief sends his regards to you both." Casio eyed me and Fab. "He's irked that there hasn't been anything new on the Seraphina Reynolds case that he sent the two of you chasing after. He doesn't like it when a case goes unresolved, and he has a bad feeling that she's probably going to turn up dead, since that's how a lot of these cases turn out."

"You went on a job interview and hooked up with the Chief…" I tapped my cheek. "It's my deduction that you're going to work for him again."

"It's not like I'll have a new boss to break in. I know what I'm getting. He agreed, before I even drove down here, that he wouldn't give me flap about needing flexibility to parent. Which I want you to know—" Casio slapped his hand down in front of me. "—I don't totally suck at."

"Knew that already." *Duh* in my tone.

"There was that one time I went off the deep end, but the kids ganged up and reeled me back in." Casio looked embarrassed.

"Oh no, you made a parenting mistake?" I asked in faux shock.

"That's not really any of your business," Fab said.

I made a face at her.

"I grounded my oldest for the rest of his life." The sides of Casio's mouth curled up. "My youngest had to sit me down and tell me it was too long." He grimaced. "Alex climbed out his bedroom window in the middle of the night to smoke and drink with his hoodlum friends. You know I did that when I was a teenager, but I sure as hell didn't tell him that."

"What kid doesn't sneak out?" I asked in a teasing tone. "I did that a time or two, minus the cigarettes. And you've got three more to go."

"I instituted a new rule," Casio said. "If they think it's going to scare me in any way, then they can't do it. I'm sure they'll forget and I'll have to remind them."

The kids jumped out of the pool and dried off. Casio laughed and smiled at them as they came up and hugged him before sitting down.

He flipped the lids on the boxes, and everyone

helped themselves. Joseph wasn't interested in food, so he claimed a chair at the end of the table, put Svet in the chair next to him, and promptly went to sleep. The kids kept the conversation going, and in between reliving the highlights of their day, they wrangled a promise out of their dad to jump around in the pool with them before they went home.

Once finished, the kids asked to get back in the pool. Casio gave the go ahead, and they cleaned up after themselves before jumping back in and taking Crum with them.

"I'm late because, on the way back, I stopped to look at a house," Casio said. "The location was the prime selling point, as it would be a short drive to work. But the inside was a complete fixer-upper, and I don't have the time or patience the repairs would require."

"So, we're going to be neighbors... of sorts," I said. "I'm surprised that you'd want to be away from your extended family. I assumed that you'd kissed and made up?"

His brother, Brick, had supported his wife's decision to wage a custody battle for Casio's kids, declaring him unfit after his wife died. He'd fought them and won, and their once-close relationship took a huge hit.

"Hardly." Casio snorted. "Told my bro not to call unless he grew a pair big enough to stand up to his wife. Brick knew trying to steal my kids was wrong. I may call him and gloat that I had dinner with this one." He winked at Fab.

For years, Brick Famosa was Fab's only client. He'd professed to care about her but didn't think twice about putting her safety on the line. I didn't want to think about all the cases of his that came with ducking bullets.

I stood and cleaned up the table.

Mac and Casio wrestled Joseph out of his chair, and Casio helped the man back to his cottage, drunk-mumbling all the way. Mac followed with Svetlana.

"Don't even suggest that I go home to my husband," Fab said. "I know you're getting ready to have a talk with Casio, and I'm not going to miss a word."

Casio walked up, grabbed a beer, and sat in one of the chairs I'd pulled around to face the pool. "Mac helped me get Joseph on his bed; he was snoring before we left the room. Hot girlfriend." He grinned.

"Don't you be romancing Svet," I admonished with a smile. "Since she came into Joseph's life, he hasn't been to jail." I took a fortifying breath. "I have a few questions for you."

"I've got answers." Casio winked.

"This is about Creole. I want to know what happened to him while he was being held by the criminals you were paling around with. His personality has changed, and not for the better. Thus far, there's been little improvement—parts of his memory are still missing, and he doesn't remember anything about the kidnapping."

"I was in the warehouse the night Creole and Didier were dragged in. Both had been drugged." Casio paused, lost in thought for a moment. "Trigger appeared to be caught off guard and was extremely annoyed, which led me to believe he didn't make the call to pick them up and had me wondering who did. I knew it wasn't the two grunts that brought the guys in, as neither would risk their neck without being told directly to go collect them."

"I'd thought all this time that Trigger ran the show and called all the shots," I said.

"That's what he wanted everyone to believe, but he had a partner, who didn't get arrested when the raid went down. Or he did and wasn't fingered as one of the brains, but if one of the other men had known, they would've traded that information for a lighter sentence." A beach ball rolled up to his feet, and he gently kicked it back to his daughter with a wink. "I've kept in touch with a few local informants and have it on good authority that no one's attempted to resurrect Trigger's operation."

"I have a few sources of my own that I asked for any updates, and so far, nothing," Fab said.

"Creole and Didier were separated and held in different rooms." Casio nodded toward Fab. "I saw Didier a couple of times, and he was treated well, considering he was being held hostage. No signs of abuse." He finished off his beer, setting the bottle down. "No one was allowed in the room Creole was being held in, and now that I think of it, I never saw Trigger come or go, either."

"Where were you when the raid went down?" I asked.

"Standing downstairs when the door got kicked in. Law enforcement had surrounded the place and a number of them rushed inside, and most everyone gave up peacefully. Trigger decided to shoot his way out and was taken down."

"You talk to Creole since the rescue?" Fab asked.

"Didn't talk to him at the hospital. He'd been taken for x-rays when I got the boot," he said.

"What has Creole's doctor told you?" Fab asked me.

"The last I talked to his doctor was at the hospital as he was being signed out. I asked to accompany Creole to his appointments, and he said no. 'Head injuries take time to heal' is the only thing I get from him, which echoes the sentiments of his doctor. Come to think of it, he hasn't mentioned an appointment in a while." I didn't share that it was a subject that annoyed him."The last time I saw him was at the family dinner, and on the way out, I told him that if he needed someone to talk to, give me a call," Casio said. "He told me we were never friends and let's keep it that way. I felt like sticking my foot up his ass but refrained." He chuckled. "Creole's name briefly came up today. The Chief said he doesn't answer when he calls and doesn't return messages. So he stopped bothering, thinking Creole would get in touch if he needed to talk."

I reached for another water bottle, passing one to Fab and a beer to Casio. If only I had a pitcher of margaritas, I'd have sucked them down already.

"Did I answer all your questions?" Casio asked.

"I had an ulterior motive. You saved me a trip to Miami to track you down. I would've treated you to my best cop knock." I laughed, then sobered and told him about Creole's nightly treks. According to the tracker I put on his car, he was going to the warehouse.

Fab hissed, and I knew she was thinking about all the secrets I'd been keeping and still was.

Casio's eyebrows went up. "Every night?"

I nodded. "At first, I thought maybe another woman, but settling for middle-of-the-night rendezvous would be weird. Then I came up with him suffering survivor's guilt, except no one died except Trigger. But Creole didn't know the drug dealer before everything went down, other than by reputation, and I can't imagine they bonded in any way."

Casio hesitated before offering, "You want me to check the place out?"

"Not without me," I said adamantly. "I don't

want to go by myself, which is where you come in. At night is out of the question; Creole would be sure to catch me, and it would be the end of my marriage." Or me. "I don't want any kind of confrontation. I'm thinking of checking the place out in the daytime, when I know he's otherwise engaged."

"What do you think you're going to uncover by snooping around?" Fab asked.

"I'll admit it's probably a waste of time, but I'd feel like I was doing something," I admitted. Stupid, probably.

"I'll do it," Casio said. "I'll give you a tour, answer your questions, and even if nothing comes of it, it will be one less thing for you to overthink about. You set the time and date; I'll come back down, bring the kids, and we'll stay overnight. I'll hire the professor to keep them entertained."

"I have access to Didier's schedule and can let you know when they're going to be out of the office for a couple of hours," Fab offered. "They always have outside meetings. I agree with Casio—one less thing to worry about. No matter what, you'll feel like you're doing something."

"Thanks to both of you," I said.

"So this means we're friends." Casio held out his knuckles.

"Yeah, sure." I made a face at him and smiled.

He laughed.

Chapter Twenty-Seven

The next morning, my phone rang and Fab's face popped up. I'd known she wouldn't be happy since she didn't know where I was staying. She'd left The Cottages the night before to go home, and I'd stayed while Casio and the kids played in the pool. Casio had offered to follow me back to the warehouse, and I'd jumped at the offer, not anxious to go back by myself.

"You're not at The Cottages," Fab grouched.

"I'll text you the address. But you need to bring something to eat. Also, if you don't want water or coffee mix, you need to bring your own beverage."

She readily agreed and hung up.

I rolled off the bed and fed the cats, who'd jumped down and were staring expectantly. They hadn't launched into their usual morning howls, so they were also getting used to the new digs.

I'd left my open suitcase leaning up against the wall and dumped my garment bag on the floor next to it. I hadn't given a thought to where I'd hang anything, as there wasn't a rod in either of the storage closets. I rooted through my suitcase, tossing clothing over the top, until I decided on a full skirt and top.

The cats preferred a rumpled bed, but I straightened it anyway. I found the remote under the comforter, turned on the television, and flipped to the screen showing the front gate.

It didn't take long for Fab to drive up. Another first—answering the buzzer for the first time. I pressed the speaker button. "Who's there?"

"Food delivery."

"Yum. The code is Mother's birthdate, for future reference." I buzzed her in. "Pull around the back." I watched as the gate closed behind her, then went out and stood at the top of the steps. "There's an elevator." I pointed.

Fab climbed the stairs, pink box and shopping bag in hand. "I like what you did with the exterior. A little paint and some landscaping, and it doesn't look like the rundown pile it was before."

"Such a gracious compliment." I laughed and flourished my hand. "Come in."

"You've got the minimalist thing going on." Fab looked around and approached the table, setting everything down. "Must have slipped your mind to tell me you bought this place." She raised her eyebrows.

"It was meant to be a surprise for Creole, since it was his idea. I didn't tell anyone except the person who orchestrated the deal so I could remain anonymous during the transaction, and I want it to stay that way for now."

Fab walked around the space, checking out the bathroom and opening the cupboards in the kitchen and the refrigerator. "You need to go shopping or eat takeout." Her nose went up at the sight of my suitcase on the floor.

"No place to hang anything."

She sat on the bed and bounced, then stroked the cats. "How long are you staying?"

"I haven't given any thought to a long-term plan... or a short-term one. I had hoped that Creole would've calm down enough to call me by this time. That hasn't happened. He may be waiting for me to apologize, but I didn't hit him or accuse him of things he didn't do." Since he'd never acknowledged his awful behavior, I didn't hold out any hope for an apology. I motioned her over to the desk and looked in the shopping bag. "Good thing you brought napkins and utensils."

"Is it legal for you to live here?" Fab went over to the window and looked out.

"You know it isn't. But no one except you, Casio, Toady, and Xander knows that I'm here, and I'm certain that none of you will turn me in."

"You should've come to my house."

"Since Creole spends so much time there, I was certain that if I did that, it would've ended any hope of us sitting down and talking."

Fab opened the pink box and set a pecan roll on a napkin, shoved it across the table, and handed me a cup of coffee. "Isn't it unnerving here at night? Knowing you're the only one in the building?"

It was, but I didn't want to talk or think about it, so I ignored the question and took a bite of the roll. "This is sweet of you," I said, and moaned my appreciation.

Not deterred, Fab asked, "When do you plan on telling your family? You know it's impossible to keep anything from them for long."

"I'm not thinking about that today."

Fab didn't roll her eyes, but it was clear she wanted to. "It's my opinion that you should only get back together if Creole's going to get help for his anger issues, and only if it's what you want."

I nodded noncommittally.

"I'm serious about you coming to my house." Fab took the lid off her coffee and downed half of it. "You'll have your own room, and as you know, it's on the opposite side of the house and Didier and I don't go over there."

"What are you going to do? Hide me?" All the ways that could go wrong flashed through my mind. The fact that she didn't have a ready answer meant she was thinking about doing just that. "When Didier finds out, and he will, he'll flip out about all the sneaking around."

"If you haven't heard from Creole in a couple of days, then you're moving in with me. I'll figure out what to say to Didier so he won't get mad and how to do it so Creole won't find out."

"If I haven't gotten a call from Creole by then, I'll contact him and suggest a neutral place to meet and talk. See what comes of that." I felt a deep sadness that our marriage was on the rocks.

We finished our breakfast in silence. I stood and flipped up the lid of the bakery box, licking my lips at the sight of the two rolls still inside. "These for me?" I grinned.

"Score you. Leftovers."

I cleaned up, came back with water, and sat down.

"I got an interesting call from Essie Newman, that friend of Sugar's," Fab said. "She actually asked to speak with the 'red-headed one.' That would be you."

"What did you tell her?"

"That I'd pass along the message and you'd get back to her."

"As a good assistant, did you write down the number? And perhaps the gist of what she wanted?"

Fab made a face.

"What surprises me is that you didn't pull a con on her and morph into me," I said. "It wasn't like she could see you. You could pull it off for a short time... but then you'd get frustrated and hang up."

Fab's cheeks pinkened, and guilt momentarily crossed her face.

"You did, didn't you?"

"Too loud. Echoes in this place." Fab rubbed

her ears. "Essie didn't buy it for a second."

I laughed.

"After that… which was a bit embarrassing—" Fab shook her head, appearing to relive the moment. "—I told Essie that I'd need something to motivate you to call, and all she would say was that it was about Sugar. Asking for a bigger hint irked her immediately. She snapped, 'Just have her call me.' and hung up."

"You should've told her that it was your case, which would be true, and I tagged along because… you'd have come up with something nice."

Fab made a face. "I wouldn't count on the nice part."

"Why me? I barely contributed anything to the first conversation."

"And still you came off as the more approachable one," Fab faux grouched. "I know you're about to ask…" She pulled her phone out of her pocket and flicked through it, hit redial and the speaker button, and handed it to me. Essie answered on the second ring.

"This is the red-headed one," I said. "What can I do for you?"

"I'd like you to trot on over here so we could have a chat," Essie said in a demanding tone. "The sooner the better."

"You need to give me a reason," I said. "We're talking Miami, after all, which is a long drive from where I'm located."

"It's about Sugar, and that's all you're getting."

"Why not have this conversation with Fab — you know, the other one — although I'm fairly certain that she doesn't trot."

Essie snorted. "She's intimidating. You coming or not?"

Today? I mouthed at Fab, and she nodded. "We'll be there in two hours," I told Essie. "This better be good and not some time-waster, because I'd be tempted to rough up an older lady."

"I'll be waiting." Essie cackled and hung up.

I handed Fab back her phone. "You need to get hot on the phone with the Chief and make sure you're getting paid."

"I owe him a freebie for not getting anything concrete the last time."

"You can't guarantee results. A few freebies, and you'll stop taking his calls. Better not call me; I'll tell him he's cheap." That made Fab laugh. I got up and strapped on my Glock, slipped on a pair of slides, and shoved a pair of tennis shoes in my tote. "What do you suppose Essie wants?"

"Bugs me to have no clue." Fab picked up my purse and handed it to me.

Chapter Twenty-Eight

Fab pressed her foot down on the gas and made the trip to Miami a short one. She pulled up in front of the art deco apartment building and parked. Once again, the restaurant that shared the property wasn't open. It was a quiet neighborhood and such a beautiful day, you'd think you'd see people out enjoying the sunshine, but there was no one.

The furniture on the patio had been rearranged since our last visit. In a colorful ankle-length dress, Essie sat under a large umbrella on a wicker couch facing the entrance, her bare feet on a stool. She waved us over as we entered the courtyard.

"This better be good," I said, and sat in a chair opposite her, Fab next to me. "It would be horrible if I asked my friend here to beat the heck out of you."

Essie laughed. "When you two showed up the first time, I don't know what I thought, other than that you could be trusted, which is what I told my friend. I talked her into asking for your help, because she needs it and she can pay. If she couldn't, I'd ante up."

Friend? I looked around the property.

"What kind of help are you talking about?" Fab demanded.

Before she could answer, the exterior door to the apartments opened, and a woman in a form-fitting red-striped sundress that hugged her ample curves, large sunglasses, and a wide-brimmed sun hat stepped out and looked around. She nodded to Essie, then walked over and sat next to the woman.

I stared at her hard, recognizing her from the pictures I'd seen, and checked her out from head to toe, taking note of the bruising covering her arms and face that was now yellowed and fading. The deep slit in her mid-length dress showed evidence of more bruising and cuts and scrapes that were scabbed over. I noticed Fab doing the same thing and was certain that she also recognized the woman.

"Sugar, these are the women I told you about," Essie said.

Fab made introductions. "Essie says you're in need of help. If it's not something I think we can handle, I'll refer you to someone else."

"Happy to find you alive, because honestly, we didn't think you were," I said.

"There were times... Before I tell you anything, I want assurances that this conversation goes nowhere unless I give permission." Sugar smiled grimly. "I understand that you're private investigators, but I need to be sure that I have confidentiality."

"I never discuss my clients with anyone," Fab assured her. "If I did, I wouldn't be in business long."

"Fab is the licensed investigator; I'm her bodyguard." I smiled, amused at my choice of words. I didn't dare look at Fab.

That garnered stares from both women.

"I'm hiring you." Sugar stuck out her hand and shook Fab's. "How much?" She took a wad of cash out of the front of her dress.

Fab waved off the money. "Why don't we wait and see if I can be of any help and then discuss payment?"

"It's quite the story. I might not have believed it if it wasn't coming from Sugar," Essie said. "You two need anything to drink before she gets started?"

We both declined.

"I was kidnapped," Sugar said, getting straight to the point, and drew in a long breath. "I'd gone to the mall that day and was coming out to my car, focused on where I was going next and not paying attention to my surroundings. I unlocked my car, and before I could get the door open, I was grabbed from behind. A rag was pressed to my mouth, and the last thing I remember was the terrible odor and my knees giving way."

Essie reached over and enveloped her in a hug.

"When I woke up in the back of the van, I had no idea how long I'd been there. I'd been blindfolded with a smelly rag but could see out of the corners. There were two men arguing—one wanting to have 'a little fun' with me and the other insisting that they didn't have time. That man reminded the other that they needed to get out of town, call, and report the job done. One of the men realized I'd come around and jumped on me, ripping my clothes, and I fought back. I wondered later whether if I hadn't and just lay there and let him have what he wanted, he wouldn't have beat me so badly."

"Now, didn't I tell you no blaming yourself over the what ifs?" Essie admonished in a light tone. "I know it's hard not to do. Instead, share your feelings with me." Her love for the younger woman shone in her eyes.

"I honestly thought some greedy person had found out I had money and I'd be held for ransom and let go once it was paid," Sugar said. "Wrong. The van hit a rough patch and came to a sudden stop, the door slid back, and each man grabbed an arm and a leg. The next thing I knew, I was airborne. I hit water and floated in between two huge boulders, where I got hung up on the rocks. After I heard the van rumble away, I yelled for help until I went hoarse, but nothing. When the darkness came, I never believed I'd survive."

Essie snuggled closer to her.

"Take all the time you need," Fab said.

I nodded, watching as she struggled to tell the story.

"It took most of the next day to work myself free of the boulders and climb up the rocks. If I hadn't been in top physical shape, I'd be dead. That's when I realized the men had driven out to the end of a jetty, gave me the heave ho, and lucky me, they didn't stick around to see where I landed." Sugar blew out a broken breath. "I didn't have it in me to move any farther and laid down to die on the gravel and rock. No one was around, and I gave up."

"Just a little more." Essie patted her hand.

"I don't know how much time elapsed before the cops found me. I tried to tell them what happened, but nothing made sense. I woke up in the hospital, hooked up to machinery. It was another few days before I was completely awake. When the cops came back with more questions, I gave them a phony name and claimed to be homeless." Sugar grimaced.

"Why not call your husband?" Fab asked.

Essie snorted.

"You don't know how badly I wanted to go home and still do." Sugar laid her head on Essie's shoulder. "I was able to hear parts of the conversation when the driver called to report the job done. I had this feeling that he was talking to my husband, but hard as I try to remember, I don't know why I thought that. I could be wrong, but what if he was involved and I show up at home? He'd never let me live."

"What do you want us to do?" I asked.

"I want my life back. To not have to wonder what would happen if someone saw me alive and walking around," Sugar said.

"Are you aware that your sister is the one who hired a private investigator to find you? That would be me." Fab smiled. "Or rather, the company I work for."

"More red flags. My sister and I aren't that close. We talked on occasion and maybe got together for lunch once or twice a year. So how would she know I was missing?"

"Why not go to the police?" Fab asked. "They'd at the very least question your husband and sister. It would be easier to get him out of the penthouse if he were in jail."

"Fear. I'm not sure exactly what I heard and can't swear to anything definitive. I figure that once I admit to that, the cops won't waste their time," Sugar said.

"How did you get here?" I asked.

"When I improved enough that they wanted to release me from the hospital, I heard talk of sending me to a homeless shelter. I called Essie, who rushed over with clothes and brought me here." Sugar paused, turned to her friend, and smiled. "I've been here for a week."

Essie picked up a sketch pad sitting next to her hip and flicked through the pages. "Here's a likeness of the two men who abducted Sugar. She described them as best she could, and I drew them until she was satisfied." She handed it to Fab, and I leaned over and checked the two men out.

"Why abduct me, then kill me for no reason?" Sugar mused. "Do you know if there was a ransom demand?"

"None that your husband or sister reported." Fab shook her head. "Do you have a will?"

"I don't. Under Florida law, that means that everything I have goes to my husband."

"Eventually," I said. "Your sister might get a portion if she contested. But that could take years, and without a body, there's a long waiting period before they could have you declared dead. Seven years, unless it's changed."

"Why did you marry Bowman?" Fab asked.

"Truthfully?" Sugar studied her hands. "When I woke up in the hospital, my wedding ring was gone, and I felt sad that I didn't care one way or the other. The only thing I remember about the day I exchanged vows was having a couple of drinks at my favorite casino and being about ready to head back to the poker table. The next thing I remember, it was morning. I stumbled to the bathroom and, on the way back, saw the marriage license. Shock doesn't quite cover my emotions. Then the guilt. Bowman talked me into giving the marriage a chance, even saying he'd sign a pre-nup, which I never followed through

on. He morphed into the perfect husband, catered to my every whim, and backed off to give me time to get used to the idea."

"What do you want us to do?" Fab asked.

"I want these two men found." Sugar poked at the sketch pad. "Then I want to know who hired them and why and for everyone involved to go to prison. Until that happens, I plan to stay hidden."

"I know you were originally hired by Sugar's sister, and I took a chance that you wouldn't feed her to the wolves," Essie grumped.

"We'd never do that," I assured her.

"This might help in your investigation," Sugar said. "When the two men got into an argument in the van, one called the other Harold, and boy, did he get mad, screaming at the top of his lungs to 'shut it.'"

Fab took out her phone and made a couple of notes. "The man who owns the investigation firm I work for is a retired cop and a straight-up guy; he would never do anything to put your life in jeopardy," she said. "I'm going to call him and tell him what's going on. I'll also suggest that he pass the drawing of the two kidnappers around to a couple of his old contacts and see what he can come up with. If either can be found, then it's highly likely that they'll spill all they know in exchange for a lesser sentence."

"I know her boss, and he's a good guy," I said. "You can trust him."

"If you ever don't feel safe here, we can hide you in the Keys." Fab handed Sugar her business card. "If you remember anything else that would be helpful, don't hesitate to call. Anytime."

"Do you mind if I go inside and lie down?" Sugar stood. "I still feel like I was run over by a truck."

"We'll take it from here and be in touch soon," Fab said.

"I'll be right back," Essie said, standing and putting her arm around Sugar's shoulder to walk with her back inside the building.

Fab flicked through her phone.

"I suppose it's too nervy to ask you to put it on speaker." I scooted my chair next to hers. "Don't start—I learned the trick from you." I doubted I'd hear a thing and sat back. "Tell the Chief I said '*Bonjour*.'"

"Your French is terrible."

"Yes, I know." I gave her a smirky smile, which made her laugh.

Fab relayed everything Sugar had told us to the Chief. He asked questions, and based on her answers, he wanted to know if she thought Sugar was truthful, which she did. She hung up and said, "He's calling Casio to come question her, since he's in the area, and he wants me to stay and introduce them so she knows he's not some weirdo. Even though he is."

"In the past, I've trusted Casio and the Chief to do the right thing by me, and they've always come through, so you can reassure Sugar."

It was less than five minutes before Fab's phone rang again. I knew from her tone that it was the Chief, and the conversation was short. "Weirdo is on his way over. Lucky us, he lives fairly close, so we won't have to sit here all day."

"Would I be wrong in thinking that this case will eventually end up being a police affair?" I asked.

"No, and that's fine with me. If the husband or sister is involved, I think the only way to get a confession would be to beat it out of them. I'm thinking that's not legal."

"Probably not." I laughed and nudged her. "Here comes Essie. You should have her give Sugar a heads up that Casio is on his way."

Fab stood and walked over to the woman. Their conversation was short. Fab came back and sat down. "She's going to tell Sugar."

"Hiring on to do a job that involves kidnapping and murder will get these two men life in prison." I stared at the sketches.

Fab reached over and grabbed the sketch pad, snapping a couple of pictures with her phone.

"I wouldn't think murder for hire would be cheap. It'll be interesting to see where the money came from," I said. "From what Sugar told us, it doesn't seem like a random job. I wasn't a Bowman fan, but for Sugar's sake, I hope he wasn't involved."

Twenty minutes went by before Casio roared

up in his SUV and parked behind us. He came sauntering up, a small bag in his hand, a big smile on his face, and full of himself. "Hello, ladies." He bowed.

Sugar and Essie reappeared. One of them must have had an eye out. Or perfect timing. Fab introduced them.

Casio oozed charm, which I'd not witnessed before. I turned and rolled my eyes at Fab, who bit her lip to keep from laughing. He held out the bag to Sugar. "I've had my ass kicked a time or two, and my granny swears by this all-natural lotion to take away the pain."

Granny? I mouthed to Fab. She shrugged. We both knew he didn't have one.

Casio put his arm around Sugar and escorted her to her chair. She smiled at the big man. He sat across from her, pulling his chair to where their knees almost touched. He started by reciting his credentials— "I'm a retired Miami detective with so many awards it's embarrassing." —and went on to reassure her that he was just the man to lock up the "cretins" responsible. "Now, tell me what happened and start from the beginning."

Fab and I sat back and listened; the story didn't vary from the first time.

When Sugar was done, he asked questions and also to see the sketch, and Fab handed it over. "No need to worry. I'll get everyone involved locked up. That way, you won't have to look over your shoulder." He pulled out a business card. "This is an old one, but my cell number is on the back." He handed her his phone. "Put your number in, and I'll call every day and keep you updated, even if there isn't anything new. First thing I'm going to do is pass this sketch around; I'd bet these two have had run-ins with the law before and someone will recognize them."

Fab stood. "If you don't need anything from either of us, we'll be leaving. You've got my number," she said to Sugar. "If for any reason you can't get ahold of Casio, you can call me."

We said our good-byes and walked to the SUV.

"I'm amazed that Sugar survived — there's barely a place on her body that wasn't bruised," I said.

"She only thinks she gave up; she didn't, and I admire her will to live." Fab pulled away from the curb, checking out the neighborhood as she headed to the corner.

"I'm happy Sugar's alive and this case didn't go down the way we thought it would."

"Agreed."

Chapter Twenty-Nine

As Fab passed the "Welcome to the Cove" sign, my phone dinged, signaling a text message. "Bastard is dead," I read to Fab, adding, "It's from Rude," before she could ask. My phone dinged again. "This one's from Mac," I said. "'Cops are here. Can't say I didn't give you a heads up.' Be nice to know who's dead." I pointed for her to turn. "I need to find out what's going on at The Cottages."

"I've got an idea…"

I groaned.

"That's not very nice."

"I can't believe I'm going to say this, but do you think you could step on it? Wouldn't want the body to get hauled off before you get a picture or six."

Fab squealed around the corner. "Happy now?" She turned the next corner before she slowed and turned into Mac's driveway.

"No pics for you today." I pointed at the two cop cars.

Fab pointed to the coroner's van as we got out and claimed chairs on Mac's front porch. "A body fell out of the back of one of those the other day and into traffic."

"That's why making up stories is my forte and not yours." I shook my head in disbelief. "In the future, try for a kernel of truth to make the story believable."

"When I get around to forwarding you the news article, I expect an apology."

"Oh, okay." I pointed to a woman running up the middle of the street. "Showtime. Here comes Mac."

Mac ran up the steps, skidded to a stop, and leaned against the railing. Fab and I looked down at her feet; she'd donned low-heeled sandals shaped like peeled bananas. She sucked in a couple of breaths. "Canton hung himself on the doorknob. Drunk as a skunk, according to Pastel. The last time she saw him was before she went to bed."

"Canton? Pastel's boyfriend?" I asked Mac. "Guilt over the crimes you fingered him for? Did you ever get proof or a confession?"

Mac squinted at me in annoyance. "Rude and I were still investigating." Hands on her hips, chest thrust out. "We didn't come up with anything more for the cops. They took Canton in for questioning, but he lawyered up and nothing came of it."

"Apparently you forgot that the reason you two got an introduction to Bouff was so you'd stop sticking your nose into something that could get you killed," I reminded her.

Mac scuffed one of the bananas on the concrete. "If we could solve our first big case, we'd be in hot demand."

I turned on Fab. "This is all your fault— chasing criminals and making getting shot at look all sexy."

"You need to calm down," Fab said with a smirk. "More coffee?"

"I'm telling you now, Mac quits and you'll be sitting in the office." I snapped at Mac, "Where's Rude?"

"She's finishing up questioning the rest of the potential witnesses." Mac tossed her wrist in the direction of the street, meaning the woman could be anywhere. "It's good to talk to these folks while their memories are still fresh."

I leaned over and peered down the block. "If Kevin over there—" I pointed across the street. " —gets a whiff of what you two are up to, he'll have you both in cuffs, and you probably won't get the scenic ride to the hoosegow. He's short on patience anyway, but it will completely evaporate when you try to do his job."

"Where's Pastel?" Fab asked.

"She was inconsolable after finding Canton and was taken to the hospital," Mac said.

"If the apartment needs cleaning, then have it done for her," I said.

"I already put in a call," Mac said. "While I was consoling Pastel before the paramedics

arrived, Rude snuck in and had a look around."
Mac waved off my irritated retort. "Before you
flip, she was quick and didn't touch anything."

"I'm unclear as to where the two of you were
that you could respond so quickly," I said.

"We were chatting it up with one of the
neighbors, heard Pastel screaming, and went
running," Mac said.

"That's what I pay the two of you to do? Stand
around and gossip with the neighbors?" I almost
laughed at her irritated expression, as we both
knew the answer was yes.

"Who do you know in the neighborhood?"
Mac snapped.

I pointed to Fab. "She knows all the men. Does
that count?"

"If I weren't the friendly one, you wouldn't
know squat about what happens on this street."
Mac spit on her finger, bent down, and rubbed
the toe of one banana.

"You go around asking questions, any killer
you're chasing may find out, and you'll be a
target," Fab said. "You're lucky that this one died
and didn't take you with him."

"Be nice if Canton had left a signed confession
so we'd know for sure he was the murderer,"
Mac whined.

"Did he scribble a note for Pastel?" I asked.

"Didn't look for one, and Pastel didn't say,"
Mac said. "I didn't think to ask, but that might've
come off pushy in her time of grief."

"You think?" I asked.

Mac crossed her arms and scowled.

"The cops are going to want to know what Pastel knew, since she lived with the man," Fab mused.

"Pastel insisted that Canton didn't live there… except he was there every day," Mac said.

"If you want to be helpful, get Pastel to move," Fab said. "In the meantime, be prepared for a lot of drive-by lookie-loos."

"I'll suggest to Rude that we make it a stop on the next tour about town." Mac looked pleased with her idea.

"Canton wasn't famous, so I'm not sure people would care," I said.

"Spoilsport," Mac mumbled.

Fab poked me in the arm and laughed.

Kevin whistled, yelled, "Mac," and waved her down the street.

Mac cleared the steps in her excitement and tottered back and forth before regaining her balance. She grinned and took off running.

Fab nudged me and pointed to the coroner's van. "There goes the body." She jerked on my arm. "Let's go."

"You waited too long to make that call." I nodded as Crum strutted across the street, flinching as he got closer. He wore a form-fitting scooped-neck bodysuit, tie-dyed glittery high-tops, and mismatched thigh-high socks. I wondered if he was planning a trip to Key West.

"At least, the bell sleeves are in fashion," Fab said with a straight face. "He could use a wax."

I choked down a horrified laugh. "Please don't bring up grooming issues."

"Ladies." He twirled the cheap beads around his neck on his finger, then had to tug to get them to come loose. "If you have a few minutes, I have a business proposition to pitch you. Business partners, wouldn't that be fun?" He pointed between me and him.

I didn't look at Fab to try to figure out the noise she made. Retching?

"Mac said I was on my own, that she didn't have the intestinal fortitude to bring it up and wouldn't anytime soon. One thing about business—you've got to jump on a good idea while it's hot."

Fab bent over and made a choking noise. I knew she was laughing. I slapped her back… a little hard. She tipped her head to the side and glared.

"Have a seat." I waved my hand at an empty chair. "Just know upfront that I won't feel the least bit obligated to jump on one of your infamous once-in-a-life time opportunities."

"Would I steer you wrong?" Crum waggled his brows and threw himself in the chair, which rocked from side to side.

In a word, yes. "Pitch away."

Crum leaned back and kicked his feet up on the railing. "The guests are loving the Barbie car.

Except for that slight close call when someone barreled into the driveway. Almost splat." He made a choking noise. "You know me, always getting one good idea after another, so I made a rule that the Jeep could only be ridden on the beach. Worst that can happen is it tips over and the occupants get sand in their shorts."

"Happy that you had the foresight to move the fun out of the driveway before anyone died." Trying to anticipate what Crum would say next was exhausting.

Fab fake yawned.

Crum glared and then ignored her. "My idea is for you to add a couple more to the inventory and rent them to guests."

"We have beach cruisers available, and so far, they've sat in the shed unused," I reminded him.

"That's why having something unique to ride would make it a hot ticket." Crum pulled a sheet of paper out of the front of his body suit and handed it to me. "Here's two of my ideas, and I have a couple more sitting on the table in my cottage."

Fab coughed again and leaned toward me.

They were both pictured on the page. The top image showed a three-wheeled cruiser with a partial smart car body. The other was a bicycle with a toilet for a seat and a tool box attached to the back that I imagined would hold beer or... whatever.

I laughed and handed the paper to Fab for a

closer look, but she waved it away. "A drunk gets on the toilet bike—" Fab pointed. "—who cleans up?"

I looked down and did my best to scrub that image from my brain. "How do you see this business partnership working?"

"I find them, and you buy. I'll organize the rentals, and we share in the profits."

"And when you get bored and go off on your next money-maker? What then? You reel in Joseph?" I felt bad when his big smile vanished. "I think your idea is fun, but I don't see it making any money, as we don't nickel and dime the guests. And to offer to the public at large would require licensing that I doubt we'd get, not to mention the inventory that would be required." Not to mention the whack-jobs loitering on my property.

"You buying them and humping free rides works for me." Crum looked hopeful as he tapped his gnarly tennis shoe.

"Did you ever plan to make an investment of your own?" Fab asked. "As in kick in some of your own cash?"

"You're not part of this deal." Crum glared at her. "An old man has to watch his pennies."

"You should be embarrassed to cry poor mouth," I admonished. "You can't be buried with your dough, and your heirs are going to party it away." His cheeks turned red. "Run Plan B by Mac, and if she thinks it's a good idea, have her call me. If you're going to buy the cruiser, I suggest you take Mac because she's good at grinding down the price. The toilet thing…" I made a face. "You're going to need to find something else for the reason Fab mentioned. You find the rides, Mac and I will discuss it *before* you purchase and get back to you."

"You can't drag your feet on these deals," Crum said.

"When do I ever?" I ignored his raised brows. "I need you on another job and hope your schedule is flexible."

"Aren't I always available to you?"

"For a price. That said, Casio is bringing his offspring and staying the night. I'll need your kid-watching services again. I can get back to you with the date, but it will be sooner than not."

Crum saluted. "No worries. Me and the kids are simpatico. Smart little things; must get it from their mother."

Fab laughed, much to her disgust, I'm sure.

Crum stood and kicked his chair back. "Thank you for your time. Got to go; got me a date."

"Are you going to finish getting dressed?" I asked.

He grinned, turned, and wiggled his butt. "The babes are hot for me."

"My retinas have been burned," Fab said as he sprinted across the street.

"That thing he was wearing was a vulgar display of his… and Mac needs to add it to the list of items in his wardrobe that he needs to cover up when he leaves his cottage." I squirmed. "And never wear around the kids."

"There are a lot of reasons I couldn't be manager, but he's definitely one of them. He'd work my nerves in a second. I'd shoot him and have his body dragged off somewhere."

I banged my head on her shoulder and laughed.

Chapter Thirty

Mother called the next day and invited me to lunch at the Bakery Café. When I attempted to put her off, she made me feel guilty, so I accepted. I hung up and immediately called Fab, who begged off, saying that she needed to finish updating her report on Sugar for the Chief and get it to him before the end of the day.

It was a short drive from the warehouse, and I amused myself by cutting through alleys over to the restaurant. I spotted Mother as soon as I pulled up in front and parked. She'd claimed an outside table on the patio. I sucked in a deep breath, got out, and crossed the sidewalk.

"You look fabulous." I eyed her sleeveless black sundress, leaned down, and kissed her cheek.

Less than a minute later, my brother showed up, kissed us both and sat next to me.

"Don't you have a job?" I squinted at him.

He squinted back. "How could I pass up the opportunity for a family affair, just the three of us? It's been a while."

Now I knew Mother was up to something, and I'd bet it had everything to do with me, and probably my personal life, judging by her conspiratorial smile with Brad.

"Let's order first." Mother flagged the server over, and we all chose a variation of the same thing—sandwich and iced tea. "I should have chosen a restaurant with a bar, but then we'd need rides home and Spoonee has a big client coming in today."

Brad gagged.

"Mother, you know *Spoonee* likes you to save that nickname for the bedroom," I reminded her. Her cheeks burned red.

"*Please* stop," Brad whined.

I shook my head. "Sometimes it's just too much fun to watch you squirm, bro."

The server set down our drinks.

Mother patted my hand. "I was disappointed that you didn't come and share your problems with me. You know I'm always here for you."

"What are you talking about?" I asked, knowing fulling well where this conversation was going but holding out a scintilla of hope that I was wrong.

Brad shot me a slight grin.

"Creole came over for dinner last night." Mother smiled. "He confided that the two of you were having marital difficulties and said that his long recuperation was to blame."

I ground my teeth so hard, I expected them to snap off.

"We want to be of help any way we can,"

Mother continued. "Creole feels guilty over how long it's taking him to heal and regain his full memory, which he's not convinced is a sure thing anymore, despite the doctor saying otherwise."

The arrival of the food gave me a minute to breathe. I hoped that we could change the subject but knew that wouldn't happen.

"Creole takes full responsibility for his mercurial moods," Mother said as soon as the server left. "I told him not to give up, his hard work would pay off."

What I wouldn't give for a drink. I'd barely had an appetite when I sat down, and now it'd vanished.

"You thought an ambush lunch to discuss my marriage was a good idea?" I said to Brad, struggling to stay calm and not rant about siblings having each other's backs.

"You could appreciate that I was in a bad position." Brad gave me a wily smile. "I could hardly rat out Mother. I also wasn't going to deprive myself of a possible girl fight, with Mother going to jail for beating up someone younger."

"You're hilarious."

"Don't be mad at your brother." Mother smiled at him. "You know how persuasive I can be."

"Isn't this the exact kind of thing you'd do to me—for my own happiness and all?" Brad said with a smug smile.

"Don't forget this, because I owe you one. More like six." I glared at Brad.

"We both love you and want to be here for you," Mother said in a conciliatory tone.

"You need to let me and Creole work out our own problems." I couldn't imagine what he'd said, and would bet that Mother didn't get the whole story and that whatever Creole told her, she'd only repeated half of their conversation. I wasn't about to add my half. What had me grinding my teeth again was Creole's back-handedness. My husband was rapidly becoming a stranger.

"I was thinking that you and Creole could come for dinner," Mother said, looking pleased with her idea, which I'd bet she already had planned out. "Afterwards, the two of you can slip away and go for a walk. You two just need some alone time."

Brad gave me a cheesy smile.

I kicked him under the table. Hard.

To his credit, he didn't flinch, but his smile disappeared.

"It's hard to work on your relationship when you're not living together." Mother patted my hand. "Moving back home would be a start. I don't know how you can stand staying at The Cottages."

So that's where Creole thought I'd moved to, and now so did the rest of the family. "Does

Spoon know that you've donned your marital-advice hat?"

"He didn't think it was one of my better ideas but didn't stop me," Mother admitted with a sigh.

"You have any marital advice?" I asked Brad, my words dripping with sarcasm. This ought to be good, coming from a man that had never been married and only dated nutjobs.

"I feel compelled to contribute some words of wisdom." Brad grinned. "It wasn't long ago that you and Creole were really happy, and if you want it to work out, then I hope it does."

If I dropped the bomb that Creole had hit me, it would be the end of any conversation. And before long, I'd be getting a call that Creole was in the hospital. "I didn't tell you that we were having problems because I don't want all of our relationships to change."

"Creole wants to make things right and work on the marriage, so that's a start," Mother said.

"I'm going to call him," I said, managing to dial back the sarcasm. *And tell him to leave my family alone.* "Now stop worrying and let us figure out our problems for ourselves."

Mother wasn't going to let it go, but Brad covered her hand with his and squeezed, and she stayed quiet.

"What's Mila up to?" I asked.

I didn't have to worry about any more relationship talk once we got started talking about Brad's daughter and her adventures in elementary school. I tore off pieces of my sandwich and, when Mother wasn't looking, shoved them into the napkin in my lap. Brad caught me every time and glared but didn't say anything.

The check arrived, and I was happy that Brad had to get back to the office. I made up an appointment with an electrician I needed to meet at The Cottages. Good excuse, because Mother didn't like going there and wouldn't suggest tagging along. Before standing, I shoved my shredded lunch in my purse.

Brad walked us to out to the sidewalk, and Mother and I hugged. "I'll be in touch with a date for a family dinner. I'm thinking a room full of people will make it easy for you and Creole to just relax and be together."

"Sounds good," I lied, then felt guilty because the last thing I wanted was to sit in my mother's living room with everyone watching Creole's and my every move.

I kissed Brad and waved to the two of them, then got in the Hummer and called Creole. It went to voicemail, and I snapped, "Don't drag my family into the middle of our marital problems." I disconnected and called Fab.

"How did the lunch go?" she asked upon answering.

"Did you know it was an ambush?"

"I knew Madeline was up to something and didn't want any part of it," Fab said without a hint of remorse. "I hope it wasn't excruciating."

I wasn't in the mood to rehash the lunch conversation. "Is your offer of moving into my bedroom at your house still available? More importantly, will Didier be okay with it? He and Creole are good friends, and I don't want it to be awkward."

"When are you coming? I can't believe you lasted this long in that creepy warehouse."

"The nights are the worst. All the noises are amplified in the quiet. It's too isolating." I had lain awake last night and jumped at every noise I heard. We hung up.

I knew all the shortcuts, and it didn't take me long to get to the warehouse. It only half-surprised me when Fab pulled up behind me in the parking lot. She helped me pack the Hummer and get the cats situated. They weren't happy with another car ride, but they'd like Fab's house, with plenty of room to roam and more pieces of furniture to lie on.

Before I followed her home, we stood in the parking lot. "I've got this idea for being as unobtrusive as possible," I said. "I thought I'd park in your garage; that way, no one would know I was there. I'll stay in the bedroom except to come and go, and that will be out the back way."

"I wouldn't worry about it. Creole's only been over once since you two split up," Fab said. "Besides, I already told Didier that you and Creole were having problems and I invited you to stay. I brushed it off as marital issues and said that we're going to let the two of you figure it out yourselves. I pointed out that it's a good idea— not having to choose sides and you not staying in some dump." She eyed the warehouse.

"It's not bad during the daytime." I laughed.

Chapter Thirty-One

It was easy to be low-profile in a mansion, with the master suite on one side of the u-shaped house, the guest bedrooms on the other, and the living room, kitchen, and dining room in the middle, opening out to the massive patio that overlooked the beach. When Fab and Didier bought the house, they'd remodeled a bedroom for Creole and me. We'd declined to move in but had spent several nights in the luxurious space, which even had a separate sitting area. The double-king-size bed was my favorite.

I'd called Creole again and this time, when he didn't answer, left a calmer message, suggesting that we meet and talk. He didn't return that call either. A good reason for him involving my family escaped me, unless it was to retain his good guy status. Another thing he hadn't been concerned about in the past.

I took my laptop outside to the private patio with its own alcove and reviewed the security feed at the house for the last couple of nights. On the first night, he'd once again searched every nook, and whatever he was looking for, he'd come up empty-handed. I'd hoped that when he opened the safe, he'd see that I only took my personal items and left his untouched, but he never went near it.

We both had access to our medical records online, but I only checked mine when I wanted the results of a test. I'd never had reason to access his before. Maybe they'd tell me something. I entered his password, looked up the test results… and there were none. That was because he hadn't had any since he left the hospital. I checked to see when he had his next appointment, and not only didn't he have one scheduled, he hadn't had one since the follow-up after his release. I double-checked all the tabs in his file, and there was nothing past his hospital stay. I stared at the screen as the anger bubbled up. "What the heck?" No wonder he never wanted to talk about his appointments; he hadn't had any. My husband—who'd never lied to me in the past, or so I thought—now uttered one lie after another. I had no clue what to do with this new information. Confront him? Confess that I'd been snooping? I shuddered to think what his response would be.

"You out here?" Fab called from the other side of a hedge that afforded privacy.

"I'm over here." I logged out of the program and closed my laptop, setting it on the side table.

Fab came around from the main patio, glasses of water in hand, mine stuffed full of fruit.

I licked my lips. "You're the best hostess."

"And I come with news." She set my drink in front of me and sat next to me. "Creole and Didier have a meeting with the planning department day after tomorrow; they'll be tied up for a couple of hours."

I pulled my phone out of my pocket and called Mac. We had an available cottage, and I reserved it for Casio. I then called the man himself and heaved a sigh of relief to hear that he was also available and not going to renege on going with me.

"I'm happy that Casio didn't go back on his word and you're not going off on some wild hair by yourself," Fab said when I hung up. "I'm going to hang out and make sure that they go to the meeting and there are no last-minute cancellations." Fab took a drink of her water filled with weeds. "I just worry that if this little adventure doesn't answer at least some of your questions, then what?"

"I'm short on answers these days."

Fab peered at me sympathetically and mercifully changed the subject. "Got an update on Sugar. After her talk with Casio, the Chief called the new guy who got promoted to his job, and he assigned a couple of detectives to her case. They were able to ID the kidnappers and get warrants out."

"Sugar still at Essie's?" I asked.

Fab nodded. "And no one's come snooping around."

"The money behind this is in for a big surprise when the kidnappers get arrested and start talking. Why wouldn't they fully cooperate to save their own backsides? I'd be doing whatever I could to lessen my prison time. I wonder if people think about the consequences of criminal activity before doing the crime."

"I imagine they think they wouldn't get caught."

"It will be interesting to find out if the husband or sister is involved," I said.

"I'm happy that we're not the ones chasing down the kidnappers," Fab said. "Or trying to figure out the involvement, or lack thereof, of the other two."

"Me too."

Chapter Thirty-Two

Two days seemed to drag by, even though I had plenty to do.

Finally, the day arrived. I met Casio at The Cottages and left my Hummer parked in front of the office. He opened the door to his SUV, and I got in. I almost programmed his GPS, then laughed at myself, as he'd been to the warehouse nightly after he signed on as one of Trigger's men and knew exactly where we were going.

"I did some research on the place," Casio said as he sped down the highway. "It's still for sale, so the inside is probably filthier than it was when Trigger used it. Never sure how he knew the place was empty or why he picked that location. It's surprising that no one paid attention to the comings and goings. He'd told his men that they were not to come near the property during the day."

"That was smart of him. It just takes one nosy person and the cops would show up to investigate."

"These are the ground rules." Casio turned to make sure I was paying attention. "Once you set foot outside this car, you'll stick by my side. I'll give you the tour, answer any and all questions you have, and we're out of there. I'd say take pictures if you're so inclined, but just know that there will be no light except from our flashlights, so they'll come out murky at best."

"I'll take a few so I can show Fab I made an attempt." I chuckled.

"I take it her husband doesn't know she snooped in his appointment book?"

"No, and I hope Didier doesn't ever find out. I'm not asking for this kind of favor again. Things are already weird enough, and I don't want to cause a rift between those two or in my relationship with them." I couldn't bear to contemplate the loss of their friendship. From the start, I'd wanted to avoid anyone having to choose sides. "This is probably a waste of your time and won't answer any of the multitude of questions I have, but I feel compelled to check the place out." I confessed about my latest snooping into the medical files.

"Wonder what he's hiding, pretending to go to appointments he doesn't have," Casio mused. "No matter what, it won't be a waste of time because it will be one less thing to question."

He turned on the familiar street. It had been a long time since I'd been out there. The last time was before the night of the raid. The commercial area hadn't changed at all. There were cars parked at the rest of businesses and not a single person in sight, so we didn't attract any attention pulling into the parking lot of the vacant warehouse and around the back. He killed the engine, and I got out and looked around. It was eerily quiet. Casio took a lockpick out of his pocket and opened a smaller door alongside a pair of rollup doors. He went inside and raised one up. "So we can see what's going on, on the lower level anyway."

I eyed the interior from the doorway. It was a large space, with several layers of dirt on the walls and concrete floors, cobwebs hanging from the corners, and dead bugs everywhere. I stepped inside. There wasn't much to see. I walked from one end to the other and poked my head through the bathroom doors at the end, jumping back at the smell.

"This way." Casio pointed up the stairs. "Creole and Didier were held up here in separate rooms at the far end."

I didn't count, but it reminded me of Fab's warehouse—it was quite the hike up and at a steep incline. Thankfully, I'd worn tennis shoes.

Casio's flashlight lit the way. We walked the upper floor from one end to the other, and he narrated. The room that got the most use was originally an office and contained a broken down desk and chair. I shuddered at the filth.

Midway down the hall, Casio pointed to a door. "Didier was held in here." He opened the door, and I looked in. The only thing left was a single stained mattress propped against the wall.

"The last door was where Creole was held." He turned the knob, but it was locked. "That's odd." But the minor inconvenience didn't stop him, as he whipped out his lockpick again and shoved the door open.

It was decorated the same as the last room—a dirty mattress on the floor. Except...

I screamed. Casio pushed me back out of the room.

There was a man. Half-naked. Dirty. His ankles locked together in chains.

The man slowly rolled halfway over, his hand covering his eyes as though the beam from Casio's flashlight hurt them. "You're here..." he croaked, staring at me. Dried blood was caked on his face, one eye swollen shut. His hands dropped.

I stumbled against the doorframe and stared open-mouthed, certain I was hallucinating.

Casio shot across the room and checked for injuries. "Can you talk?"

"I..." the man rasped.

"Take it easy." Casio turned his attention to the lock on the chains. He attempted to pick the lock, and when that didn't work, he inspected it closely and pulled his weapon. "Don't move." He shot the chain, which snapped in half.

"What are you doing!" I screamed, but it was already over and the man could move his feet.

"This is going to hurt and probably a lot," Casio warned the man. "But I've got to get you out of here before whoever did this comes back."

I went weak in the knees, thinking Creole had something to do with this battered man.

It took several tries to get the man on his feet, and even then, he stumbled and Casio just barely managed to keep him from ending up on the floor. He pushed his shoulder under the man's arm and held him up, supporting him down the stairs. The man couldn't stand on his own, appearing weak and dizzy. His legs shook as he struggled to support himself.

I couldn't hear what Casio was saying, but they sounded like words of encouragement. At the roll-up door, Casio stuck his head out and swept the area before he crossed to his SUV and helped the man stretch out on the back seat.

Casio and I both got a good look at him at the same time.

I screamed again and struggled to stay on my feet and not succumb to a faint. "It can't possibly be," I whimpered.

Casio caught me and wrapped his arms around me. "Breathe," he commanded. "And again." He barked this time. "Listen to me. I'm going to get you into the car, and we'll figure this out." He helped me into the back seat from the other side.

I slid in and lifted the man's head, supporting it in my lap. "Creole?" I whispered.

His lashes fluttered.

Casio got behind the wheel and jammed on

the gas out of the parking lot. He remained sharply focused as he tore out to the highway.

Creole stopped moving completely, and it freaked me out. I checked his pulse and breathed a sigh of relief. I stared into his face and lightly fingered his cheek, knowing without a doubt that it was Creole. But who would beat him like this and leave him for dead? Someone from his old life? Someone he'd arrested?

Casio made a call and had a short conversation with someone. It was hard to eavesdrop from the backseat and could only be done if I moved Creole and scooted up, and I wasn't doing that. It wasn't long before his phone rang, and he took another short call. He drove straight to Tarpon Cove Hospital and jumped out, disappearing inside. Soon, he was back out with a gurney and two attendants. Creole was loaded onto the stretcher and wheeled inside.

"He looks like crap, but he's survived worse." Casio hugged me to his side.

"It's really Creole, isn't it?"

Casio nodded and led me to a chair. "I'll be right back." He was gone for too long. I forced myself to stay seated and not pace around the reception area. He finally strode down the corridor, and I jumped up and stood in front of him. "They took Creole to surgery. He's got broken ribs and internal bleeding. If anyone asks, I'm his brother."

I smiled faintly at that lie. "So he's going to be…"

"We're going to sit right here until they come out with an update." Casio led me by the elbow over to a chair in the corner.

It'd been over two hours, and Creole was still in surgery. There hadn't been any updates, which I decided was good news. Seeing him a battered mess, I pushed recent events from my thoughts and would focus only on him getting better.

My phone rang, Fab's face on the screen. I answered but didn't say anything.

"You better be okay," she grouched. "I called for an update."

"You're not going to believe what happened," I whimpered.

Fab groaned so loud I thought she'd be heard across the room. I was wrong; no one looked up.

I told her what had happened.

Casio stood and crossed the room, and I watched as he met up with the Chief.

"The Chief and Casio are here. I'll call you once Creole gets out of surgery."

"You need anything, you call," Fab said, and hung up.

The Chief and Casio stood at the opposite side of the reception area. After a short conversation, they talked to the woman at the desk. Casio came back and guided me to a lounge area, where the Chief was making coffee. There was only one other person, who stared mindlessly at the television on the wall. He didn't seem to notice the volume had been muted.

I struggled to calm the anxiety that riddled my body, with little success. I had a lot of questions, and most started with "What the heck..." I lowered my head to my knees and breathed slowly in and out until I was certain that I wouldn't spiral out of control. Casio leaned toward me and massaged the back of my neck until I sat up and slumped back in my chair.

The waiting was torture. I couldn't have told you how long we sat there. The two men moved a couple of chairs away to talk and avail themselves of the coffee machine.

"A lot about this doesn't add up," I overheard Casio say. The Chief's response was muffled.

I carried on an internal monologue, reminding myself several times that Creole had arrived alive, and according to what one of the nurses told Casio, his chances were good. All he had to do was survive surgery... and then what? Our lives would go back to what exactly? I couldn't think about that right now.

Stay calm was my new mantra. Patience was another.

The minutes ticked by into hours, long and painful ones. Finally, a doctor appeared, looking tired.

I shot to my feet. "Is my husband okay?"

"We finished the surgery, and he's on his way

to recovery. Everything went well. Once he's stabilized, we'll be transporting him to a room. You're welcome to wait in recovery with him."

Tears leaked from my eyes, but I managed to control myself.

"I knew he'd be all right." Casio took my hand and squeezed. "He's always been a tough one."

Chapter Thirty-Three

It took several hours for Creole to be moved from recovery to a room. I sat next to his bed. His eyes were swollen and black and blue. I lightly ran my finger over the cuts and abrasions I hadn't noticed in the SUV. The doctor had informed me that he stopped the internal bleeding and reassured me that Creole would recover. Hard as it was to look at his injuries, I couldn't imagine the pain he'd be in when the drugs wore off.

A pair of police detectives also paid me a visit and fired off questions, which I answered directly. I told them that I'd followed Creole because he'd been acting out of character since his kidnapping but didn't mention the rest of our marital difficulties. I didn't know what Casio told them, but our stories couldn't have varied by much, since we hadn't left each other's side at any time while we were in the warehouse. The Chief stood by my side, his hand on my back. I'd been surprised that he showed up, but his moral support was welcome. The person I imagined they most wanted to talk to was still unconscious. I'd also be interested in the answers to any questions put to him.

The door opened, and Casio strode into the darkened hospital room, only one light casting deep shadows across the room. "Do you mind being alone with him while I go check on my kids?"

"Go. He has enough drugs in him that he'll sleep through the night. Come back tomorrow." I smiled tiredly.

The Chief, who'd drifted off sitting in a chair across the room, straightened and grouched, "I'm not going anywhere." He stood and stretched, then walked over to the bed, standing next to Casio. Neither blinked or showed any emotion as they stared at Creole, who was hooked up to an IV and a machine that monitored his vital signs. Both continued to glower as though he were a puzzle they were trying to figure out.

The big question was why would someone beat him within an inch of his life and leave him to die? He wasn't the kind of man who made enemies. The only explanation was that it had something to do with his old days as an undercover detective, and wondered if it was one of the reasons the Chief stayed close by.

Casio waved, and he and the Chief left the room. It wasn't long before the Chief was back and stretched out on one of the couches. I kept my vigil at Creole's bedside, several times laying my head on the mattress and falling asleep as the hours went by with no sign of movement.

My eyes snapped open when I felt Creole's fingers tighten ever so slightly around mine. He muttered a few words, nothing intelligible, but never opened his eyes. His jaw clenched, and he twitched like he was having a bad dream. "Marcus…"

Who? I'd never heard that name before.

More hours went by before his eyes flew open and he stared at me, his chest rising and falling faster. "Marcus…"

There was that name again. I covered his hand with both of mine.

It didn't seem like he'd registered that I was sitting by his side, still disoriented as he slowly took in his surroundings.

I squeezed his hand, careful not to tug on one of the wires. "I'm here." My hand moved to his chest.

"Babe…"

I couldn't remember the last time he'd called me that. He'd barely used my name in the past couple of months, let alone an endearment.

He looked into my face, stared for the longest time, and sighed softly. "Am I dreaming? I thought I'd never see you again." His fingers twitched toward my face and touched my cheek tentatively.

"I'm right here and not going anywhere. The doctor says you're going to be fine." My fingers locked with his. It was hard to make out that he had blue eyes, as the swelling hadn't gone down and his face was still dark and discolored.

Creole tried to lift his head, groaned, and fell back against the pillow.

I leaned toward him and pressed a kiss to his cheek.

The Chief had stumbled up off the couch and rushed over and now stood at the end of the bed.

"Boss." Creole nodded. "Marcus… in… custody?"

I caught the Chief's look of confusion, so he didn't know this person either.

The door flew open, and Fab flew in like a gale force wind, Didier attempting to slow her down and failing.

"Did we miss anything?" She moved to Creole's bedside and peered down into his face. "You look like… well… not so great. What's the other guy look like?"

Creole started to speak, then began to cough.

I held up a cup of water, and he nodded. I fit the straw between his lips, and he drank until he sputtered.

"Happy to see you alive." Didier stared at Creole, an extremely confused look on his face.

Creole attempted to speak again.

Casio barreled through the door, looked around tentatively, and moved into the room. It was standing room only at the end of the bed. "If I missed anything, start over." He grinned cheekily.

"Good thing there's not an occupancy limit," the Chief sniped.

"We need more chairs," Fab said. "I could go take them out of rooms where the patients are sleeping."

I was the only one to laugh. I winked at her, thankful for the moment of humor.

"Who are you?" Casio's eyes narrowed in on Creole.

"Is there someone..." Creole tried to look toward the head of his bed.

"Casio's talking to you," I whispered, though everyone could hear me.

Creole reached for his water, and I helped him. He finished off the cup before relaxing back against the bed. "You're just the guy to tell me if you've got Marcus in custody."

"That's the third time you've asked about Marcus," I said. "Who is he?"

Creole groaned and squeezed his eyes shut, then opened them slowly. "My twin brother."

If someone had asked, I would have said it wasn't possible to render this group all speechless at the same time. I'd have been wrong. It was easy to see from the looks on everyone's faces that that wasn't the answer anyone was expecting.

"I'm guessing by everyone's jaw dropping that the answer is no." Creole tightened his hold on my hand. "I'm sorry..." He stared at me. "For everything he did."

I whooshed out a long breath and rested my forehead on Creole's arm. A nurse came through the door, pushing a machine to take his vital signs. "The patient needs his rest," she announced after taking a head count.

"Since I'm his sister," Fab said, and waved her hand over to the couch, "I'll be waiting over there until he's fully awake." She tugged Didier across the room.

"Thanks, Sis." Creole half-laughed and winced, lightly fingering his ribs.

I pushed my chair back from the bed, even though I wasn't in the way, just in case the nurse needed the access.

Twin brother? What the heck was Creole talking about?

The Chief and Casio, not about to be sent out of the room, joined Fab and Didier, Casio grouching "scoot over" at her. Fab waved her finger imperiously toward the other couch, the Chief's makeshift bed. He rolled up the blanket and tossed it on a nearby table. Didier grinned.

No one said a word until the nurse left, saying, "Don't overtire the patient."

As soon as the door closed, everyone was on their feet and claiming their places around the bed.

Casio edged out Fab, who looked ready to put a bullet in his butt, and stood next to Creole. "Your story is that you've got a twin and he did all this to you?"

"Pretty sure you're an only child," the Chief said.

"Yesterday, Creole and I had a meeting," Didier said. "I'm telling you, he didn't look like this; in fact, he didn't have a scratch on him."

Fab muscled Casio aside and leaned in for a closer look at Creole, who growled at her. Not to be intimidated, she growled back, then smiled. "Some of these bruises are old," she said. "I also saw Creole or whoever yesterday, and he was twenty-five pounds heavier, give or take a pound or two. If you can bottle that diet plan, you'll make a fortune."

"Turns out that my mother gave birth to twins. The old man, apparently always a bastard, didn't want two kids and sold my brother, telling my mother he died." Creole fingers tightened around mine.

"That's awful," I gasped.

"I'd never have believed the story if we weren't identical. Not even plastic surgery could create an exact match." He made eye contact with the Chief. "You need to find him. Marcus is filled with anger and rage, and he's dangerous. No telling what he'll do next." He tried to reach for his water glass, and I did it for him.

After almost downing another glass, he continued, "Marcus isn't going to leave town quietly when he finds out that I've been rescued. He'll want to create as much havoc as possible, more than I'm certain he already has. He has nowhere to vent his anger now that dear old dad is dead, although he did unleash plenty on me."

There were differences, but I'd brushed them aside and told myself they were side effects from the head injury. If I'd known Creole had an identical twin, would I have taken a closer look?

"Marcus kidnapped you? Lured you to the warehouse?" the Chief asked, scrutinizing his reaction.

"Neither, actually. How long ago now? I have no clue what day it is or how much time has passed. What I remember is that Didier and I were rear-ended. I thought it was some stupe not paying attention. Didn't occur to me to do anything other than pull over and exchange information. But when we got out to inspect the damage, guns got pushed in our faces. Two more men climbed out of the truck. One of the men came up behind me, and the last I remember was a stabbing pain in my neck. Then waking up in the warehouse, which smelled like dead rats, my lookalike grinning down at me."

Didier grimaced at the re-telling.

"I'd infiltrated the group and was there the night the two of you were brought in," Casio said. "I was restricted in where I was allowed to go in the warehouse without raising eyebrows. Sorry to say I never got so much as a glimpse to suggest that there were two of you."

"Explains why we were held separately," Didier said.

"Did your brother happen to say how he and Trigger hooked up?" the Chief asked.

"Marcus wouldn't say much about the connection; he'd only say that Trigger owed him a favor. He had an elaborate plan to take over my life and used Trigger's men to kidnap me. Marcus figured he was owed for being sold and he'd waited long enough. Sorry..." Creole said to Didier. "Happy to see you made it out in one piece. I asked and, from Marcus' laugh, figured that you hadn't."

Didier nodded to Creole. "I was dumped in a room and left alone, not sure how we were going to get out. Then one night, I heard a commotion—gun shots and the sound of boots in the hall—and the two of us were rescued. Or so I thought."

Fab leaned in and hugged Didier.

"I must've been drugged, as I didn't hear any of that," Creole said. "When I woke up, I felt body-slammed and noticed the accommodations had changed, and not for the better. Marcus laughed that it was a hidden room and to get comfortable, that I wasn't going anywhere. It was worse than before, and I didn't think that possible. The black room was unnervingly quiet, my only company the rodents running and squealing in the walls, and I lost all sense of time. I figured I'd been left to die." Creole closed his eyes and sank into the pillow before opening them again. "I don't know how many days I went with no food or water. Finally figured the end was near... and Marcus showed. He appeared relieved that I was alive. Didn't take me long to figure out why—he needed information that only I could give him." He reached for his glass and, this time, managed it himself. "He tied a rope around my feet and dragged me back to the first room. Guess he was too lazy to go all the way to the hidden room every time he wanted to question me. At first, I didn't answer his questions, so he used me as a punching bag. I decided that staying silent was stupid and bargained for food and water and fed him half-truths and a few outright lies, hoping that someone would notice and investigate."

"The night of the raid, when Marcus was found, he had a huge bruise on the side of his head. Even when they released him from the hospital, he was still claiming amnesia," I said. "There were a few times when some of the things he said made no sense, but I wrote it off as a result of his injuries. Which he milked," I added in disgust. "The guilt at suddenly not even liking my husband anymore ate at me, so I tried harder."

"I worried that by the time I managed to make it out and back to my life, you would've chosen him." Creole tugged at the ends of my hair.

"The more time I spent with the man, the less I liked him." My eyes filled with tears. "Did Marcus also report that we were such a happy couple that I left him?"

"Babe." His finger brushed at my eyes.

"I always love it when you call me that." I brushed his lips with mine. "I didn't understand why you stopped. Now I know, and I'm happy he never called me that or I'd hate it."

"I thought my brother was a dick, but yours takes the blue ribbon," Casio said. "How did he find you?"

"Marcus found paperwork showing that he'd been adopted and tracked the old man down before he died." Creole's face filled with anger as he said, "Turns out that after years of being the worst father a boy could have, dear old dad tracked my career and anything he could find out about me and kept a file. Marcus complained there wasn't much in it, and I wasn't in any position to tell him how much I couldn't care less. The best part is that he sicced an investigator on me and complained that it was a money suck to only find out that I'd relocated to the Cove."

Casio turned to Didier and Fab. "Any clue where Marcus is now?"

"We had a meeting scheduled yesterday, and just as we arrived and were walking across the parking lot, his phone beeped," Didier said. "A text, I assumed, since he spent a long time staring at the screen, barely able to contain his agitation. I asked if there was a problem, and he brushed it off. He apologized for leaving me to handle the appointment on my own, but said he'd return as soon as he could. Before I could ask any questions, he ran back to his car and flew out of the parking lot. Annoyed doesn't cover how I felt at being ditched without an explanation. I tried calling and leaving messages, but his phone was turned off."

"Probably had an app set to trigger a warning if anyone entered the warehouse," Casio said. "We've got a cop parked there, and there's been no sign of anyone."

"After getting the call from Madison yesterday while you were in surgery, I shared *everything* with Didier the second he walked in the door." Fab smiled up at him and stepped closer, and he put his arm around her.

"I'm very happy to have you back and that Marcus didn't win." All this time, I'd carried the guilt of causing the kidnapping of my husband and one of our best friends, thinking it was because I'd bested a drug dealer in a real estate deal. But it wasn't that at all.

"We're going to hold off on any more questions and let Creole get some rest," the Chief said. "Heads up—the detectives assigned to the case will be stopping by with questions of their own now that you're awake."

"We'll soon have this Marcus character in lockup," Casio said, then waved and followed the Chief out.

"Can you be tempted by a Roscoe burger?" Fab asked. "Hospital food blows."

"You do know that would mean you'd have to use a burger stand drive-thru?" I said in mock horror.

Fab wrinkled her nose at me.

The guys laughed.

Didier clasped Fab's hand in his, and they left.

"Alone at last," Creole said when the door closed.

"I want you to know that nothing happened between me and Marcus," I said. "Nothing. It was soul-eating to go through that, thinking that we were drifting apart, but now I'm happy that I don't have to scrub his paw prints off my skin."

"You're going to have to tell me how you found me." Creole attempted to pull me closer and grimaced. "I give your bald friend only minimal credit."

"Baldie didn't even hesitate when I pitched my idea to go check out the warehouse." I laughed. "The biggest flaw in Marcus's 'take over your life' plan was that he didn't like me and could barely conceal that fact. The feeling was mutual, which caused me to snoop in a way I never thought I would and now no longer feel embarrassed about." I proceeded to confess to all the things I'd done.

Creole chuckled a couple of times. "Big mistake, discounting you and how crafty you can be. I've been treated to a front-row seat on occasion. I racked my brain to come up with a cleverly coded message to send you, but the words didn't come to me in a way that wouldn't have resulted in you getting hurt if he'd figured out you were onto him."

"You must have without realizing it, as he flubbed up a few times."

"Come here." He tugged on my hand and said against my lips, "Give me a few days. I can't wait to hold my wife in my arms again," then kissed me.

Chapter Thirty-Four

The next day, two detectives showed up at the hospital, got all their questions answered, and left seeming satisfied. The Chief and Casio arrived ahead of them and stood in the background, only adding to the discussion when asked.

"I want to go home," Creole said, his broodiness on the rise since he'd been woken up by one of the nurses in the early morning hours and hadn't been able to go back to sleep because of the pain.

I'd suggested that he ask for a shot when he winced for the tenth time, but no, he thought toughing it out was a better idea. "I'm fairly certain that you're not getting released today unless you threaten the doctor, and since he saved your life, that would be unfriendly." I leaned in and gave him a quick kiss. "What I will do is go home and get you a change of clothes so when you do get sprung, you won't have to go home in a hospital gown."

"Where are you living?"

"Fab's."

"You need to be careful. Any sign of Marcus,

don't bother with niceties; just shoot him. It would easily be self-defense."

I leaned in and brushed his lips.

"Better yet, ask Didier to go—you know he wouldn't say no. Besides, you need a nap." He chuckled. "Sleeping in a chair takes a toll. Probably already has, but you won't complain."

"Didier isn't taking over my wifely duties," I playfully admonished. "I'm going back to Fab's to shower and change clothes, then a quick stop at the house. On the way back, I'll pick up something yum to eat. I checked last night before your hamburger arrived, and you're not on a restricted diet. What will it be?"

"I've missed your home cooking." He smiled cheekily. Everyone knew that I'd adopted my mother's "home cooking" skills—all that required was keeping a stack of to-go menus on hand. "Another hamburger and fries—you know how I like it—and sneak me a beer."

"No alcohol for you until you're off pain meds."

The door opened, and Didier walked in with a wave.

Creole looked between me and Didier. "You don't seem surprised to see him."

"Caught me. I didn't want to leave you by yourself. Just like you said, not one word of complaint when I asked." I winked at Didier. "If you help him escape, I won't be happy with you." I shook my finger at him, then leaned down and kissed Creole's cheek.

"Don't worry, *cherie*, I'm onto his tricks. He'll be right here when you get back."

I hugged Didier. "Thank you."

On the drive back to the compound, I unleashed all the tears I'd been holding back. To think I might not have gotten Creole back, never known about the switch. Worse yet, found him dead because I was too late. I sucked in a breath to get myself under control, and that worked for a second before the tears flowed again.

I pulled up and parked in front of the beach house, brushed away the last of my tears, and blew my nose. I hadn't been back since the morning I moved out. I got out, grabbed my tote and went to unlock the gate, and my key didn't work. "Prick. He changed the locks?" I said to myself.

I went back to the Hummer and got my lockpick out of my purse. I opened the gate and tried my key on the door, and it didn't work there either. I opened the door and walked in, gasping in shock as I looked around. The entire house was empty, only the screen divider that gave privacy to the bedroom left. I crossed to the patio doors, and not one piece of furniture had been left behind. I moved across the room and opened the closet door, and it had also been cleaned out. I crossed to the safe and opened it, relieved to see he hadn't touched it. I cleaned it out and shoved everything into my bag, then turned in a circle, not believing my eyes, my sadness replaced with anger. "Damn that bastard." I locked up, got in the Hummer, and made the short drive to Fab's.

No one was home. I went into the bedroom and showered, then put on a skirt and top. Plans had changed. I needed to stop and buy clothes and shoes for Creole. Under different circumstances, it was one of my favorite things to do.

It wasn't until I got back to the hospital that I remembered I hadn't called Mother or Brad. I'd call in a favor and get Fab to do it. I wasn't sure I could get through the conversation without crying.

I walked into Creole's room and was happy to see that Fab had joined Didier. Shopping bags in hand, I hurried across the room and set them down on one of the couches. I grabbed the smaller bags and handed one to everyone, then passed out bottled water out of the last bag. It surprised me that Fab didn't complain about hamburgers two days in a row.

"I'm cashing in one of my hundreds of IOUs," I said to Fab.

Didier laughed. "Fab always grumbles when you want to cash one in. But I'm certain she'd never say no." He kissed the top of her head.

"I'm gracious about it," Fab said in a snooty tone.

Her big fib had us all laughing.

"Would you please, oh please, call Mother and Brad… or let one tell the other about Creole? But then you'll have to play favorites, see who gets to spread the news."

"I was going to offer." Fab sighed. "Not before trying to figure out who else I could fluff the call off on, but I couldn't come up with anyone that wouldn't be drunk or weird."

"If you *fluff* it off, make sure you get a favor." Fab and I laughed. She loved the idea.

"What's with the shopping bags?" Creole asked when we finished the burgers and the telltale signs of yummy to-go food had been thrown in the trash.

I sighed. "You know I excel at storytelling, and if I had one for you, I'd go with it, but since I don't… Marcus cleaned our house out; he didn't leave a stick of furniture or a single personal belonging. I didn't check the kitchen or bathroom cupboards, but I imagine he was thorough."

"It happened a couple of days ago." Fab sighed. "I went back over the security tapes after I got your call. A couple of work trucks showed up and weren't there long. Even if I'd seen it happening at the time, I'd never have guessed he was moving." That it was hard for her to admit was audible in her tone.

"I'm so—" Creole started.

I cut him off. "Don't say sorry. In fact, don't apologize for that man ever again."

"I'll be relieved when the police call to say

they have him in custody," Fab said.

"Agreed," I said.

"As soon as we get home, we'll change the code at the entrance," Didier said.

"I just remembered that I put a tracker on the Mercedes," I said. "Let's find out where Marcus is, and I'll give the information to Casio. He can rearrange his brains, then let the cops haul him away." I took out my phone and pulled up the screen.

Fab took the phone away from me when my hands shook. "It's not showing up," she reported. "I'll send Xander a text. He can access the app and get an address." She kept my phone in her hand. "I told him to hustle. Don't worry, he knows it's me and not you, even though it's your phone."

It took about a half-hour to get the return text with an address, which Fab promptly forwarded to Casio.

"Casio's still at The Cottages," she said. "The kids are having a good time with Crum, who's back to tutoring them on their schoolwork so they don't get behind."

"The perk is that they like him. I admonished him to stay dressed, and he's complied." I told the guys about his latest bodysuit ensemble, and they laughed, not sure whether to believe me until Fab verified the story.

Fab and Didier got ready to leave, and she promised to call Mother. They both said they'd check in tomorrow and to call if we needed anything.

Now that it was just the two of us, I scooted my chair closer and laid my head on Creole's chest, turning so I could see his face. He ran his fingers through my hair and tugged on the ends.

"You didn't mention the cats," Creole said.

"Marcus and I had a fight, and when I left him, I took the children." I told him about my move to the warehouse. "Surprise. I wanted to tell you… him… but he kept blaming me for his memory issues and I never found the right time. Another thing I felt guilty about. Warehouse-living is creepy, so I moved to Fab's."

"Happy to hear that you moved to where you'd be safe."

"The way I see it, we have four housing options until we get new furniture: The Cottages, the warehouse, Fab's, or kick Doodad out of my house. It's your decision." I gave him a sneaky smile, and he did a double take. "If you choose anything but Fab's, you get to tell her."

"So mean."

"I know." I laughed. "She's wanted us to move in since they bought the place. Knowing her, she's making a list to stock the refrigerator with all our favorites." I stroked his cheek. "I've laughed more with you in a day than the whole time with Marcus. The few times I did, it was put on."

Chapter Thirty-Five

Two days later, the doctor stopped by, examined Creole, gave him one last admonishment to rest and take it easy, and signed him out. I helped him into the shorts and shirt I'd bought and was happy I'd thought to get a belt. I'd also chosen a pair of runners that I knew he'd love.

Before he checked out, Casio stopped by with an update. "Marcus sold the Mercedes to a private party for cash. The new buyer boasted he got a good deal. Do you think he's left town and is planning to lie low?"

"What I know is that he feels he's owed something, and I'm the only one in the family left to pay up," Creole said. "He stole everything of mine and Madison's that he could get his hands on. Is he satisfied? I doubt it. He wanted me dead, and he didn't get that."

The thought of running into Marcus again sent shivers up my spine. I remembered all the cold looks that I didn't understand and passed off as health-related; now I knew how much he hated me. It made me wonder whether, if his duplicity hadn't been discovered, I would have met an untimely death.

"Anyone rear-ends you in the near future, I'd suggest not pulling over." Casio half-laughed, devoid of humor.

I left the two men to talk while I went to the business office, which had left a message that my credit card was declined, much to my surprise. I'd have to call the bank and find out what the problem was when I got back to Fab's. In the meantime, I gave them The Cottages credit card.

The nurse and I arrived back at the room at the same time. I stepped back as she rolled in a wheelchair. Creole grumbled that he wanted to walk but sat down with a grunt, knowing that it was hospital rules. Judging by his grimace and the breaths he blew out, his ribs were sorer than he let on and would be happy for the ride, whether he admitted it or not.

"Anywhere you'd like to go before we go back to the compound?" I asked before we turned out on the main highway.

"Can't believe I'm tired already," he said in disgust. "I'd like a beer and to sit out in the sun with my feet up."

"You're going to have to remember that you had the snot kicked out of you and need to take it easy," I grumbled. It wouldn't be hard to shoot Marcus if I saw him again.

"I've heard that phrase before and wondered what it felt like; now I know," Creole teased.

It was a short drive to the compound. I pulled up to the security gate and hung out the window, using the new code that Fab had texted me. "When we get to Fab's, I'll pilfer a burner phone and send you the code."

"I'll be bumming a ride for a few days anyway." Creole blew out an exasperated breath.

"In the meantime, you could use the Barbie Jeep... except you wouldn't fit." I chuckled to myself and told him about my lawless joyride. It made him laugh, something I wanted to make sure he did more of.

I slowed before turning toward Fab's, and we both looked at the beach house.

"I'm sorry," Creole said.

"I was about to say the same thing." I leaned over and kissed his cheek. "It's only furniture. We'll make it easy on ourselves and go online, make our choices, and have it delivered. We'll be back in our house in a few days." I turned and continued down to the opposite end of the street. "In the meantime, we've got five-star accommodations."

I pulled into the driveway and parked. Didier and Brad walked out the front door and helped Creole into the house, laughing and joking. Didier led him over to one of the couches, and Brad handed him a beer.

"Reading my mind, dude." Creole took the bottle.

Fab waved from the kitchen, opened the refrigerator, and crossed the room, handing me a water. "In case you didn't know, Didier and I are very happy you're staying here."

Brad sat down opposite Creole and gave him a thorough once-over. "The only difference I can see is that you lost weight. You run into your twin again, you should black both his eyes, return the favor."

Creole rested his head against the back of the couch and took a long pull on his beer. "I'm not up to a fight just yet, but when I am, I'll keep your advice in mind should the opportunity present itself."

"Got invited to dinner and thought I'd show up early," Brad said. "It was Mother's idea, and you know how she can be."

"A Westin family dinner, and I'm the central attraction?" Creole grimaced. "That should be interesting."

"Twin? An imposter amongst us? Who wouldn't come?" Brad laughed. "I told her not to stare and that if you ate and excused yourself to go to bed, she wasn't to say anything."

"That sounds fun." I winked at Creole.

He clasped my hand and pulled me down next to him. "Don't leave me to fend off your family by myself. Another thought that nagged at me during this ordeal was what if they liked Marcus better—wouldn't that be nice and awkward?"

I snuggled to his side. "That didn't happen." No way was I ever going to tell him how often Marcus had been the 'life of the party' while he was impersonating Creole.

The door opened. "We're here," Caspian yelled, stepping inside as Mother and Spoon came in behind him. Mila, who'd been holding Caspian's hand, broke free and ran straight to her dad, who picked her up and twirled her around.

"Learn something fun in school today?" Brad laid a loud kiss on her cheek.

I knew that everyone had questions about Marcus and would want every detail about what Creole had been through but hoped no one would ask. That would surprise me, but one could hope. I needed to pull Fab aside and have her whisper to everyone that she'd update them later.

"It was music day." Mila belted out a children's song I'd never heard before.

When she finished, everyone clapped.

Brad set her down, and she ran to Creole. "I know you can't play today." She grinned and leaned over and kissed his cheek.

"When I'm back on my feet, I'll put you on my shoulders and we'll go for a run on the beach," Creole said, and they knuckle-bumped.

Caspian held out his arms, and she ran straight into them. They talked more about her day with their foreheads together.

Mother leaned down and kissed Creole's cheek. "Happy to see you're feeling better." At her side, Spoon nodded.

"When you've had enough, say the word," I whispered.

They all greeted Creole as though nothing had happened, but they all stared longer than normal, the same as Brad, probably trying to see if they noticed any differences. They were there, but were subtle. Now that I knew there was a twin, I'd never be fooled again.

With help from Spoon and Brad, Didier finished preparing dinner and got it on the table on the patio. For a Westin dinner, it was a tame affair, and everyone was on their best behavior. Once the meal was over, Didier refilled everyone's drink of choice, and we gathered around the pool. Creole stretched out on a chaise. I pulled over a chair and sat next to him, taking his hand in mine and squeezing. The sun was sinking low, painting the sky orange.

"Any help you need moving back into your house, I'm available," Mother offered. "You know I love to shop."

Caspian cleared his throat and looked uncomfortable. "I'm sorry to have to break the news to you... but your brother sold me the beach house."

"I just found out and wanted to tell you, but I didn't know how." Fab grimaced.

Creole sucked in his breath. "How could that have happened?"

I blurted out what I was thinking: "It would take my signature on the deed."

"Upon hearing what happened to you, I contacted the title company," Caspian said. "They assured me that you and Creole showed up and signed all the necessary documents. We now know that was your twin."

"I didn't know about it and have no clue who passed themselves off as me." That wouldn't have been easy to pull off. I'd get the name of the title company and check it out myself. I wanted Caspian not to have a single doubt that I tried to pull a fast one.

Creole pulled me closer in a side hug. "How much did you pay?"

"Two million," Caspian bit out.

The only people that didn't gasp were Fab and Didier.

"You got screwed," I said. I'd let Creole know as soon as were alone that we'd work it out. Marcus sold our home out from out under us, but we had each other.

"Did Marcus approach you?" Creole asked Caspian.

"He did." Caspian nodded. "He told me that he and Madison were interested in getting something bigger and he'd found something just outside the Cove and needed a quick close. I shared that it would be a great surprise for Fab to own the whole block. I have to tell you, the man was good; I never suspected a thing." His eyes bored into Creole. "He told me he'd sell to the first person with a good offer and mentioned that he'd had a couple of potential buyers view the property. I played right into his hands and didn't balk at the price."

"I'm not going to contest the transaction," Creole said.

I knew there was no way he'd screw Caspian, since he was a friend and business partner in the family partnership. If that wasn't enough, he was Fab's father.

No one said a word.

Mila laughed. She lay in a chaise next to Brad, headphones on, watching a movie.

"I've got an announcement," Fab said. "I've got a tenant for one of the floors of the warehouse that Madison bought."

Really? I glared at her.

Just go with it, her return look said.

All eyes flew to her.

"What warehouse?" Mother demanded.

"Madison shared the good news while I was in the hospital," Creole said, his tone conveying that he approved. "I'm sure you all remember when she pitched buying the warehouse near the Boardwalk as a good investment to the partnership and it was voted down?"

I pasted on a stupid smile.

Creole continued, "I encouraged her to buy it anyway. I had the ulterior motive of wanting her to be busy with real estate projects, with no extra time for chasing down degenerates."

"I was working on the deal when Creole got

kidnapped, and it finally closed." No one needed to know how long I'd actually owned the building or that I'd slept there a few nights.

"I'm surprised you got one of the Michaels brothers to sell to you." Brad laughed. "I approached the other one about the three that are about ready for demo, but he knew you were my sister and cussed me out."

"Everyone knows I'm more charming than you." I smirked at Brad.

He wasn't buying it, but also wouldn't call me out until we were in private.

"Word has it that the city is forcing Michaels to clean up the property, so it won't be an eyesore much longer," I said.

"Any more business?" Spoon asked, and didn't give anyone time to answer. "Madeline and I are going out on the boat for a few days," he informed us all.

"That sounds fun," I said. "You'll have a great time."

"Do I get a drum roll for my news?" Brad asked with a laugh. "My daughter is cutting her first day of school tomorrow. She's going to hang out with the professor and Casio's brood. When I told her that they'd hit town, she asked a dozen times to go to The Cottages." He smiled at his daughter, who'd crawled into Fab's lap and fallen asleep.

"It surprised me, but not only is Crum good with the kids, they like him, for all his eccentricity," I said. "Don't be surprised if Mila learns something useful, as he likes to boast."

The talk drifted back to business. Brad and Didier talked about the family business and caught Creole and everyone else up with what was going on down at The Boardwalk. It was good to know that Marcus hadn't screwed up anything there. I hoped there wouldn't be any more shocking news and thought back to the rejection of my bank card. It was just a glitch, I tried to assure myself. It was too late to get it straightened out now, and I'd take care of it in the morning.

"I'd like to sneak back to our room and lock the door," I whispered to Creole.

He chuckled. "Make that happen and I'll owe you. Big."

Chapter Thirty-Six

The sun shone through the sliders, signaling it would be another warm day. I smiled at waking curled up next to my husband. It had been forever. Thankfully, Marcus had discouraged any kind of intimacy.

"You awake?" Creole nibbled on my ear.

"Hmm…" I cuddled closer.

"I'm thinking we should get dressed before Fab kicks in the door."

I winced along with Creole as I watched him slowly get to his feet. Dressed and on our way down the hall, I heard my phone ring and went back to get it. I sat on the bed and made several calls before following Creole out to the kitchen and sliding onto a stool next to him at the island.

"Good morning." I smiled at Didier, who handed me a cup of coffee, which I smelled, even though I knew with one look it was my pedestrian brand. Didier laughed.

"Like old times." Fab sidled up next to Didier and put her arm around him.

Creole fisted his fingers in my hair, lifting my face to his and staring intently. "What are you thinking about so hard?"

"I got a call from Mac, and when I answered, I could tell the line was open but she didn't say anything. Then suddenly, it went dead. I called back, but she'd either turned off her phone or it died because she didn't charge it, which is unlike her."

"Simple solution: take a drive over to The Cottages to check on her and the rest of the place," Creole said.

"Great minds." I tapped the side of my head and snuck a peek at Fab. "I thought to cash in on another favor from Fab, as I still have quite the stack." I turned to her with a pleading look. "That way, I can play nurse to my husband."

"That sounds like a great idea, except that the guys are having a meeting," Fab said, not meaning a word of the first part. "The best I can offer is chauffeur service."

Like she'd ever let me drive. It had happened, but not often. "Meeting?" I looked up at Creole with a frown.

He held up his hands and pointed to Didier. "You were on the phone when Didier told me."

"We had a meeting planned a couple of days ago to go over Boardwalk expansion plans, but Marcus had some lame excuse about a doctor's appointment, so we rescheduled." Didier grinned at him. "Brad's bringing food."

I glared at Didier, softening it with a slight smirk. "If you corral Creole into a run or some other high-intensity fun, whether or not he gets hurt, I'll shoot you."

Didier looked down at Fab, who grinned back. "That's not very supportive, wife."

"The good thing about Madison is that she doesn't shoot to kill. At least, not every time," Fab said.

Creole hooked his arm around my shoulders. "I promise, nothing adventurous today. And probably not for a couple of weeks." He scrutinized me as though trying to read my mind. "I suspect you're withholding something from me."

"Wifely concern," I said, trying to deflect the question, and knew I sounded lame.

Fab snorted. "You're a better actress than that."

She was lucky I didn't have anything to throw except my coffee mug. That would make a mess.

Not one to let anything drop, she continued, "It's easy to see something's bothering you; might as well blurt it out. You'll tell me sooner or later, and then I'll tell Didier. We're all here, so why not now? Besides, you know I prefer sooner." She shot me a sneaky smile.

I thought briefly about a girl brawl. The guys would enjoy it until one of us got hurt… probably me.

Didier snapped something in French that sounded like a reprimand.

Creole laughed.

"None of the French business," I said. "Not

fair that I'm the only one here that struggles with even one language."

"I told her to mind her own business." Didier smiled.

"I bet that's never worked." I laughed at the heated scowl she leveled at me and Didier. "I... uh..." All eyes were on me now. I let out a long sigh. "It's about your dick brother. Sorry." That wasn't very nice, since he knew without having to be reminded.

Creole hugged me. "What did he do now?"

"He cleaned out our personal checking and savings accounts."

Fab gasped.

Anger filled Creole's and Didier's faces.

"When he asked for the password, I didn't think anything about it since he'd just gotten out of the hospital." I patted Creole's hands, which had curled into fists. "Good news: he didn't have access to our business accounts."

"I'm—" Creole started.

I cut him off. "It's fixable. We need to get to work on replacing your identification. Then we'll go to the bank together and set up a new personal account. In the meantime, we'll both have to pay cash. I cancelled all the credit cards." I didn't tell him that one had been maxed out already.

"Once I found out about the switch, I went over the Boardwalk accounts and found no irregularities," Didier said. "He didn't have access, and I'm surprised he didn't figure out a way to ask without raising eyebrows."

"He had me fooled," Fab said, which obviously irritated her.

"Considering the man came in cold and took over your life, there were very few glitches, and nothing that stood out," Didier said.

"Wonder if Marcus has some acting in his background?" I half-laughed despite my loathing. "He assumed the role of 'Creole' and wore it well. He was smart to keep me at bay with his coldness or I might have caught on."

Fab refilled everyone's coffee cup except mine; she knew that I restricted myself to one cup and instead set a bottle of water in front of me. "So, Creole…" She waved her hand theatrically. "Tell us how you and Madison met?"

It took me a minute to realize what she was doing, and I chuckled.

"You need to prove to us that you're not a triplet," Fab joked with a note of seriousness.

All of us laughed.

"Madison's Aunt Elizabeth kept an eye out for me when I was a kid. I'm certain she didn't know I had a twin; she'd never have kept that kind of information from me," Creole said. "When I moved to the Cove and needed a place to stay during my undercover activities, she rented me a cottage. One day, this amazing redhead showed up and took control, accepted cash with no questions, and didn't boot me to the curb. As

soon as she dumped that other guy, I moved in."
Creole kissed me. "You've been mine ever since."

"I did a little lurking of my own in the early days, eager for a glimpse of you and that fine backside of yours coming and going." I winked. "I don't need to grill you. The differences between you and Marcus are glaring."

Chapter Thirty-Seven

Before heading to the car, I gave Creole one last admonishment not to overdo it and sealed it with a kiss, and he made me promise to call if there was a hint of a problem.

"How long will it take before I stop having a foreboding feeling when leaving Creole, hoping that when I see him again, he won't be someone else?" I asked as Fab drove out of the compound.

"Probably a while. We both know that the same scam would be impossible to pull off a second time," Fab reassured me. "Marcus had some big ones and never showed a lack of confidence in assuming someone else's life. And the way it's all played out, he had an exit plan in place."

"Marcus genuinely liked you and Didier and, I believe, loved my family, considering how territorial he acted at times. I can't help but wonder if he'd given thought to making disappear. Then there wouldn't have been a risk of me ever finding out." I stared out the window at the handful of white fluffy clouds that dotted the blue sky.

Another driver honked at Fab as soon as the light turned green. She sat there until the car went around with more honking.

"Jerk," I said.

"Didier and I were shocked when Caspian told us he'd bought your house. It happened at the same time we heard about Marcus. We talked it over and decided that we want you to stay at our house."

"I haven't shared this with Creole, but I don't want to live in the beach house anymore. Too much happened. Besides, the only way would be to buy it back, and it's not a good deal anymore." I laughed and shook my head. "We've got other choices, but none as classy as your house."

Fab turned off the highway. "Settled then. You'll live with us. Plenty of room." She pulled into the driveway of The Cottages and parked in front of the office.

A quick perusal of the property told me that all was quiet, but that could be deceptive.

As we got out, Crum crawled out of the bushes. He slapped around the corner in a pair of flip-flops with the soles wrapped with electrical tape and a skirt of two yellowed pillowcases pinned together. "You looking for Mac?" He brushed his hair back from his sweaty forehead. "She and the sidekick had words with the looney broad next door, and you know how women are—they made up in that noncommittal way. Then the three huddled together in an intense conversation and went that way." His finger pointed one way and then another.

"Where exactly?" Fab snapped.

"The apartment building." Crum's tone implied she was a stupe. "That chick's manic, and you never know which personality you're going to get. I know because she took a swing at me for no reason and started screaming that I was the instigator. I go out of my way to make sure I don't share sidewalk space with her, even if she's a block away."

"If she's half-crazy, she fits right in," I said, thinking she'd been at the center of more action than most and none of it good.

"Mark my words, she's trouble on a stick." Crum shifted from one foot to the other, nervousness overcoming his usual snooty confidence.

"Anything else I should know about?" I hesitated to ask, but better to be forewarned.

"You need to corral your two managers before something bad happens. They're strutting around, imitating you and your friend here, as if one pair of you wasn't enough. They're asking questions about murders of people that may or may not have anything to hide. Not smart." Crum tapped his temple.

"How many times did I tell them to stop?" I sighed. "They're worse than children."

"Your sex never listens." He backed up at Fab's growl and added, "In my experience."

I hooked my arm in Fab's. "I'm taking her out of here before she beats you up. You can thank me later." To my surprise, Crum didn't say anything, just saluted and walked away. "I think you scare the man."

"Crum thinks he can out-snooty me, and I'm more than happy to show him he's wrong."

"I'd definitely put my money on you." I led her out to the sidewalk and let go of her arm. "Since I know you're going to ask, we're going to knock on manic chick's door and ad lib. The goal is to fetch my two managers home, and then they're grounded."

"Since it's your plan, you first." Fab pointed to the steps.

Pastel lived at the far end of the building on the second floor. I listened, hearing what sounded like the television, and knocked.

The door opened a crack, and Pastel stuck her head out.

None of the tenants knew that I owned the building. Word had been spread that it was now under the control of a management company.

"Pastel?" I pasted on a smile to appear more sincere. "I own the building next door, and I'm here about my manager, Mac."

"This isn't a good time; I have a really bad headache." Pastel shut the door in my face.

"That wasn't friendly," I grumbled.

Fab hissed and stepped around me. She kicked the door. No answer. She kicked again.

I tugged on her arm. "Maybe Crum was wrong about them being together, but he's so snoopy, it's hard to believe."

The door opened again, Pastel opening it enough to slither out, a gun in her hand. "The law gives me the right to defend myself in my home if I feel threatened. This is your only warning. Go. And don't come back."

Fab drew her weapon and shot the gun out of her hand.

It clattered to the ground, and I kicked it out of the way.

Pastel screamed, blood dripping on her jeans.

Fab's leg shot out and made contact with Pastel's midsection, sending her flying back through the door, where she landed on the living room floor. Fab went to stand over Pastel. "You move, and I'll shoot you again. You might want to wrap your hand in your shirt."

Muffled sounds drew my attention to the far corner of the room, where Mac and Rude were tied to dining room chairs, rags stuffed in their mouths. I ran around Fab and removed the gags, tossing them on the floor. "Anyone have a knife?" I inspected the knots. Pastel had used a jump rope to secure their hands.

"Pastel killed Canton." Mac coughed.

"The serial killer?"

"Canton killed the two women," Rude said, and spit on her sleeve. "Bonnie, the first one, was just a pain in the twat, and when he told her flat out that their relationship was sex and nothing more and it was over, she wouldn't go away. So he made her." The woman shuddered. "Number two—Kay—was an accident. Some kind of 'get your rocks off' suffocation game."

"Call 911 before this one bleeds out," Fab snapped.

"I'm always the one that calls; you do it," I said, and Fab glared. I pulled my phone out of my pocket and called. "What's wrong with this neighborhood? They hear gunshots and no one calls the cops. If they had, sirens would be ripping up the street."

"You think you can untie us?" Mac asked in exasperation and jerked from side to side.

Fab crossed the room and inspected the knots. "Sorry ladies, I forgot my knife, so you're tied up until the cops get here. Besides, them finding you tied up will back up your version of events."

Pastel rolled over and attempted to crawl toward the door.

Fab ran back and kicked her in the butt, and she landed face down. "Where do you think you're going?" Fab barked, and Pastel answered with a string of curse words.

I turned to Mac and Rude and, in an irritated tone, told them, "You two know that you're indebted to Fab for forever, now that she's saved your life, don't you? Knowing her, she won't let you forget." I moved to the front door, hearing the squealing of tires, and peered over the railing as two cop cars pulled into the driveway. Kevin had drawn the short straw again. I whistled. He looked up, and I waved. The other cop, I didn't recognize.

"Don't you ever stay out of trouble?" Kevin asked as he climbed the steps.

"Once you get the whole story, you can thank me. A couple of times." I ignored his snort. "You should be happy that Pastel wasn't able to follow through on her plan to kill Mac and Rude, because with Mac gone, who would keep you in snacks?"

Fab had come outside and stood next to me. "Careful of that one," she said to the other cop and pointed to Pastel on the floor. "Mac and Rude are inside."

"Give me the quick version," Kevin barked.

I told him what happened.

"Self-defense," Fab said when I got to where she shot Pastel.

"Wait downstairs and don't wander off anywhere," Kevin ordered, then skirted around me and into the apartment.

He didn't need to tell us twice. We hustled down the steps and out to the sidewalk, where a few people had gathered, one of whom wanted to know, "Who died?"

"No one," Fab told them.

They were clearly disappointed.

"I don't want to sit in the street." Fab yanked on my arm and nodded towards Mac's house.

"We can sit on the porch. Kevin will spot us from here."

"You were impressive," I told her. "Once again."

"Mac and Rude are lucky that you care enough to check on them. If we'd been much longer, they might've been dead."

We crossed the street and made the short walk, claiming the best spot for people watching, according to the owner.

"They're also lucky that locked doors irk you, especially when they're shut in your face."

Fab smirked. "How do you suppose Pastel planned to get two bodies, each bigger than her, down the stairs without being seen?"

"My luck, she'd have blown town and left the bodies to rot. They wouldn't have been discovered until the smell seeped out from under the door."

An ambulance pulled up, and two EMTs unloaded a stretcher and disappeared from sight. It wasn't long before they were back, Pastel strapped on the stretcher, and flew off down the block.

Kevin and Mac came out and stood in front of the building, him with an uncharacteristically sympathetic look on his face.

Fab stood and let loose with a shrill whistle. Kevin turned, and she waved like a crazy woman. "Just in case he's looking for us." She sat down, amused with herself.

Kevin shook his head. He and Mac walked up the street. "I left Rude at her apartment. She called Cootie, who's on his way home. Almost getting murdered gave her an attack of nerves. You might want to check on her later."

His partner whistled and waved him back.

"Pastel doesn't have all her oars in the water," Mac said on a ragged sigh. "Thank you for showing up when you did, or we'd be toast." She got teary-eyed and wiped them away with the bottom of her shirt.

"How did she get you into her apartment?" I asked.

"We went willingly." Mac rolled her eyes. "Pastel told us she'd heard that we'd been asking questions about the murders of the two women. She wanted to make sure that the cops had the right man in Canton and there wasn't another murderer or two on the loose. She had personal belongings of Canton's and wanted help going through them."

"Good ruse," I said.

"As soon as we walked in, she pointed a gun in our faces. I cussed myself for not bringing my own."

"How did she get you both tied up?" Fab asked.

"Pastel held the gun on us and made me tie up Rude, then tied me up. I thought about making a run for it immediately, but I figured she'd put a bullet in one of us. Out of ideas, I thought I could talk her out of killing us." Mac shuddered. "But then, when she confessed to drugging Canton and planning his murder to look like suicide, I knew we were toast."

"Did Pastel say why?" I asked.

"She'd overheard him on the phone, making plans to leave town with another woman."

"I'm happy that we got there in time," I said. "You should take a nap, go for a swim, walk on the beach. Any problems come up, ignore them."

Mac flashed a small smile.

Fab and I left as Mac went inside and stretched out on the couch.

Chapter Thirty-Eight

Instead of turning onto the main highway, Fab cut through residential streets to her office. "I need to pick up some paperwork."

"While you're doing that, I'm going to stop in and see Xander. I've rapidly become one of his best clients."

"What are you up to now?" Fab demanded.

"Multitasker that I am, a bunch of stuff. I'd like to stop by the title company that handled the closing of the house and demand a few answers. I'm going to prove that I wasn't the one at the closing. I don't want Caspian to have any doubt that I was in on pulling a major con on him."

"Don't you need an appointment?"

"I bet if I were to create a scene in the reception area and tell anyone sitting there that I'd been defrauded, I'd be ushered into the manager's office in short order."

"Or out the door in handcuffs." Fab shook her head, clearly not liking my idea. "If it were my company, and I hadn't been part of a con, I'd be hot on the phone to the cops, reporting a lunatic on the loose."

"If fraud can be proven, Caspian would get his money back."

Fab punched in the code, and the security gates opened. She pulled inside and waited for them to close before parking. "Wait for me, so I don't miss anything." She pointed to where I stood, then flew up the stairs and unlocked the door, leaving it open.

I took out my phone and texted Creole on the burner phone he was using until he replaced his old one. "I'm cooking."

"We're having a party here, so make sure you order extra," he texted back.

Cook was my next call. I placed an order for one of his amazing sampler platters for a dozen and laid on the charm. Then I sent Fab a text, telling her that we'd need to stop for dessert. She reappeared, folder in hand, and came down the stairs reading her phone, then looked up and frowned at me.

"Shindig at your house." I chuckled. "Unless Creole exaggerated, and if that's the case, we'll have leftovers for days. We need to stop at Jake's."

We cut across the parking lot and up the stairs of the other warehouse. Fab stepped in front of me, lockpick in hand, and I slapped her hand down. "You can't barge in with two guys inside. They might be naked." I scrunched up my nose, then reached around her and unleashed my best cop knock.

Xander threw open the door, laughing. "I know that knock." He threw out his hand and ushered us inside.

"Got a job for you, and super pronto." I slid past him and claimed a stool at the island.

"Is there any other speed?"

"I'm sure you're well aware of what's been going on," I said.

"I was happy to hear that you got your husband back." Xander slid onto a stool at the far end in front of his open laptop and a pile of paperwork that he'd spread out.

"Need you to do a background check on Marcus Towers. His last name was Baptiste at birth, before he was adopted. I'd also be interested to know whether it was a legal adoption, with all the appropriate paperwork filed."

"While you're digging around," Fab said. "Research the real estate transactions on Madison's beach house."

"This next request might not be very legal, so feel free to foist it off on one of your black hat friends," I said. "In addition to getting a cool two mill for the property, Marcus also cleaned out Creole's and my bank accounts, and I'd like to know where the money went. I know the payment for the house was probably wired and wonder if it's still sitting in the same account. Though it's hard to believe that Marcus didn't move it immediately. I would. When you're a criminal, the harder you are to track, the less chance you'll get caught."

"I'll get on it," Xander assured me. "I've got a couple of great connections that have offered to help me out anytime. Before you ask, they made it clear they'd never ask for anything in return."

"I'm preapproving whatever the cost is," I said.

"This is going to be fun." Xander grinned.

"Your warning that I'll probably end up in jail has me thinking I should call my lawyer," I said to Fab.

Xander got wide-eyed. "You're always telling me to avoid jail; you need to do the same."

I told him about my idea of confronting the title company.

"You don't have to do any of that," Xander said. "The transaction is a matter of public record, and I can get a copy of the paperwork."

"Whoever impersonated me had to show valid ID, and I'd like to see a copy of it," I said.

"That's not a slap on the wrist, if we're able to identify the person and turn the information over to the cops." Fab turned to Xander. "You get a picture, forward it to me. If the woman lives in the Keys, someone will recognize her."

"Calling Tank." I scrolled through my phone and hit the number for my lawyer. No surprise, it went to voicemail, and I left a message. "We're out of here unless you need anything," I said to Xander.

"All's good here. No one would lurk around here now that Toady spread the word he owns the property and lives here." Xander smirked at Toady's exaggeration. No one was going to contradict him if it kept criminals away.

"Where is Toady?" I looked around the large living area, where two leather chairs had been added to keep the couch company. Nothing out of place; even the coffee table was spotless. I suspected the men conducted all business at the island, as evidenced by a basketful of remotes.

"He's out boosting a car," Xander said. "The finance company who wrote the loan isn't happy that the guy never made a payment. Took a while to track the fellow down, as he kept moving around."

"I've done a couple of those jobs." Fab grimaced. "You'll be happy to know I won't be taking another one," she said to me.

She was right; it did make me happy. Some jobs you knew would be trouble from the start, and car repossession came with a big red flag.

"Behave and all that." I slid off my stool and headed to the door, Fab behind me.

"You too. I'll keep in touch and let you know where I am in my investigation." Xander waved.

"Who would have thought a pickpocket would turn out to be such a great employee? Even now that he's gone out on his own, he hasn't dumped us," Fab said as we hiked down the stairs to the car.

We'd met Xander while he was attempting to relieve Fab of her wallet. A chase ensued, and it took a couple of days to track him down, but we did. Then I'd made him an offer that was good for all of us.

Fab turned off the highway.

"Wait!" I tugged on her sleeve. "We need to pick up the food."

"Took care of it. I texted Cook and asked for delivery service. He texted back that he'd send his nephew."

"Did you call the guys and report in?" I asked. "I'm out of the habit, as Marcus didn't want to be bothered."

"I called and gave Didier a bare bones version, giving credit to Mac and Rude for nabbing a murderer. Not in the mood for a lecture, I waited until after I hung up, then texted, 'More details to follow.'"

"That's a good one." I beamed at her.

Fab rolled through the security gates and slowed at her driveway. Like me, she inventoried the cars and matched them to the owners. She opened the garage door, edged around an Escalade, and pulled in.

"Interesting group," I said. "Hope we didn't miss anything good."

"We're sticking our necks out for our fellow man and the community at large, and the guys are partying it up!" Fab grouched with a trace of a smirk.

"You be sure and lord it over them in just that tone." I laughed and got out of the SUV.

Brad opened the door and pointed us toward the kitchen. I paused and hugged him.

Creole, Didier, Casio, and Tank were seated at the island drinking beer.

I slid onto a stool next to Creole, kissing his cheek.

"That took longer than I thought," Didier said, and enveloped his wife in a hug. "I shared our conversation with the guys, and it was the consensus that I got a watered-down version of events."

"What kind of trouble did Mac get into?" Creole asked.

Tank waved his hand. "She need a lawyer?"

"The murderer chick needs one, but the case would probably be a freebie," I said. "Doubt she can afford your fees."

"I suppose you were right in the middle of whatever you're talking about?" Creole arched his brows.

"The middle?" I squinted, and my attempt at a delay got me a frown. "Wanting to follow in the footsteps of Fab, Mac and Rude teamed up to solve a couple of murders in the neighborhood. Thanks to Superwoman, those two are still sucking air. I told them both that they owe her big." I winked at Fab. "Huge." I held out my hands.

All eyes turned to Fab.

Fab relished retelling the takedown, ramping up the danger and excitement.

Didier wasn't happy but wrapped his arms around her.

"Happy you're okay, Sis," Brad said. "I call dibs on telling Mother."

"And for once, Kevin didn't threaten to arrest either of us," I said, and turned to Casio. "Where are your kids?"

"Happy to say that they're back home and missed all this drama," Casio said with a shake of his head. "I got one of my aunts to come stay until I get back to Miami."

Didier fixed Fab a martini and me a margarita. Brad handed out more beers.

"Got a couple of updates for you, one better than the other," Casio said. "First one is about Marcus. It's not much, but something. He dropped out of sight the same day Creole was found. He hopped a flight to the Cayman Islands, and we lost him after that."

"If he had the money wired directly to a foreign country, that would raise red flags," Creole said. "Wouldn't be surprised to hear the money got transferred a couple of times and the Caymans is a ruse."

"I've got my Information Dude following the money trail; I'll let you know what he finds out," I said. "What other good news do you have for us?"

"There've been arrests in Sugar's case," Casio

said, looking pleased with himself.

"Who?" Creole asked.

Fab gave him the rundown on the case.

"Turns out that the sister, Laurie, drained her family's accounts with frivolous shopping, and her hot idea to replenish the coffers was to kidnap her sister, thinking the new husband would pay up," Casio related. "She thought that by calling in an investigator, she would look concerned and not be considered a suspect. When the call was made to the husb, he whined about not having access to the money. He claims he didn't call the cops because the kidnappers threatened to kill Sugar if he did."

"So it was the sister," Fab said. "She was cold as icicles, but I pegged the husband."

"When the cops hauled Laurie away in cuffs and her husband heard what she'd done, he beat it to a divorce lawyer," Casio said. "The kidnappers agreed to a twenty-five-year sentence in exchange for their testimony. They were looking at life, which is what the sister will probably get."

"How's Sugar taking it all?" I asked.

"She's a tough one." Casio grinned. "I helped her do a little house cleaning. She insisted that piece of… get two days to pack up and get out. I wanted to throw him off the balcony."

"Thirty-eight floors. Splat!" Fab accentuated that with sound effects.

"Let me guess," I said. "You had a little sit-down with Bowman, and he cleared out?"

Casio brushed his hands together. "I hooked her up with a lawyer to expedite the annulment." He pointed to Tank.

"Tank's here to discuss legal options with regards to the property," Creole said. "And in no way screw Caspian."

"You can ignore the message I left on your office phone then, since I called for the same reason," I said. "I thought about going to the title company and creating a scene. Thankfully, my friend here talked sense into me, and I called you instead. I'd be interested to know if this particular company is one that does things by the book and turns away criminal opportunities. If that's the case, then they were also fooled."

"Unfortunately, real estate fraud is big business," Tank said. "Forward me anything Xander finds out."

Boy did I know that, having had a couple of experiences in the past. At least, those transactions had been halted before I lost the property and had to fight it out in court.

"What about the dog custody case?" Fab asked Tank. Before he could answer, she ran down the highlights of that case for Creole.

"Happy ending, including the pooch."

"You mean Max, the recently deceased beloved animal?" I asked.

"Turns out that the pictures of dead Poochy were a ruse. Yes, he got hit by a car, but he survived surgery and those were pics of his recuperation. With both the dog and my client recovering from untimely accidents, the loving couple bonded and ended up getting back together." Big eyeroll in his tone.

"Wasn't the wife a suspect in the husband being mowed down and left to die? And let's not forget the neighbor woman who got shot," I reminded him.

"The cops questioned her after she lawyered up, and not with me, by the way. I have it on good authority that she's a person of interest, but there isn't enough evidence to make an arrest."

"Did you at least warn him that hooking back up might shorten his lifespan if they weren't able to agree on something else?" Fab asked.

"Better yet, tell your client to grow up and tell his little friend to stay out of his life decisions." I snorted.

The guys laughed.

"Madison suggested no more animal custody cases, and I agree with her, Fab said.

"Did you guys manage to stay out of trouble while we were gone?" I eyed Creole and Didier.

"Not as exciting as your morning," Didier grouched.

The compound gate bell rang. Fab walked over and checked the screen, then opened a drawer and took out cash. "Going to need some help carrying in the food."

Didier and Brad followed her outside. They

came back in with several shopping bags and set them on the counter.

"You order enough food to feed an army?" Creole chuckled.

"Just following orders." I smirked. "It's in the Westin DNA to overbuy when it comes to food. Plus, you have to factor in leftovers."

Chapter Thirty-Nine

It was a quiet couple of weeks, with less drama than usual. I drove Creole around so he could replace his identification and start to get his life back on track. He researched a new ride and chose an oversized black pickup truck—Casio had a connection for a great deal, surprisingly not his brother—and it was being delivered to the house on a flatbed from Miami.

Now that Creole was almost back to his old self, I suggested a trip to the warehouse and said I'd give him a tour. There wasn't much to see, since all the floors looked the same and I'd had the few pieces of furniture I borrowed returned to The Cottages.

"You did a good job on the renovations," Creole said as he walked around and checked out the upgrades.

"Toady and his crew really came through." I hooked my arm in his.

"Knowing you, you had a hand in every decision."

I stood on my tiptoes and kissed his cheek. "Your idea and encouragement, and I made it happen. I'm going to make sure that it isn't a money suck or a haven for illegal activities."

Creole cupped my chin. "That's why I want veto power in selecting tenants. Any serious applicant has to pass a background check."

"I'd prefer that prospects come with a recommendation from someone we know; even a friend of a friend works for me." I laughed at his grimace. "Xander's got an artist friend that's looking for space, and Fab's got someone but needs to verify that said person is interested before divulging the name."

"I'll ask Didier, and if he doesn't know who it is, he'll find out and give us a heads up."

"In ten days, we close on the other three buildings," I reminded him.

"Can't believe that Toady got both brothers to sell."

"He made the last standing Michaels brother a 'take it or leave it' offer, and he accepted because it was the best offer on the table and avoided a courtroom showdown with the code department."

Creole clasped my hand in his, and we walked down the stairs and back to his truck. He swept me off my feet and slid me onto the front seat, something else I'd missed.

"Since we're in the neighborhood, I want to stop by Toady's. I've got a few questions," Creole said.

It took all of a couple minutes to make the short jaunt down the street. Creole drove up to the security gate, punched in the code, then pulled in and parked. He got out and walked around to help me out.

"I'm going to get with Xander and have him make us universal gate openers," I said.

"Or change all these security pads to open with our thumbprints."

"That's a better idea." I smiled at him. "One less thing for someone to steal and use to gain entrance to our properties." I tugged on his hand and led him up the stairs. At the top, I kicked the door.

"Babe." Creole smirked.

"Learned that trick from Fab," I said as the door flew open.

"We both lose," Xander called over his shoulder, then stepped back and ushered us inside. "Toady and I were sure it was Fab."

I grinned at Creole, who hadn't believed me.

We slid onto stools at the island.

"We stopped by because I've got a few questions about the warehouse deal," Creole said to Toady.

"Coffee, beer, something stronger?" Toady offered.

Creole nodded at the coffee. I passed.

I ran the idea for easier access to the security gates by Xander.

He nodded and said, "Did you get the queen's permission, including for any changes you want on your property? She's head of security, in case it slipped your mind."

Creole barked a laugh and took the mug Toady handed him. Toady set his own down and retrieved some paperwork from the far end of the island.

"I'll run it by Fab, and when she tells you to get on it, you can act like it's the first time you've heard the idea," I said.

Toady laid out several pictures of the interior and exterior of the three buildings. Creole examined each one and asked questions. "We'll want to use your crew on these properties, since they did a good job. There's no need to advertise our involvement and stir up unnecessary trouble."

While Creole talked business with Toady, and Xander worked on his laptop, I excused myself and went downstairs and across the driveway to retrieve a set of keys that Didier had mentioned forgetting on Fab's desk. I scooted up the stairs and inside, and was reaching for the keys when the hair on my neck rustled, and I knew I wasn't alone.

I spun around and was confronted, entirely too close for comfort, with the menace radiating from Marcus's eyes, the same icicle blue I remembered. How had I missed the difference? He looked every bit the arrogant bastard that he was.

"I'm surprised brother dear let you out of the house by yourself. Should have assigned you a bodyguard at the least, or maybe he finally sees you disappearing as a path to his freedom," Marcus hissed, slamming the barrel of his gun into my stomach, hard enough that I hit the floor and rolled into a fetal position. "Get up. Now." He motioned.

Until I tried to stand, I didn't realize the hit my knee had taken when it met the floor. As steadily as possible, I hobbled to my feet. He marched me to the door, grabbing my arm and thrusting me in front of him, his gun poking square in my back. He shoved me forward, and if I hadn't already had one hand on the railing, I'd have tumbled down the steps. I shrieked.

"Shut up," he barked in the angry tone I remembered all too well. He fisted his hand in my hair and dragged me out of the garage and around the side of the building, where he'd found the one space he could park an SUV without it being noticed.

It surprised me to see it was an older model, and I wondered if that was because he didn't plan to stick around and didn't want to be easily spotted while in town. I had no intention of getting in, knowing it would be the last mistake I'd ever make; he'd make sure of that. He forced me toward the back driver's side door. I struggled to control my panic, dropping to the ground and opening my mouth to yell as loud as I could, while at the same time attempting to roll away. Something white-hot jabbed me between

the neck and shoulder, and my world went black.
My last thought was of Creole and that I'd never
see him again.

Chapter Forty

I slowly opened my eyes and stared into pitch darkness, my heartbeat thundering in my ears. I lay on a cold concrete floor, my hands and feet tied together in front of me. The creak of rusty hinges startled me, and my attempt to scoot toward the corner failed as a faint light cast a shadow into the room.

Marcus kneeled down in front of me. "How many times did you dream that I'd be found dead? Or perhaps you wished to kill me yourself?" He chuckled, a harsh sound.

I kicked and twisted, much to his amusement, then ceased to struggle for now, not seeing a path for escape. "What do you want?" I choked out, wondering where I was but not wanting to ask. Creole would never find me in this dank hole, wherever it was. I hoped to outsmart Marcus and get the heck out of there but didn't want to dwell on my chances of success. "It can't be money; you stole it all." Not quite, but he didn't need to know there were accounts he could still get his greedy fingers on if he had the passwords.

Marcus glared. His jaw hardened as he cut the

rope away, jerked me to my feet, and shook me witless. "I want what's due me. What I've always wanted. Creole's life. His friends, family. But not you." He fisted his hand in my hair, yanking my head back to stare into his lifeless eyes. "*You*, I can't stand. I don't know how Creole tolerates you. You bitch." He spit in my face. "You ruined my plans. But not this time. I'm using you as bait to reel in my brother. I haven't decided which of you dies first."

My attempt to move away failed when he tightened his hold until my scalp burned. "You're not going to be able to fool our family and friends a second time."

"Your interference was what derailed my plans," he ranted as he dragged me across the floor by the hair. "Not this time."

Despite the stabbing pain in my scalp, I threw myself against him, rocked back, and kicked out, making contact with his lower leg. He heaved me across the room like a sack of garbage. Electric pain tore through my body, so sharp and sudden that my lungs burned. I rolled to my side, screaming from the shards of pain that ripped through my shoulder and wound down my arm. I turned from his gloating stare as tears rolled down my cheeks.

Grabbing my arms, he picked me up and threw me against the wall, where I slid to the floor. "Do you know what it's like to have a great life and one day find out that it's nothing more than a pack of lies? That's what growing up was like for me."

I attempted to wipe my nose on my shirt, which sent more pain tingling down my arm. "Did you ask Creole about his life growing up?" Keep him talking, I thought, as I slumped over. "From what I heard, you had it way better than he ever did. Your bio dad was a vicious drunk." *Kind of like you, except you were sober.* "Daddy dearest took his wrath out on his son with his fists. There were many occasions that Creole hid from the man. And you're sorry you missed all that?" I snorted in derision.

"Lies. I got the real story from our dad. Creole grew up wild, and without Dad's intervention, he'd be in jail."

"If that's what he told you, then the man had gone senile by the time you met him."

"Now, I've got a second chance. Madeline and Spoon will be the family I always wanted and support me through the loss of my dear wife." He sneered.

I choked on my disgust. "When Spoon figures out what you've done—and trust me, he will—you'll die one piece at a time." He'd never fool Fab a second time, but I wouldn't point that out. I wanted her safe and off his radar. Marcus would never overpower Spoon, unless he hit him from behind, and he wouldn't get the opportunity if Spoon was onto him.

Marcus yanked me to my feet, giving my arm

and shoulder another twist as he shoved me forward.

I detected noises in the distance. Inside... outside, it was hard to tell. I took a deep breath, knowing there would be pain, and tugged as hard as I could against Marcus's hold. I felt his hold loosen as he again pitched me against the wall. This time, I hit my head. I fought to keep from succumbing to darkness.

He chuckled. "Party time."

Every fiber in my body hurt, and I screamed as he tugged me to my feet. He wrapped his arm around my neck, using my body as a shield and jamming his gun against my temple. "I left a trail that even my dumb-ass bro could follow... unless he didn't want you back."

The footsteps came closer... Creole darkened the doorway, gun in hand.

My insides quivered at how evil Marcus's laugh sounded in my ear. I turned my head slightly and watched as his smile grew.

Keep calm, I told myself. *Think strategically.*

For a second, everything went still as the two men locked eyes.

Marcus breathed like he might collapse. I hoped he would.

"Drop it," Creole ordered. "It's the only way you're getting out of here alive."

"Some family. Shoot your own brother." Marcus got momentarily distracted as Casio came up behind Creole, sticking his head over his shoulder and flashing a manic grin. "What the—"

Creole used the moment to grab my hand, shoving me into Casio's arms and wrenching Marcus's gun away. It went off, tearing a chunk out of the wall. Creole tossed it out the door and delivered a fast punch to Marcus's face that, judging by the crunching noise and the blood that splattered over the two men, broke his nose. And another punch. As Creole yanked Marcus's head back to plant another fist in his face, a plainclothes cop grabbed his arm.

Marcus wrenched free, holding his face, and managed to stumble out the door, leaving the sound of his maniacal laugh in his wake.

"Go after him," I screeched.

"I'll take it from here," the cop said. "There's more cops downstairs. They'll get him. And no worries about him making bail anytime soon."

Creole pulled me into his arms and ran his hands over my arms and down my body. "The terror on your face... I really wanted to kill Marcus, but I'd be the one to end up in jail." His expression hardened when I winced. He drew his finger down my cheek. "You okay? How badly did he hurt you?" He kissed my temple. "I'm getting you checked at the hospital and then taking you home." He scooped me off my feet, and I sagged into his chest and rested my cheek against his shoulder. "Marcus has a tenuous grip on reality, and I, for one, hope he never gets out of jail." Creole tightened his hold and carried me out the door.

As soon as we stepped outside, I recognized the warehouse and shivered, even though it was another steamy Florida day. I bit back the pain in my head as it rippled through my body.

We both watched as Marcus, smirk firmly in place, was driven away in the back of an unmarked car.

Chapter Forty-One

Creole had a surprise for me, and I was excited, pulling on a loose-fitting turquoise spaghetti-strap sundress and sliding into a pair of nude sandals.

Thankfully, I'd only spent a few hours at the hospital and been released with an admonishment to take it easy—that my bruised ribs and shoulder sprain would take time to heal.

"I don't suppose you know what's going on?" I eyed Fab in the floor-length mirror.

She shrugged, the picture of innocence.

"You flitting around, somewhat nervous and half-excited, is a dead giveaway." It didn't escape my notice that she refused to make eye contact.

Fab came up behind me and twisted my hair into a knot, holding it with a clip.

"Can you give me a hint about where Creole and I are going?"

"You think Creole shares his plans with me?" Fab laughed. "You look great; now, go have fun. You two deserve it."

Knowing that Marcus was in jail wasn't comforting to me because I expected to hear at any moment that he'd broken out. Fab and I knew from past experience that people we thought were locked up, with the key tossed in the Gulf, could come back to haunt us. Creole had forbidden me to worry about the what ifs and asked Tank to keep us updated as the case progressed through the courts. I let Creole know that he'd better have plans to keep me very busy.

Creole and Didier stood in the kitchen and watched as Fab and I walked down the hall. Creole whistled and gave me a wolfish once-over. Didier grinned.

Creole closed the distance between us and hooked his arm around me. "Don't wait up." He ushered me out the door and into the Hummer, pulling a blindfold from his pocket and tying it around my eyes before closing the door. He went around to the driver's side and climbed in, taking my hand in his. "We're not going far."

That was the truth. Less than a minute later, he parked and shut off the engine.

"Do I get a clue?" I asked.

"Nope. You're way too good at that game." His door slammed, mine opened, and Creole scooped me into his arms. He set me down and hooked his arm around me, holding me close and walking me forward.

We stopped, keys jingled, and a door opened. He scooped me up again, took a step, and the door banged closed; then he set me back down. There was a slight gap at the bottom of the blindfold, and it gave me a glimpse of hardwood flooring.

"Are you peeking?"

"I swear, I can only see the floor."

"Careful." He wrapped his arm around me and led me forward. "Slight step down." He tightened his hold, then turned me slightly and took the blindfold off.

We stood on a large wraparound deck that overlooked the waters of the Gulf. The waves were gentle as they lapped the shore. The sun sat low and bright on the horizon. The view was amazing, and the ocean looked bluer than usual—almost aquamarine from this vantage point. We'd had the same view, but a different angle when we lived in our beach house just down the sand.

Creole left me standing at the railing and went back inside the house. He came back with a tray of cold drinks and set it on the table, then pulled me down on a chaise, handed me a margarita, and sat down next to me, taking a beer for himself. "To us being back together," he toasted.

"I never want to live my life without you in it." I gripped him by the front of his shirt and kissed him, letting him know there was nothing I'd rather be doing.

"Nothing and no one is going to come between us again."

I craned my head around and saw that the house was empty. Except for a couple of barstools in the kitchen, the only furniture was the chaise we were sitting on and a small table off to one side. "Did you buy this house? Is that the surprise?"

"It's on the short list." Creole chuckled. "Your friend threatened my life if I didn't show you this property first. She doesn't like the idea of us moving out of her house, but she'd be content as long as we were only several hundred feet away."

"Fab can be quite the whirlwind when she wants her way and doesn't easily take no for an answer."

"And snoopy."

"There's nothing that annoys Fab more than not knowing something... and the detailed version. Last to know doesn't work for her. I get it, because last to find out... sucks."

"Well... I'd planned an end run around her and was going to keep my plan under wraps until I wanted people to know, and certainly, you would be the first."

I puffed my lips into a frown, trying not to laugh, knowing Fab would immediately sniff out that something was happening without her input and be all over it.

"Thinking that we needed a house of our own—and how we'd talked about getting something bigger—I searched the real estate sites and came up with a handful of listings that I printed out, planning to do a drive-by and weed out the unsuitable ones, then take you on a house-hunting excursion." Creole shook his head. "My big mistake was leaving them under my keys and phone on the counter when I went back to the bedroom to grab something. Coming down the hall, I saw that she had them in hand and was flicking through, more annoyed than I've seen her in a while. I thought Didier would step up, maybe a polite 'mind your own business,' but heck no."

I laughed, knowing that would never happen because he didn't want us to move far away either.

"Great. Even you knew Didier wouldn't have my back on this issue." He refilled my glass. "Fab gave me a grilling equal to that of a hardened detective. I figured she'd kill me on the spot if she got an answer she didn't like."

I bit my lip and asked, "Didier didn't attempt to rein her in at all?"

"He only laughed, and I was happy to get out the door in one piece." Creole snorted. "I told him later that there'd be payback."

After selling the beach house, Marcus moved the money several times, and Xander hadn't found it yet. He'd gotten a copy of the identification of the woman who impersonated me. Her driver's license information matched mine, except for the picture. No one that I asked recognized her. Tank awaited our decision about whether or not we wanted to get into a legal showdown with the title company's insurance company.

"Is the house next door in the running?" I asked and crooked my head to the right.

"Turns out that Fab is entertaining the idea of a short-term rental. Couldn't get any details out of either her or Didier, even after I told them that it would affect our purchasing decision. Let them know I wouldn't tolerate *another* weirdo for a neighbor."

I laughed, wishing I could've seen their faces. "Did your house-hunting turn up other options?"

Creole held up two fingers. "They're here in the Cove, but not close enough for Fab." He grinned at me. "I'm leaving the choice to you. Just know that any house you choose is fine with me, but you're going to be the one to tell Fab if it's one of the others. 'Nice house, but we found something better.'"

We both laughed.

"Thumbs up?" Fab's voice rippled across the sand from where she stood, megaphone in hand.

Creole took my drink, set it down, and pulled me to my feet.

I moved to the railing and leaned over it, yelling, "I haven't gotten a tour yet." I hoped she could see that I was smiling back at her.

Creole nudged me and nodded down the beach.

Didier came barreling down the sand and

tackled Fab. The two rolled around, and after a tussle, he came up with the megaphone in hand. "Sorry," he yelled into it.

Fab made a grab for it, and he moved it out of her reach. She jumped on his back. Didier pitched the megaphone and shook her off. He scooped Fab off her feet and threw her over his shoulder, retrieved the megaphone, and started back to their house.

Fab looked up and waved, then smacked his backside. He returned the gesture.

"The neighbors are crazy," I said, and started to laugh.

Creole pulled me back down next to him and told me that he'd looked at a dozen properties and whittled it down to three, including this one. He got out his phone and showed me pictures as he ran down the pros and cons.

The doorbell started ringing continuously.

"Wanna bet who that is?" I asked.

Creole stood and stomped into the house. He came back and held his hand out to me, helping me to my feet. "Fab brought food."

Didier stood in the kitchen, looking apologetic. "The delivery guy was knocking on the door before I found out what Fab was up to."

I recognized the boxes, which were from The Crab Shack. Yum!

"I figured the best way to get my foot in the door was to bring food," Fab said, not the least bit repentant. "I asked for the sample platter, found out that they had two, and got them both."

"You're shameless." My admonition fell short, since I was laughing and so were Creole and Didier.

~*~

PARADISE SERIES NOVELS

Crazy in Paradise
Deception in Paradise
Trouble in Paradise
Murder in Paradise
Greed in Paradise
Revenge in Paradise
Kidnapped in Paradise
Swindled in Paradise
Executed in Paradise
Hurricane in Paradise
Lottery in Paradise
Ambushed in Paradise
Christmas in Paradise
Blownup in Paradise
Psycho in Paradise
Overdose in Paradise
Initiation in Paradise
Jealous in Paradise
Wronged in Paradise
Vanished in Paradise
Fraud in Paradise
Naive in Paradise

Deborah's books are available on Amazon
amazon.com/Deborah-Brown/e/B0059MAIKQ

About the Author

Deborah Brown is an Amazon bestselling author of the Paradise series. She lives on the Gulf of Mexico, with her ungrateful animals, where Mother Nature takes out her bad attitude in the form of hurricanes.

Sign up for my newsletter and get the latest on new book releases. Contests and special promotion information. And special offers that are only available to subscribers.
www.deborahbrownbooks.com

Follow on FaceBook:
facebook.com/DeborahBrownAuthor

You can contact her at Wildcurls@hotmail.com

Deborah's books are available on Amazon
amazon.com/Deborah-Brown/e/B0059MAIKQ